BY LOVE REDEEMED

CROSSWAY BOOKS BY
DEANNA JULIE DODSON

IN HONOR BOUND
BY LOVE REDEEMED

BY LOVE REDEEMED

DeAnna Julie Dodson

CROSSWAY BOOKS • WHEATON, ILLINOIS
A DIVISION OF GOOD NEWS PUBLISHERS

By Love Redeemed

Published by Crossway Books
a division of Good News Publishers
1300 Crescent Street
Wheaton, Illinois 60187

Cover design: Cindy Kiple

Cover illustration: Laura Lakey

First printing, 1997

Printed in the United States of America

Library of Congress Cataloging-in-Publication Data

Dodson, DeAnna Julie 1961-
By love redeemed / DeAnna Julie Dodson.
p. cm.
ISBN 0-89107-947-5
I. Title.
PS3554.03414B9 1997
813'.54—dc21 97-14531

05 04 03 02 01 00 99 98 97
15 14 13 12 11 10 9 8 7 6 5 4 3 2 1

DEDICATION

To the One who calls me His own—
Thank You for loving me.

ACKNOWLEDGMENTS

To Jacky Chappell and Shawnita Lusk, who suffered through a million revisions and a billion questions—

To Rosie Barrow, who took the time to read when she already had too much to do—

To my mother, Katherine Hiebert Dodson, who brought creativity and an artist's vision into the family—

To the army of prayer warriors who are interceding for me still—

May God reward your love and faithfulness in the same generous measure you have given them.

PROLOGUE

"THAT WAS NOT OUR AGREEMENT, MY LORD OF ABERWAIN," KING Philip told the heavy-set man that stood before his throne. The king's voice held the soft tautness that Simon Taliferro instantly recognized as displeasure. Doubtless King Philip meant to be heeded when he spoke in that tone, but Aberwain's expression smacked of insolence rather than respect.

"The agreement I made was with your father, your majesty," Aberwain replied. *You will have to be taught respect for your elders, boy, no matter how royal your blood. No king, especially a pup of three-and-twenty, is stronger than the nobles who support him.*

Standing beside him in the great hall, awaiting his own audience with the king of Lynaleigh, Taliferro could read the words in Aberwain's eyes as clearly as if he had spoken them aloud. He had listened to this man most of the afternoon, listened to his demands, to his petty quibbles over what was rightly due him as a lord of Lynaleigh. He had listened to the king's voice grow colder and tighter as his patience thinned. All that day he had listened . . . listened and watched and taken note of everything.

They make quite a contrast, Taliferro thought, amused behind his grave demeanor at the fierce politeness of their contention. The young king was all lithe muscle, the fine scar high up on his left cheek adding a martial touch to his strong-willed, aristocratic handsomeness. Aberwain was a dark bear of a man, bearded and brawny, big boned, heavily muscled, and fat to the bargain.

Both stubborn, Taliferro decided, but there was something solid and unshakable in the king's assertions that the other man could not match. *Aberwain will lose this debate*.

"Then you admit to the contract," the king said.

"I admit to an agreement with King Robert," the burly man allowed. "He was willing to fight for my lands in exchange for my loyalty. You, if you will pardon me, my lord king, have given my lands away."

"I gave away nothing," the king said, an uncompromising lift to his square jaw. "That part of the Riverlands belongs to Grenaver. It was meant to be so and Lynaleigh held it unjustly."

"A good two-thirds of that land you 'did not' give away, my lord king, was mine."

"Land you took, my lord," the king shot back, "without thought for what would be just."

"That land was a sturdy buffer between Grenaver's attacks and the rest of Lynaleigh, your majesty. Since you have let the finer points of law take precedence over the defense of your kingdom, surely you cannot expect my poor forces to keep that border safe. And I cannot speak for those nobles who, seeing how you have abandoned my cause, might question the desirability of allegiance to so changeable a monarch. What might our enemies do should they know how weakly we are defended?"

"I will see to my kingdom's defense, my lord," the king said tightly. "You see to those duties that belong to you. Loyalty, for one, and obedience. You agreed that, once the war was ended, you would bring your daughter to her husband. They have been apart too long already."

Taliferro studied the young nobleman who stood beside the throne, a dark-eyed near-copy of the king's long-limbed, powerful grace, and reviewed the details he had of him: *Thomas Chastelayne, Duke of Brenden; brother to the king, younger by a scant ten months; staunch supporter of the crown; married two years ago to Elizabeth Briesionne, Aberwain's daughter*.

Since arriving that morning, Taliferro had seen him at the king's side, had watched the two confer together in answering the day's petitions, and, though Brenden said little for the ears of the court, there was sharp intelligence behind his warm affability, and his dark eyes missed nothing. Taliferro suspected it was the influence of this even-tempered brother, sweetened by the gentleness of the angel-faced queen at the king's left and combined with Philip's own passion for justice and truth, that made so young a ruler able to govern a war-ravaged kingdom and forge a reputation for wisdom and strength in doing it.

A *threefold cord*, Taliferro mused, *not quickly broken*.

Aberwain gave his son-in-law a dismissive glance. "Your majesty, the marriage of my daughter and your brother was agreed upon in exchange for support of my rights in the Riverlands. Now that your majesty has, shall we say, grown delicate over the matter of right and wrong . . ."

The king's frown deepened. "Lynaleigh never had true claim to the south of the Riverlands, my lord, and, had I been the one to make this agreement with you, it would never have included aid in so wrongful a cause. But that has no bearing upon this matter. They are married and the lands you want cannot be given you."

"Suppose I grant your majesty the justice of returning those lands, might not my loss be replaced to make good the agreement between your house and mine?"

"Replaced?"

"There are rich lands belonging to the crown that might make me see your willingness to keep your father's word and properly value my daughter . . . and my loyalty."

"Where?" the king asked, his blue crystal eyes narrowing.

"Kingslynne touches my land on the north side."

"That is the richest land in the kingdom!"

"It is less than half the lands I lost, your majesty."

"That land you lost, that we fought over for mere vainglory, is no more than wasteland now. The war has stripped it bare. You cannot compare it to Kingslynne for richness."

"The land I lost will be rich again someday, your majesty. What value might I put on it? I counted it worth my daughter once, and I cannot give her for naught."

"You *have* given her, my lord. She is my brother's wife already and there is no changing that. We have been patient thus far, but there is a limit to what patience will bear. You will bring your daughter to her husband here before the middle of this month. That is not a request."

Aberwain's insolent expression did not change, had not all this while. "Surely you would not endanger the girl's life, your majesty."

"Her life?" the king demanded, and there was a flash of concern in his brother's dark eyes.

"She lies ill even now. To bring her here in the dead of winter and she so sick . . ." Aberwain shook his head in a show of regret. "I would be less than a father."

"Sick," the king said with contempt. "A very convenient sickness. And I suppose she has suffered this sickness these three months since the war's end?"

Aberwain shrugged apologetically and the king's eyes turned colder.

"And I suppose she would return to health were I to grant you Kingslynne now?"

"I shouldn't wonder."

The king drew a sharp breath, his tongue ripe for an oath, but he stopped himself when he saw the look on his brother's face, a look that counseled discretion.

"Do not imagine, my lord, that I am too young or too raw to this game to play it well," the king said, his voice icy with control. "As to your request, I will give it my consideration. Who is next, Tom?"

"The Baron of Warring," Brenden murmured.

Pretending he did not notice Aberwain's indignation at the summary dismissal, Taliferro straightened his narrow shoulders. Then he heard the scribe read his name aloud.

"Simon Taliferro, Baron of Warring."

He stepped forward and bowed low, humility in his deep-set eyes, eyes that were so black it was hard to distinguish iris from pupil.

"Your majesty."

"My lord of Warring."

Taliferro made his expression properly abject. "Your majesty, I have no demands for you, only a simple plea for charity."

"Charity, my lord?" the queen asked. For the first time, she lifted her eyes to his, and their emerald luminance held him momentarily speechless. He had received reports that she was a woman of inestimable beauty and unassailable virtue. Now he could vouch for the first, and he wondered if he might sometime have opportunity to make trial of the second.

"Yes, royal lady, for the people of Warring. There is such destruction there, such barrenness from the war, that every day more and more go hungry and naked, the old die, mothers have no milk for their little ones. It is a sight unfit for such lovely eyes as your majesty's."

"I have heard it so, too, Philip," Brenden said, "though not to such a degree."

Taliferro could almost feel his thoughts being sifted in the young duke's dark eyes. There was no animosity there, only a piercing search for truth that the baron found vaguely unnerving.

"It *is* so, my lord," he said earnestly, "and worse than I have said."

"And have you made an account of what your people will need to set them toward prosperity again?" the king asked, catching up the soft hand the queen had laid on his arm in a silent plea for pity.

"I have, your majesty. I fear it is rather a prodigious amount, considered all at once."

He handed the king his list and waited for reply, hoping it would be the one he sought.

"Prodigious, as you say, my lord," the king said finally, handing his brother the list. "Can we do it, Tom?"

"With God's help," Brenden said after a moment. "Perhaps not all at once, but enough that the people of Warring needn't suffer so bitterly all the winter."

"You will have to stay here in Winton, my lord, to oversee the collection of what you need and the transport of it back to your people," the king said and Taliferro bowed his head, concealing his sly satisfaction.

"I thank you, my liege. I could not have asked a fairer answer. I thank you, as well, my sovereign lady, and you, my lord of Brenden. I shall make good use of my time here."

"You are most welcome, my lord," the king said. "Come to me tomorrow and I will have direction for you in starting your venture. Who is next, Tom?"

"Warring's 'charity' will drain the store we have from this year's northern harvests," the king told his brother as they conferred alone later. "But my lady will have no refusal of any beggar's plea."

Tom smiled. "I think the harvests were bountiful enough to share with the south. The war did hit them hard."

"Well, we will grant Taliferro's request, but I do not know that I can say as much for your father-in-law's."

"Give him what he wants, Philip," Tom said. "Has it not been long enough?"

"I cannot." The exasperation came back into Philip's expression. "Am I to let him dictate to me? He held those lands wrongly. I could not justly keep them from Grenaver, and I cannot now give him what rightly belongs to the crown. He has no right to keep her from you, and I'll not allow it any longer."

"We cannot just take her from him."

"She is your wife, Tom."

"And as such, she is worth any amount of land to me. Give her father what he wants and take Brenden in its place. I care not, so I have Elizabeth."

"You hardly know her. Why should you give up your dukedom for her?"

"Two years is a long time; I am tired of the waiting. She is Aberwain's heir. When he dies, I will have back anything you give him, and I will give it back to you."

"And meanwhile I let him bully me into what is unjust? No, Tom, I cannot even for you. But he will bring her. I promise you. Before Christmas."

"That's not even two months away."

"I will see to it."

Tom was too familiar with the inflexible resolution in his brother's face.

"Philip, I would keep peace with my lady's father as well."

"Trust me," Philip said, and then he smiled. "What good is it that I am king if I cannot get you what you want?"

When court was held the next day, Tom was surprised to see all the nobility gathered in the great hall. In times of peace, they usually only met together in the council, or, if they attended court all at once, it was at the king's command on some great matter of state. Tom was unaware of anything of such consequence on today's agenda.

Aberwain was called first, and Tom watched him make a swaggering bow before the throne, certain that such impertinence would not urge his proud brother toward compromise. Tom wondered how much longer his wait was to be made because of it.

"I have considered your request, my lord of Aberwain," Philip said, "and have this in answer: If you wrong me, I am bound in Christian charity to forgive you; but, if you wrong Lynaleigh, I am bound to defend her with every means in my power. You know, and every man here knows, what she has suffered from the war we have just fought. With every one of my nobles loyal, she will have difficulty enough recovering. If one of them, just one, puts himself ahead of her and leaves her weak before her enemies, she will be lost. Would you, my lord Darlington, leave her so?"

Darlington bowed his head. "God judge me, your majesty, not I."

"And you, Lord Ellison?"

"Never, my lord," Ellison swore, a look of contempt on his young face. His father had been killed in the war little more than a year ago, and he had little patience for those who did not uphold the king for whom that sacrifice had been made.

"My lord of Eastbrook?" Philip asked, and Eastbrook put his hand on the hilt of his sword, the gesture serving both as a pledge and as a warning.

"You have my oath already, my liege. You will never find me slow to defend your right against any enemy."

"And you, my lord of Aberwain?"

Before the calm authority of the king's words, Aberwain's smugness dissolved into uncertainty. A swift glance at the rest of the court showed him only suspicion verging on hostility, and Tom could see that he realized only now that he had overplayed his hand in braving this king in his own throne room, before the solid support of his nobles.

"Your majesty—"

"I must refuse your request for Kingslynne, my lord of Aberwain," Philip said, "in the best interest of the kingdom and independent of your threats."

"Threats, your majesty?" Aberwain sputtered.

Refusing to acknowledge Tom's silent plea for restraint, Philip numbered them on his fingers: "Disaffection of the nobility, attack from the south, my deposition . . . Shall I go on?"

Aberwain flushed red, then white. "My lord, your majesty, I never so much as dreamed—"

"In whatever words you couch them, my lord of Aberwain," Philip said severely, "are these not the promised results of your defection?"

"Defection?" Aberwain protested with another glance at the grim faces surrounding him. "My liege lord and king, on True Cross, I swear there was no thought of defection, nor anything else you have charged, ever meant in my words or my deeds." He smiled thinly. "Surely *you* never thought so of me, Thomas, my son."

"For my lady's sake, my lord," Tom said, "I hope I never need think so."

Philip's gaze was still stern. "Then I may conclude that your daughter's health will improve so much that she will be with us at court before Christmas."

Aberwain bowed in shamefaced defeat. "She will, my liege."

"And, of course, I need not question your loyalty in defense of my southern border."

"Of course not, your majesty. I swear it and overswear again my oath to you as my king."

Philip let his expression soften. "Do not swear to me, my lord; I am but a servant of this kingdom. Swear, rather, to Lynaleigh herself, whom I know you love."

Tom saw surprise and then relief in his father-in-law's face as he looked up at the king and realized that Philip was willing to put this failed attempt at coercion behind them and let him prove his trustworthiness.

"I do, your majesty. Most truly, I do."

Philip smiled a little at his fervent reply. "Have we not always found it so, my lords?"

There was a grudging murmur of assent from among the nobility and some of their animosity lessened. Tom exhaled a sigh of relief and rather poorly concealed a smile. That last touch of gentleness reminded him just how changed his brother was since the war's end. The Philip of a few months ago would never have stooped to that, not before his court.

Tom breathed his thanks heavenward. He would have his Elizabeth and peace with her father, and Philip's sovereignty was intact. He could not have asked much more.

With a final word of gratitude, Aberwain bowed and left the court, apparently unaware of the piercing black eyes upon him. Tom noticed the tall, angular figure that glided toward the doorway after him. Then Philip asked him who was next to be called and the rest of Taliferro's movements went unnoticed.

CHAPTER

ELIZABETH LEANED OUT OF THE CARRIAGE WINDOW AND SHADED her eyes against the orange sun that was sinking behind the imposing towers of Winton Castle, throwing their long shadows across the rutted road ahead. She had watched these towers for miles now, watched them grow larger and larger with every jolt of the wheels. She would be inside the city walls soon, and then in the palace itself, and then her life would forever change.

"Give me my glass, Ellen," she said, frowning, and the gaunt, middle-aged woman sitting across from her rummaged in one of the bags piled at her feet and brought out a little golden mirror, no more than the width of her hand across and set with matched pearls. Elizabeth had had it as a Christmas gift just a year ago, from this very place, from the near-stranger who was her husband.

She took the mirror and studied herself in it. Her mahogany hair was pinned back close and plain like Ellen's, tight enough to pull her dark brows into a severe line. The gown she wore was an unflattering mustard yellow, one she knew made her fair rose-tinged complexion look sallow and older than her scarcely eighteen years.

"Do you wish your hair changed, my lady?" the serving woman asked with a disapproving pucker around her mouth. Even when her face was relaxed, her upper lip was lined with the gesture. It was as habitual as the skepticism in the small eyes that were set close to her sharply pointed nose.

"No," Elizabeth answered, unconsciously copying the older woman's expression. "I've been sent for under constraint, and that is how I will come. I'll not make myself fair for it."

"I should say not, my lambkin," Ellen agreed. "Prince or no, what is my lord of Brenden but a man? Best show him from the very first that though you are his wife, you'll not be his fool."

Elizabeth laid the mirror in her lap with a sigh. What was she to say to him, this husband of hers? He had written her often in the past two years, his letters full of sweet words and lavish oaths of love, but she had sent him only the most perfunctory answers, and only for the sake of decorum. The serving girls who had come here with her the first time had sighed and giggled over him, telling her how fortunate she was to have such a man as Thomas of Brenden for her husband, but they did not understand. Besides Ellen, no one understood, no one cared.

No, she reminded herself, *I have one friend at court I can trust.*

She looked once more over the snow-laden fields toward the city. The gates stood invitingly open, and a steady stream of peasants and merchants ambled in and out, carrying the wares they had bought or were to sell, cheerful and festive in celebration of the season. No doubt there would be much revelry at the palace, too, for Advent. The thought wearied her. As a princess, she would be expected to be in constant attendance, and she knew the people would be especially eager to see her, now that she had finally come. She closed her eyes and wished for the convent.

Elizabeth stood outside the enormous double doors that led to the great hall, waiting to be presented to the court.

"It will be just a moment, my lady," Lord Darlington told her. He had been sent to meet her carriage and officially escort her to her husband, and she remembered him from her first time at court. There was a touch more silver in his hair, a deepening of the wrinkles around his eyes, but that only made him seem all the more suited to be one of the king's chief councilors.

"You mustn't fear, princess," he told her kindly. "Many arranged matches turn to love. The king had no say in choosing the queen, you know, and I dare say you'll not find a truer love than they've come to. I will tell his majesty we are ready."

"The king too much loves himself ever to love anyone else," said a cynical voice once Darlington had gone, and Elizabeth turned.

The woman standing beside her should have been beautiful. She was young yet, still in her middle twenties, with a comely shape, a fair face, and hair the color of new honey, but there was a deep bitterness in her green eyes and a tight, haughty downturn to her mouth that soured any attractive qualities she possessed.

"Princess Margaret," Elizabeth said as she made curtsey.

"Oh, no, your highness," Margaret corrected, making a mocking curtsey of her own. "It is you who are a princess. The king suffers me no title but 'Lady' now, and I think even that chafes him."

Elizabeth remembered her, too, remembered seeing her not long after the funeral of her first husband, the king's elder brother and then-heir to the throne, Richard of Bradford. She had scandalized the whole kingdom shortly after by marrying her late husband's cousin, his rival for the kingdom, Stephen of Ellenshaw. But Stephen had been killed in the final battle of the war, crushing for a second time Margaret's high-reaching aspirations.

Her father had disinherited her for her faithlessness, and it was only because she was the queen's sister that she was allowed now at court. There were those who said she should have been imprisoned for what she had done . . . even put to death.

"But you mustn't let that fret you," Margaret continued. "The king would do anything for your precious Prince Tom. So long as you are a submissive little wife, willing to put your hand beneath your husband's foot and serve his pleasure, the king will have no quarrel with you. It pleases him to see a woman who knows her place and does as she is bidden." She smiled. "He has my sister well trained."

"Pardon me, Lady Margaret," Darlington said coldly. He turned to Elizabeth. "It is time, princess."

"The Princess Elizabeth," she heard the herald announce. Trying not to hold too tightly to Darlington's arm, she let him lead her into the great hall.

Every eye was on her, every low murmur was about her, assessing her clothing, her hair, her person, comparing her, she was certain, to their beautiful and much-loved queen.

She had not met the queen before, of course, but she had heard much of her piety and her beauty. Little wonder the king was smitten with her; beautiful women were always beloved. These two were a good match, though, Elizabeth thought, looking at the king. Doubtless there was much love between two such flawless creatures.

Until that beauty fades, she reminded herself. *Then we shall see that love fade with it*.

"You are welcome to Winton, Princess Elizabeth."

The king came down from his throne to kiss her hand, and she curtsied deeply.

"I thank you, your majesty."

"My lord of Brenden has been eager for your coming, my lady," the queen said with a welcoming smile, as she came to Philip's side. "I believe he's been dressed for it since before noon."

"He wanted to ride out to meet you himself," Philip added, "regardless of the conventionalities. Even so, I think I'd best call him in now or I may have an open rebellion on my hands. My lord Darlington, if you please."

Darlington bowed and in another moment Thomas of Brenden, her husband, was standing before her.

"My lady Elizabeth," he said, bowing to kiss both of her hands.

His voice was gentle and deep and still had that soft northern touch to it that she remembered so well. He was a little broader in the shoulders since she had seen him last, and the handsome lines of his face were a little more mature, but there was more than a hint of boyishness left in the warm depths of his eyes and in the heavy lock of dark hair that fell over his forehead.

"How good it is to have you here," he added, looking up at her through his thick lashes, and she saw he was still quick to smile and that there was still a sweet hint of a dimple in his cheek when he did.

Take care you are not made a fool of for a smile, she warned herself. Then she made a stiff curtsey.

"Good evening, your highness."

He stood straight again and drew her to his side. She could not help noticing how well the simple richness of his crimson doublet suited him and the way his boots hugged the long line of his legs. King Philip was always held to be the fairest thing at court, and Elizabeth could not argue that. Tom was very like him in looks, but there were differences, too.

There was something formidable about the king, despite his youthful handsomeness and flashing smile. There was a searching watchfulness about him, a guardedness that made her feel there were only a precious few allowed close enough to truly know the man inside. It was not so with Tom.

He welcomed her now as he had that first time, as if she were truly dear to him. Despite all his Chastelayne beauty, despite her lack of anything to match it, there was warm acceptance in his dark eyes, something hopeful that drew her more than she felt right.

"How I have missed you, my lady," he said, lowering his voice for her alone to hear, and her heart began to pound harder.

Take care, she thought once more. She found no more time for contemplation as she was presented to an almost endless line of lords and ladies, all showering her with appropriate welcome and felicitations, all still appraising her suitability for their beloved Lord Tom and, she was certain, finding her sadly lacking.

Once the formalities were over, Tom squeezed her hand and pulled her a little closer beside him.

"Would you care to rest before supper, my lady? I know your journey was long and you are no doubt weary."

"I thank you, my lord," she said and he turned to the king.

"If you will pardon us, Philip, I will take my lady to her chamber now."

"Of course," Philip agreed. "So many introductions would exhaust anyone."

Rosalynde took her hand briefly. "We are so pleased you have come, Lady Elizabeth. I pray you will find happiness here in as much abundance as I have. If my lord of Brenden has his way about it, I know you shall."

Philip smiled and bent to kiss Elizabeth's fingertips. "I pray you will see to his happiness as well, my lady," he said lightly. "Anything less might prove treason."

Tom laughed, but Elizabeth could see that the king's words were not entirely frivolous.

"I shall try to keep within the law, your majesty," she said with an overly-formal curtsey, and Tom put her arm through his own.

"Come, my lady. I will see you at supper, Philip, Lady Rosalynde."

He made a slight bow and led Elizabeth into the corridor.

"Your ladies have doubtless made things ready for you by now," he said as they walked along. "There is a banquet planned for tonight in your honor and some other entertainments as well. You needn't attend if you had not rather."

"I would not wish to seem ungrateful, my lord. I know it is the custom."

"We seemed to have sidestepped more than one custom, you and I, my lady," he said with a touch of a smile. "If you would prefer—"

"Lady Elizabeth, you are come already."

She turned at the smooth voice and her eyes lit in recognition. She smiled her first smile in days.

"My lord Taliferro! How good it is to see you here."

"You are acquainted," Tom said, surprised, and Taliferro took Elizabeth's hand.

"My lord of Aberwain and I are neighbors and allies, your highness," he explained. "Your lady is quite nearly a daughter to me. In fact, her father asked that I look after her when I am able." He brought Elizabeth's hand to his lips. "I had hoped to return in time to see you presented to the court, Madonna. You must forgive my absence, but I am forced to go back and forth from here to Warring, sometimes without much warning. Still, I trust your stay here will allow us a great deal of time together."

"Oh, I pray so, my lord," she told him. "My father told me to count upon you, should I need a friend here, and I know I may do so."

His thin lips curved up slightly. "No doubt with my lord of

Brenden to champion you, Madonna, you will never have need of me, but I am here in the event you should."

"That is very gracious of you, my lord," Tom said, taking Elizabeth's hand from him and leading her again down the corridor. "We will both remember your kind offer."

"I will see you at supper, then, Madonna," Taliferro said with a bow. "My lord of Brenden."

❧

"My lord of Brenden," Ellen said, dropping a rigid curtsey when Tom and Elizabeth came into the room.

"How are you, Mistress Ellen?" he asked affably, taking a look around. "It seems you have done well in putting my lady's things in order."

"It mostly was done already, my lord. I had but to arrange the things we brought in the carriage today."

"I am to attend a banquet tonight, Ellen," Elizabeth said. "See my blue velvet is made ready."

"At once, my lady. As soon as I've settled you for a nap."

Ellen looked pointedly at Tom and began unbinding her mistress's thick hair.

"Let me, Ellen," Elizabeth said wearily. "You go find out what they've done with my dress."

Scowling, Ellen curtsied again and left the room. There was a moment of quiet before Tom went to Elizabeth's side, watching as she loosened the tight coil at the back of her head and let a few soft curls escape.

"Shall we talk a moment, my lady, while you do that?"

She stepped back from him. "Of what?"

"Why, of anything," he said with a disarming smile. "Of everything. You made such scant replies to my letters, I feel I hardly know more of you than before we met."

"There is no need, your highness. I am here. The king has commanded it, and I know my duty now. You needn't coax."

He touched her cheek, and she pulled away from him in such haste that one of the clasps that held her hair fell into the deep basin of water Ellen had brought for her to wash in.

"Allow me, my lady."

Tom pushed his sleeve up to his elbow and fished out the clasp. She stepped back from him again as he handed it to her. A handful of dark auburn hair fell down the back of her neck as she did.

"Please, my lady. You needn't fear me. I told you long ago I would never harm you."

He had told her that and had kept his word.

Any man may pretend gentleness for a week, she warned herself as she watched him dry his hands and push his sleeve back into place. She had left him two years ago almost convinced he truly meant what he told her, but she had been fresh from the convent then, still not sixteen, and had not known so much of the world.

It was only on their wedding day, as they stood before the archbishop, that they had met face to face. He had given her an encouraging smile when he caught her stealing a glance at him from under her lashes, but she had snapped her eyes straight ahead at that and had not looked at him again until they were at the banquet that followed. Even when he had touched his lips to hers at the end of the ceremony, she had not lifted her eyes from the floor.

Sooner than she had expected, the hours of feasting and dancing were over, and she was lying in the bridal chamber, waiting for her husband to be brought to her, waiting for the archbishop to come and bless the marriage bed, witnessed by all the court. It was the same room they were in now, with huge glassed windows that were overrun every dawn with the sun's glory and a high ceiling ornamented with painted saint's rose and intertwined *T*'s and *E*'s. *Thomas and Elizabeth*.

"No one ever calls me Thomas," he had told her that night, once they were alone. "No one but my father and then only when he is vexed with me."

She had made no answer to that. She had not spoken to him at all. She had merely lain there with the coverlet pulled high around her, wishing she had been allowed at least a shift for the sake of modesty, trying to breathe evenly and not tremble.

He had tried all that day to become acquainted with her, to coax her to dance or eat or drink or at least smile, but she had scarcely even looked at him. Even then, alone with him, she had not.

"I hope you will call me Tom," he had said, reaching out for her hand, and she had pulled back from him in sudden terror.

His expression had turned bewildered. "My lady, you needn't fear me. I would never hurt you."

He had tried again to take her hand, but she had only shrunk further away from him.

"No, please," she had whispered, her eyes filling with tears. "Please, please, no."

"Listen to me, my lady. I swear you needn't fear. Truly. I want only for you to be at ease. I have vowed to love and protect you. You are my flesh now as much as this hand of mine."

His tone had been gentle, but it had not stilled the fearful pleading in her voice and in her eyes.

"Please, my lord, let me go back to the sisters. It is wrong for me to be here."

"Wrong? You are my wife. It is holy and right for you to be with me. We pledged each other in the sight of God Himself, who made marriage to be an honorable thing." He had held out his hand once more. "My lady—"

"Please, let me go back."

"My lady . . . Elizabeth, please do not fear me. You vowed just today to obey me. Now give me your hand."

"No, please, my lord," she had begged, even as she did as he asked. "I cannot—"

"Shh," he had said, as he tenderly kissed her trembling fingers. "Listen to me now. You are my wife. My beloved. I know you are afraid, but you need not be. I would never force you." He had pressed the hand he still held. "I will touch you no more than this. I swear it. Not until you ask it of me."

She had slipped her hand out of his, a little of her anxiousness calming. "You are very kind, my lord."

"We are strangers yet, my lady. I understand."

That same patient kindness was in his eyes now. How well she remembered those eyes.

"You will want to rest awhile, Bess," he said, breaking her long silence. "I understand."

The familiarity surprised her.

"I am not called Bess," she told him, though he had called her that just once before—on the day she had left him.

He smiled at her again, and she had to remind herself not to smile in return. How well she remembered that smile.

"I pray you forgive me that, my lady. I have always called you so in my heart."

"In two years, surely you've had dearer things to hold there."

"No, Bess, truly." His face was suddenly solemn. "Nothing dearer than the hope I have of the love that will be between us. I pledged you my love the day we wed, and I mean to prove it true, and not just in words."

He had done that, too, in the short time they had had together before. After she had passed their wedding night in sleepless silence and the dawn had flooded the windows, she had wondered what her father would say, what his father the king would say, when they learned that the marriage contract had not been fully implemented. When Tom woke beside her, she had made a stammering attempt to ask him what they were to do, and, without a moment's pause, he had braced his forearm and made a quick cut across it with his dagger.

"Now there will be no questions," he had said, letting a few drops of blood fall onto the still-pristine sheets.

She had sat on the other side of the bed, swathed in the ornate velvet robe that had been made especially for her wedding morning. For all its lace and fine stitchery, it might have been sackcloth.

"I know you are angry with me, my lord," she had whispered, tears in her eyes.

"You must not think so," he had said as he bound the cut with a handkerchief. "I told you last night that I understand. I do. I want nothing of you that does not come willingly."

There was still a scar inside his arm. She had seen it when he pushed up his sleeve to retrieve her clasp. After so much time had passed it was slight. She would never have noticed it had she not known, but he carried forever that mark of his protective sacrifice.

He did it merely to save his pride, she told herself, *not for love of me or anyone but Thomas Chastelayne*.

She began searching for her comb, saying nothing, and he smiled again, this time a little ruefully.

"Until I have made you sure, Bess, we shall leave things as we had them before. I promise you."

They had spent the remainder of that allotted week sleeping side by side, never touching by so much as a handclasp, but she remembered the tenderness in his words as he tried to put her at ease. And try as she might, she had never been able to forget how he always told her he loved her.

"There is something of the angel in him when he's asleep," she had told Ellen, a shy hope in her eyes, but Ellen had merely laughed and called her a little goose.

"There is something of the angel in all men . . . sleeping. I had a trusting heart myself once, lady, true enough. Until I met a honey-tongued minstrel the summer of my sixteenth year. He was full of pretty words, too, and oaths of love. He was able to play a young girl's will as nimbly as he did the strings of his lute. I gave him my heart and my innocence. In return he gave me a bastard child and the back of his heels when I told him of it."

"Oh, Ellen!"

"I lost the child a month of weeping later. Afterwards, I realized he had done me a great service, teaching me so young what men are. I'd have you learn that lesson, too, lamb, without the pretty price I paid for it. Men are all the same, mark me well."

"But, Ellen, surely not all—"

Ellen had laughed again. Bitterly. "Ah, but you're such a raw young thing yet. You will no doubt believe me one day, after it is too late."

Elizabeth had said no more of it, but she was careful not to think any more soft thoughts toward her young husband after that. When, by the terms of the contract, it was time for her to return to her father's home, he had come to the carriage to bid her farewell.

"I would I could have made you happy here, my lady," he had

said, a touch of wistfulness in his expression. "I promise one day it shall be so. The war will end and you will come back to me, and I will prove you my love."

She had made him no answer, and, with a brief clasp of her hand, he had helped her into the carriage and then signaled the driver. She had watched him as they pulled away, watched him standing there with an unaccountable sorrow in his handsome face, deep longing in his dark eyes. To her amazement, he had begun to run, his long legs fleetly closing the distance between them. Though the horses had picked up speed, he had taken a running leap and braced himself against the window frame to reach in to her. His desperate hands had clasped hers, and he had briefly lifted his feet off the ground. Holding tightly, he had pressed her hand with a passionate kiss. She had heard the thump of his boots as he took a couple of running steps and pushed himself free of the carriage.

"Bess!" he had cried, his chest heaving as he stood there in the road. "I do love you!"

She had lain back against the cushions, breathless, too dazed to move. Then she had realized there was something in her hand. It was a bracelet of linked violets and saint's rose, delicately wrought in gold and, like the ceiling of the bridal chamber, adorned with intertwined *T*'s and *E*'s, another sweet pledge of his truth. It shamed her to remember all this now.

What a child I was then, she told herself scornfully. *What is he but a man? I needn't fear him unless I am fool enough to let him deceive me with his practiced words*.

She would not be so easily led, not even with this man who claimed such love for her. From what she could tell, all men spoke so. Well, her husband might by law be master of her body, but nothing more. And even that, perhaps, could be avoided.

She gave Tom a hard look. Then she opened the jewel chest one of her women had placed on the table and took the bracelet out of it.

"Take this back again, my lord. I cannot wear it. I know the meaning it holds for you."

He clasped her hand around it and would not take it from her.

"Wear it, Bess, for my sake. For the promise of what we will have."

"I cannot promise that, my lord."

"Then for my promise to you. Please."

"If you command it, your highness."

"No," he said quickly. "I'll not have you wear it but freely."

She looked away from him, feeling her resolve soften at the longing in his eyes. "I cannot."

He held her hand a moment more, then released it with a squeeze. "I will keep it for you. For when you want it."

He took the bracelet from her, looking on it as it lay coiled in his hand, admiring its perfection, saddened that it, too, would be left wasted.

"I needn't sleep here, my lady, if you would prefer I did not."

"You know what a scandal that would be in the court, my lord," she told him, searching again for her comb. "I do not know how you could even suggest such a thing."

"What do I care for gossip, Bess? They will talk anyway. My only concern is for your happiness." He found her comb, which had fallen under the table, and handed it to her. "Tell me how you would have it be, my lady, and it shall be so."

"Stay here, my lord," she told him hesitantly. "Until enough time has passed that there will be no talk."

"Very well." He touched her hand with the gentlest hint of a kiss. "I will leave you to your rest for now and come for you at supper."

"He is gone so soon?" Ellen asked, scurrying back into the chamber once he had left it. "That's a wonder."

Elizabeth shook her hair out loose, letting it fall to her hips.

"There were matters we had to settle before tonight, but they took only a moment." She rubbed her hand, still feeling the warm caress of Tom's lips against it. "He was most considerate of me."

"Doubtless he wants you well rested," Ellen said, pursing her withered lips. Fighting sudden tears, Elizabeth did not reply.

CHAPTER

ELIZABETH COULD SEE THE ADMIRATION IN HER HUSBAND'S EYES when he came for her later that night. She was dressed in a sky-colored velvet gown trimmed with rich ermine and cut low off her shapely shoulders. Her hair cascaded in dark auburn ringlets down her back. She knew she looked far more attractive than she had earlier, far more attractive than she wanted him to see, but she could not again stand before the appraising eyes of the court, beside the unaugmented perfection of the queen, looking less than her best.

"How lovely you are, Bess," he said warmly, but that same warmth had been in his tone when her dress had been harsh and plain, and it made her wonder.

"I thank you, my lord," she murmured.

She took the arm he offered, and they said no more until they reached the great hall where, between the many toasts and speeches and other diversions, there was little need for conversation. She was glad for the chance to look over the nobility again, to try to place names with faces, to try to remember those she had met before.

She remembered the brawny, brown-bearded man who was standing behind the king's chair, Philip's personal servant, Rafe Bonnechamp. Tom had told her his father had given this man charge over him and his brothers while they were growing up. Now, of course, Tom and Philip both had a host of servants to wait on them, but it was obvious from the way Rafe watched over his master that he still considered the king his particular responsibility.

She knew, too, that it was with reluctance that the older man had relinquished his responsibility for her husband to the man who stood beside him now, the one-time soldier who was more Tom's friend than servant. Rafe was nearing sixty and Tom's man, Palmer, was, her best guess, in his middle thirties, but both of them were fiercely loyal and took a gruff pride in the service with which they had been entrusted.

Her eyes moved from them to a fair-haired girl her own age, perhaps a year or so younger, sitting a few places down from the king. Elizabeth recognized her as the daughter of Edmund Dunois, Baron of Paxton, Lord High Chamberlain to the old king and the king before him. Dunois had turned traitor, she had heard, secretly supporting Ellenshaw's attempted overthrow, using his position to betray those he served. He had even tried to take King Philip's life, but he had been killed in the attempt.

After that, he had been attainted for his treason and all his lands and goods were forfeited to the crown. By law, his daughter, Marian, could have been imprisoned or banished as well, even though she had repudiated her father's rebellion, but the king had forbidden that, and she was given a place of honor at court, despite her impoverished state.

Elizabeth noticed that she seemed to be spending most of the evening in shy conversation with one of the king's pages, a lanky, sharp-featured boy with dark blond hair and a crooked smile.

"Mary and Joseph, may I never sink so low," she murmured.

"Something does not please you, my lady?" Tom asked her.

"Who is that boy that he dares speak so freely with a noblewoman?"

"That is Jerome, my lady, and I would advise you not to speak ill of him before the king or the queen. He did them great service of late, and we are all grateful for it. Philip would do much more than employ him as a page if Jerome would allow it." Tom smiled. "Besides, I've never known him to overstep his place, especially with a lady. Especially with that lady."

"You sound as if you would approve if he did."

"Anyone with eyes can see they love each other, but neither of them is bold enough to say so."

"But, my lord, even if her father was a traitor, surely the king would never allow some peasant—"

"You may be surprised at the king's views of peasants marrying nobles, Bess."

"As you say, my lord," she replied, a cynical edge to her voice, "I may be surprised."

"I beg your pardon, my lord."

Elizabeth looked up to see Tom's serving man standing at her shoulder.

"What is it, Palmer?" Tom asked, and Palmer leaned a little closer, putting up his hand to keep his long hair from falling into his face.

"The king would speak to you a moment, sir."

Tom stood up and covered Elizabeth's hand with his own. "I beg your indulgence, my lady. Palmer will bring you anything you need."

She looked up at the man, trying to read something in his imperturbable, olive-skinned face that would explain why her husband had been called away. Something told her that simply asking would yield her nothing, that it would take a command from his master or from the king himself to unseal his firm lips.

When she turned again to her plate, she saw that Taliferro had slipped into Tom's place beside her.

"Oh, my lord, good evening."

"Good evening, Madonna. I dare say the angels of heaven do not shine so fair tonight as you."

She smiled at him, feeling some of her tenseness dissipate. "I was just wondering if I was to see anyone familiar tonight."

"And here I am to keep you company. But where is the groom this evening? Surely he's not found another already."

"Oh, no," she told him, laughing at his exaggerated concern. "He's merely been called away to the king for a moment."

"In the midst of your banquet, Madonna? How very odd. But, of course, he's told you the reason for it."

She sighed. "No, merely that he would be back soon."

"Secrets already, my lady, and just your first night returned. Tsk, tsk."

She laughed again. "How good it is to speak to someone from home, my lord. Tell me, what is it you are doing here and in Warring?"

"The king has graciously granted us relief from our losses in the war. He has provided food and clothing and other supplies for the poor, to allow us to rebuild and become self-sufficient once more. I am overseeing the distribution of it."

"How noble of you, my lord, to see to such a thing yourself."

"Yes," Tom said, coming back to the table, "the baron has already taken almost half of what we have in store for the winter. Warring should be quite prosperous come spring."

"I trust it shall be so," Taliferro said as he stood up and smoothly offered Tom's chair back to him.

Tom sat down. "I thank you, my lord, that you kept my lady company while I had to be away, but I would not want to keep you any longer from your friends."

"Not at all, my lord," Taliferro replied, his black eyes narrowing almost imperceptibly. He kissed Elizabeth's hand. "Good evening, my lady."

Elizabeth watched him move to the other side of the room and strike up an animated conversation with the queen's sister, Lady Margaret. She took a taut sip of wine, not looking at her husband.

"Forgive me being away from you, my lady," Tom said after a moment.

"What did he want, my lord?"

"Philip? Oh, merely a matter of state, nothing more."

"That could not wait until tomorrow? Do you not think it odd, my lord?"

"I grant you, yes, but it is an unusual thing."

"And can you not tell me of it?"

"Really, my lady, it cannot be of interest to you."

She lifted her eyes to his. "Are we to have secrets between us already, my lord?"

He smiled and slipped his hand over hers once again. "Well, I will tell you then, though there is little enough of it yet to know. Lord Darlington's aide, a man called Ralph Mowbray, has been missing almost a month now. He was given some papers to deliver about the treaty we're to make with Grenaver, but he never came there. The rest is merely a blank."

"Do you think he's betrayed you, my lord?" she asked, a spark of excitement in her eyes, and he laughed.

"There was little in what he had that could be used in a betrayal, even did we suspect he could not be trusted. That was what Philip wanted to know. He and Darlington happened to be discussing it, and, since I drafted some of the papers, they merely wanted my assurance that what he was carrying was nothing of strategic value."

"Oh," she said, disappointed.

"I am sorry there was nothing more intriguing than that, love. Come, dance with me."

The next few days passed quickly, and Elizabeth found her husband scrupulously true to his word. They had danced that first evening of her return and on several occasions afterward, but, although she could feel the quickening in his pulse as he held her and see the light of passion in his dark eyes, when they went to bed he did no more than hold her hand in his, or touch his lips to it in gentle good night, and then sleep in perfect chastity beside her. She found it faintly disturbing that she felt a tinge of disappointment when he made no attempt at anything else.

She watched him sprawled out next to her with one arm unwittingly draped across her pillow and his head turned toward her, and she recalled the feel of his arms around her.

"*Let him kiss me with the kisses of his mouth*," she thought. Startled, she murmured a quick prayer for forgiveness, remembering from years before the solemn beating and the stern lecture she received when she was caught reading that most beautiful of songs, the Song of Solomon.

"It is wickedness to think such things or to desire such things,"

Sister Margaretta had told her. "A modest, godly young woman does not soil her thoughts with such things. When you are a wife, you must submit to your husband, but you must not indulge your flesh. Marriage is for the propagation of children. Nothing else."

Elizabeth had been too ashamed even to look at her, much less reply, so Sister Margaretta went on.

"Do not let the devil steal your soul for such wickedness. He will tell you that you will find pleasure in a man's embrace, but men desire women only for their own selfish reasons. As a woman, you must submit to that as your duty, but do not fool yourself to imagine that you are eager for it . . . like any harlot."

The hard words had stung her more than the blows.

Like any harlot, she thought once more, looking at her husband as he lay there breathing soft and deep, his lips moist and alluring. More of the forbidden words came back to her. "*His mouth is most sweet; he is altogether lovely. . .*"

Do not let the devil steal your soul for such wickedness, she heard Sister Margaretta warn again.

Elizabeth wondered at the wisdom of having Tom in her bed, even for appearance's sake. The short time she had been at court now had been nothing like the week she had spent with him before. Then she had been weary and afraid. Now, knowing he would show her only kindness, knowing he could be trusted so near, she began to mistrust herself. Even innocently asleep, he radiated a tantalizing masculinity that drew her, instinctively, undeniably.

She could have submitted to him as his wife, but she was so afraid that the sinful passions that burned inside her would draw her into hell if ever she let him kiss her with that sweet mouth, if ever she allowed herself to be taken into his embrace. And then, once she was lost to him, there would come betrayal, as sure as winter followed summer or night, day. And she would be left the fool.

He turned over, smiling faintly in his sleep, and her eyes grew cold.

"Do not even imagine it, my lord," she said. She pulled the bedclothes more closely around her and tried to sleep.

A few nights later, Tom sat in the great hall, sipping the last of the wine he had had at supper, watching lovers nestle in pairs before the fire as the musicians played. He felt again the empty ache in his heart. Even Philip and Rosalynde were there, cuddling together, punctuating their soft talk with an occasional sweet kiss.

It would be Christmas soon, and it seemed so many of Tom's Christmases held this hollowness, especially these last two, when he knew Elizabeth was his but he could not be with her. He had thought this Christmas would be different. She was with him now, but still she was not. She did not want him and the love he had to give.

"God, be with me, Lord," he prayed. "Fill this emptiness. Let her know just a part of the love I have for her."

He saw her near the fire, bathed in its flickering light, the white purity of her satin dress glowing orange from the blaze. It was a wonder that she did not burst into flame, standing so close. Taliferro was there beside her as always, drinking in her naivete and, after a few minutes, the two of them wandered out onto the balcony, talking still in low whispers.

Tom did not wait long to follow after them, but, when he stepped outside, Taliferro had somehow melted away and Elizabeth was by herself, leaning on the low wall, watching the full moon.

"A fine, fair night, is it not, my lady?" Tom said, coming up to her. "Warm to be so near Christmas, but perhaps a trifle brisk for standing alone."

He put his arm around her, just lightly, but the moon was cold-hearted that night and disinclined to play matchmaker. She stiffened her back and moved out of his embrace.

"It suits me very well," she said. "Alone."

He glanced at his empty hand and let it drop to his side. "Bess, love—"

"I trust you do not object to my taking the air, my lord."

"Of course not, as I trust you do not object to my standing with you."

She said nothing, and, after a moment, he looked back into the night sky.

"It is almost light as day out here with that moon," he observed. "Does it look so in Aberwain?"

"Some nights," she said, leaning on the wall again. "The stars are the same."

He smiled and leaned down beside her. "You can make pictures of them, if you look at them aright. They say God wrote all the story of man's redemption in the stars. See, there's a perfect cross."

She looked up where he pointed. "So it is," she said, surprised. "I have never tried to make pictures of them, but . . ."

She did not finish, and he looked into her eyes, his own encouraging her to continue.

"I have one I wish on," she admitted finally.

"Truly? Which one?"

"That one there," she said, pointing to the bright star that peeped over the highest spire of Winterbrooke Cathedral. Noticing his half-hidden smile, she flushed slightly. "It is a childish thing, I know."

"I know," he said, slipping his hand into hers. "That is my star, too. I hope you will share it with me. It is not only children who need something to dream on."

Her mouth turned up just the tiniest bit, and he was sure she was unaware of the soft wonder in her eyes. Such beautiful eyes.

"I suppose you think me a silly thing," she said after a moment. "It's no wonder you smile."

"I think you a precious thing, and should a man not smile on the one he best loves?"

Seeing her startled expression, he turned her to face him.

"Hear me now, Bess. I do not say lightly to you what I have never said to anyone else. I do not believe I have yet given you cause to doubt my word."

"No," she admitted.

"While you were in the quiet shelter of the convent or at your father's house, I was on the battlefield or captive or in hiding. I've seen enough yet, my lady, to know what it is I want from my life and what a misery it is without love."

"Everyone loves you, my lord, from the kitchen wenches up. No one could stay long at court and miss that."

"That's not the love I mean, Bess. I want that special love one man has for one woman and she for him, above all other earthly loves. I want what my brother has with his lady."

"I think it ill becomes the king of Lynaleigh to do his whoring before the whole court."

Tom laughed. "Whoring? They were but kissing, Bess. Faith, she is his wife."

"Then he should treat her as a wife, not a slut," she said, her mouth in a prim line. "Though I suppose any man would desire such a wife. Pity there is but one of her."

"The queen is a beautiful and sweet-tempered saint. Philip would be lost without her, and she has loved him with as pure a love as I think it is given for one mortal being to have for another. I cannot choose but love her for that, because she loves him so, but that is all."

"And you can truly say you do not envy your brother his wife?"

"I envy them their love, Bess, I'll not deny it. I covet such a love from you and for you." He squeezed her fingers. "I believe we could have it, too, in time."

For a while she was silent, weighing his words and the fervor in his eyes. She looked away.

"Will you take me in, my lord? The night's grown cold."

"Of course, my lady."

He said nothing more to her that night beyond the simplest of pleasant courtesies, but he could tell she had not forgotten his words. He prayed she would come to believe them, too.

"Give them time, love," Rosalynde told Philip that night when they were in bed. "They are strangers yet."

"He says nothing of it, but he is breaking his heart over her and I can see no reason in it. Why should she not love him?"

"We know there is no reason, but she does not know it yet." She linked her fingers into his. "Every maid has some hesitation at first."

He frowned in impatience. "She's not been a maid in better than two years. Faith, when they were married—"

"I think you mistake in that, my lord," she said softly, and he looked startled.

"Truly? Well, I grant you she was a trifle young then, but, faith, she is not now. It is time she was truly his wife."

"Let them work through this themselves, love. He loves her, and she'll not long be able to resist that. She does not know him yet, not truly." She smiled and snuggled against him. "I was more than a little afraid when we were first married, and I already loved you."

"How did you ever love such a brute?" he asked, leaning his cheek against her dark hair, and she reached up to caress his face.

"I loved the gentlest, truest-hearted man in this wide world. I love him still."

He put his arms around her and pulled her close to his heart.

"What a sweet, blind wonder you are, Rose," he murmured. She drew his mouth down to hers and he said no more.

"I'll not stand for it, Franklin."

Tom stood beside his brother's throne the next morning, listening to Philip reprimand one of the captains of his guard. The man had roughed up one of the girls in one of the inns the night before, but he had had too much to drink to do her much harm and seemed to think that excuse enough for his behavior.

"I'll not stand for it," Philip repeated. "You have been warned before."

"But—but, my lord—"

"Keep silent," Philip commanded, looking as if he might strike the man. "I have told you before, I'll have none of this among my men, especially among my captains."

"But, some peasant slut—"

Ignoring Rosalynde's restraining touch on his arm, Philip grabbed a handful of Franklin's jerkin, tightening it around his throat.

"That *slut* is one of God's creatures, not some beast you may seize and use at your pleasure!" He shoved the man away from him in disgust. "Would you stand before Him and say what you have said to me?"

"No harm was done her," Franklin muttered, hanging his head.

"That was no fault of yours. I should have you whipped and turned out of my service for this, but I will be satisfied instead with your apology to the girl."

"Apology, my lord? Would you shame me before the court?"

"You have shamed me and all Lynaleigh!" Philip lashed back at him. "You *will* beg her pardon." He nodded at Rafe. "Bring her in."

A moment later, Rafe returned, bringing with him a slight, trembling girl, cloaked and hooded.

"You are well treated now?" Philip asked, and she nodded.

"I thank you, your majesty. I am far unworthy your kindness."

Something in her timid voice tickled Tom's memory, but he could not quite say why.

"Captain Franklin has something to say," Philip prompted.

Franklin looked at him and then at Tom, but their faces were alike in stern reproof.

"Your pardon, girl, for my forwardness," he said sullenly, and the girl nodded again.

"Go now," Philip commanded Franklin. "If ever you dishonor Lynaleigh again, I will not hear of leniency, even from the queen."

"No," Rosalynde agreed, uncompromising strength in her delicate face. "You will certainly not hear of it from the queen."

"Forgive me, your majesty, my sovereign lady, I beg you, and I'll not wrong your trust."

"See you do not," Philip said, and Franklin bowed and slunk from the room.

"Again I thank you, your majesty," the girl said, turning as if she, too, would creep away. This time Tom did recognize her voice.

"Molly?"

Her voice dropped even lower. "My lord."

Tom went to her and took her hands.

"Molly, I can scarce believe it! I had men looking for you for weeks after I left Breebonne, and here you appear at my own door!"

She ducked her head and he could hear the tears in her voice. "Can you forgive me for what happened, my lord?"

"I told you before it was no fault of yours."

She looked up at him and the hood fell away from her face.

"Oh, Molly! Who did that to you?"

There was a long, raised scar across one side of her neck, coming from somewhere down her back and ending under her chin. Only a whip would leave such a mark.

"Men from the village," she admitted, pulling back from him and covering it with her hand. "When they found out what my father had done, they came and burned our house. They beat me and turned me out into the woods. My father they hanged in the village square, God forgive him."

"Now you must forgive me," Tom said regretfully. "It was for me they did this and left you with nothing."

She shook her head. "I had nothing before. You know what my father was, what he had me do. Now I can begin again, in some honest place, please God."

"Tell me what you would have, Molly. If money or a word of favor will help you, you shall have them from me." He studied her thin face. "When did you last eat?"

"I had some bread and cheese, my lord."

"When?" he pressed and, in spite of herself, she sighed.

"Yesterday."

"Come with me. Philip, my lady, I trust I may be excused for a moment."

"Do not be long, Tom," Philip said, a touch of severity in his tone, but Rosalynde smiled and Tom bowed to them both.

"Thank you, my lord king, my lady," Molly said with an unskilled curtsey. She followed Tom to the kitchen.

"So that is the girl you told me of," Philip said that night at supper, and Tom nodded.

"I can feel nothing but pity for her. She had no part in what her father did, less in what Weatherford did."

"Who, my lord?" Elizabeth asked.

"During the war, after we lost so badly at Grant, I had to take shelter in the woods," Tom explained. "Molly was kind enough to take me in."

"But what did her father do?"

Tom shrugged a little. "Ellenshaw had set a reward for my capture. Her father brought the Duke of Weatherford and some of Ellenshaw's other men to their cottage to take me prisoner, but, as I said, that was none of Molly's doing."

"Did one of the cooks feed her, my lord?" Rosalynde asked.

"Yes, my lady. I doubt she's eaten much in the past few months. Philip, I was thinking she might have some work to do here in the palace to earn her way now that her home is gone."

"I take it she has taken up another trade since you saw her last," Philip said, keeping his eyes on his plate as he prodded his meat with his fork. He looked as if he did not care for the idea of having the girl at court. Elizabeth had no doubt why that was or what this Molly's profession had been.

"She will be glad for something else, I am certain," Tom replied. "Philip, can we not help her begin again? Surely I owe her that much."

"I will leave that to you," Philip said after a moment. "You had the most wrong at her hands."

"At her father's," Tom said, "and she paid for his wrongs with all she had. Is it not enough?"

Philip looked at his wife with a reluctant smile. "You'd not have us turn her away, would you, Rose?"

Rosalynde put her hand over his and looked up into his face. "No, my lord, you know I would not."

"How can I stand against that, Tom? Do as pleases you, then. Between the two of them, Lady Elizabeth, we'll have every stray in the kingdom right here in Winton in another month."

Elizabeth answered him with only a polite smile.

"Tell me again about this girl who came to court today, my lord," Elizabeth said when she and Tom were alone that night. Ellen had already taken down her hair, but she sat before her glass still, combing through it one meticulous handful at a time, certain he was watching her.

"Who? Molly?" he asked, stretching himself the whole length of the bed. "What's to know?"

"Why did the king not want her here?"

"He never said that."

"Only in every way but words." She came from the mirror to the bed, still holding her comb. "Why is that, my lord?"

"Bess—"

"Because he knows her for what she is, is that not so?"

"Was," Tom corrected, sitting up. "Bess, you must understand, she was only doing what her father forced her to do. She told me he often sold her, sometimes for little more than the price of a cup of ale."

She could see in his face the tenderness he had for the wench. Was it only pity or was it something more?

"You've not told me everything of what happened when you were with her, have you, my lord?" she asked as she sat down on the bed beside him and crossed her legs under her.

"There is hardly any more to be told," he said, but she saw a touch of added color in his face.

"But there is *something* more, I see," she said, folding her hands in her lap, telling herself it made little difference to her what he did now or had done then.

"Her father told her to get my ring from me in payment," he said reluctantly, looking at the ruby he always wore, the one that, like his brother's and like the smaller version the queen wore, was a symbol of Lynaleighan royalty. "She did not know he had recognized me by it and meant her to keep me occupied until he returned with Ellenshaw's men, but she dared not disobey him. Faith, she was hardly more than a child."

"They go to it easy enough, these children," Elizabeth observed with forced calm, pulling her comb through her thick curls again. "So she seduced you for no more than the worth of the gold in your ring, though I see it must not have cost you even that."

"You are wrong, Bess. There was nothing between us in that way. True, she tried to do as her father bade her, but I told her I belonged to another."

He took her comb and laid it beside her. Then he captured her hand in his, her eyes in his.

"I told her I belonged to the sweetest lady in Christendom and that I could not betray her."

"You never said so," Elizabeth retorted. Then she looked at his hand, gentle and persuasive on hers, and once more into his eyes, his fascinating, undeniable eyes.

"My lord, did you?" she asked, biting her lower lip.

"In those very words, sweetheart."

A smile of shy pleasure touched her mouth, and he drew her hand against his heart.

"Do you feel that?" he asked softly. She could not help but feel the strong, steady beat under her fingers. "That belongs to you, Bess. No one else."

She swallowed with difficulty, too well aware of the warm, muscled bareness of his chest, unsure now if the too-rapid pounding she felt came from his heart or hers. The pounding only increased when he bent down and pressed a slow, expressive kiss against the hand he held.

"Good night, love."

Long after he was asleep, she still thought of what he had said and, more, of how he had said it, with his eyes and with his gentle touch, with the brush of his lips. Could he be so true as he claimed? She watched him as he lay beside her, one arm flung over his head and his other hand under his cheek.

There's something of the angel in him when he's asleep, she remembered, and she could still see Ellen's sour lips pursed in disgust.

"There's something of the angel in all men . . . sleeping."

He did look like an angel, as innocent as grace itself. The hypocrite! He looked so and yet she knew he was not. He could not be. No man was.

She watched his mouth, his softly parted lips, and thought what it might be like to kiss him, to be kissed by him as he had no doubt kissed this creature Molly or who knew how many others. Dare he sleep beside her now in such conscienceless peace?

He took a deep breath and rolled over onto his stomach, and she found herself admiring the broad sleekness of his shoulders and the soft, dark thickness of his hair. He was close now. If she reached out even a little, she could trace the handsome line of his jaw, feel the warmth of his skin.

She stretched out her hand, but faltered before she ever reached him. Instead, she moved carefully closer, laying her head near his so she could study his face.

Deceivers all.

The black fringe of his lashes lay lightly against his skin, but she knew the frank openness that would have been in his eyes had he been awake. Could there be something hidden in their velvet depths? More and more she could not believe it. Taliferro's eyes held such mysteries, things dark and secret, things forbidden, but not Tom's.

He was close now. She could feel the warmth of him and the faint tickle of his breath in her hair. He slept so soundly, she was certain he would never know it if she moved just the tiniest bit closer and touched her lips to his.

She trembled as she did it, but he did not waken, and she decided to risk another taste. Before she realized it, her mouth was over his, and she was touching his cheek, stroking his hair.

He dropped one limp arm over her and then woke with a start.

"Bess?"

She pulled her hand back, a guilty flush on her face, but he caught her fingers in his and brought them to his lips. She could see the longing in his eyes, but there was understanding and restraint there, too. He would never force her. He would never even try to coax her until she showed him she was willing to be coaxed.

She leaned up on her elbow and looked at his hand as it held hers. It was a strong hand, but its touch was tender and unthreatening. He could have used the power in that hand . . . She let her eyes follow along the line of his arm to his shoulder. He could have used all the power of his finely muscled body to force her to his will. She was his by every law of God and man, but she knew he would not.

Her glance went up along the line of his throat to his well-modeled chin and came to rest again on his mouth. Could there be so much harm in just one kiss? That other, while he was asleep, had been too brief a taste. What might it be like to kiss him and be kissed by him?

She slipped her hand free of his and hesitantly touched his lips. He lay still, watching her, passion kindling in the dark depths of his eyes. What might it be like?

She leaned swiftly over to kiss him.

"Bess—"

She stopped his mouth with another kiss, and his arms went around her, pulling her to him, holding her in a tight, hungry embrace.

"No," she gasped, struggling. "Please, no."

He released her immediately and then quickly reclaimed her hand, letting her away from him but not quite.

"Shh, Bess, do not fear." He squeezed her fingers. "No more than this, sweet, I promise. Until you ask me."

She looked away from the disappointment that was only partly concealed by the gentle patience in his eyes and lay down again.

"Bess?"

When she made him no answer, he turned onto his back and looked up at the painted ceiling.

"I love you, Bess."

She pressed her face into the pillows, tears burning in her eyes until she fell asleep.

CHAPTER

A FEW DAYS LATER ELIZABETH LET TOM COAX HER INTO GOING out walking with him. There had been no reference made to the events of that night and certainly no repeat of them, and he had spent the time since slowly, steadily, painstakingly showing her his patient love. He was careful not to touch her again, even in the most casual way, but still she was wary of him.

They had walked more than a mile along the snowy river bank before he finally broke the silence.

"Bess," he began, slowing to a stop, "will you tell me something?"

"My lord?"

"That night you kissed me—"

"I have no wish to be anyone's harlot, my lord," she snapped, her face flushed and her eyes defiant, and he was astonished by the sudden vehemence in the words.

"I could never think so of you, Bess. You are my wife. Nothing less."

"As well one as the other."

"Sweet heavens, love, do you think so of all marriages or just ours?"

"Most," she said decidedly. "My mother was nothing more to my father, until he tired of her and she was nothing to him at all."

"Who told you that?"

"Ellen did, but I saw for myself as well. My father flaunts his mistresses before my mother's face, makes light of his infidelities, mocks the shame he brings her."

"And she loves him still?"

"She did once. Perhaps she does yet. I do not know. How she could, I am certain I do not know."

"If she ever did truly love him, beyond herself, she loves him still. True love does not fail because the beloved does. Even bruised and bloodied, it loves on."

In his eyes there was once more that deep promise of forever that she could not answer.

"Women may love so, my lord," she said finally. "There was never a man could keep a vow of love past a maid's resistance."

"That is true of some men," he allowed, "as it is of some women, but not all."

"So you think for all their years married, your father was always true to your mother? That your brother was never false to the queen?"

"I could never believe otherwise. Philip would die for the queen's sake, I know. We Chastelaynes, when we stoop to love, love with all that is in us. I think everything my father did, before and after my mother died, was because of her."

She looked at him as if she did not quite believe him. "And he never played her false?"

"No," he said, as if he had never considered it before. "I do not think he ever did. For all his faults, he did not fail in that. He loved her with his whole heart, and she loved nothing but his royalty." He was silent for a moment, and, when he did speak, there was an added depth of emotion in his voice. "I have never told anyone this, Bess. Even Philip and I do not speak of it. But my mother was not faithful to my father. Doubtless she had her reasons—those are easily come by if one wants them badly enough. But it does not change the fact that she was an adulteress. When my father found her so, he acted out of the pain her betrayal left him, knowing all his love for her had gone for nothing. That would go near to crush the heart out of any man."

"Perhaps so," she agreed, "and all the more reason that you should understand why I do not wish to play harlot to you, only to be deceived later on."

"I could have had any number of harlots by now, my lady, had I wanted them. I much rather would have a wife. I have told you so often that I love you. Will you never believe me?"

"I suppose your mother never said she loved your father?"

He sighed heavily. "Often."

She gave him a cynical, triumphant smile, and began walking again.

"Bess, please, hear me out." He took two long strides to catch up to her. "What of those things you said to me?"

"When, my lord?"

"The other night."

"I said nothing," she told him, feeling the blood come up in her cheeks.

"You did. With the look in your eyes, with the touch of your hands, and the touch of your lips, you spoke volumes. Did you speak false, Bess?"

"I said nothing," she insisted. "I have been raised in the fear of God, my lord. I am not one of your court wantons or some village hussy. I crave your pardon for the unseemly way I behaved that night, and I pray you will be kind enough not to make reference to it again."

"Unseemly? Bess, am I not your husband? God meant husbands and wives to feel so toward one another."

"That's not so, my lord. You blaspheme to say it."

"It is so. I will show it to you in Scripture."

"It is best to leave that to the clergy," she said after a bewildered moment. "We are like to err in our interpretation of it."

"Have you never looked into it yourself, Bess?" he asked.

"Once."

"What did you read?"

"My lord, I—"

"His mouth is most sweet . . ."

She could not look at him. "I have forgotten now."

"Have you ever heard the part that says wives must obey their husbands?"

She jerked her chin up, the defiant light again in her eyes. "I have."

"Have you ever heard what goes with it?"

"What is that, my lord?"

"That husbands must love their wives just as Christ loves His church."

A touch of wonder struggled with the rebelliousness on her face. "Does it say so, truly?"

"It does. If a man were to love a woman so, my lady, would she, to your reasoning, have any need to fear obedience to him?"

"No," she said, searching his face for some sign of deceit, "I suppose she would not, but there is no man who could love so. It is not possible."

"Not in himself, but by God's grace and with His help, he could. God would not command it if it were not possible."

She struggled to make her expression disdainful, but she could only manage uncertainty. "And I suppose I am to believe you love me so?"

"You may believe as pleases you, my lady, but I mean to come as near that as I am able." He took her hand. "I pledge it."

"That is easily said," she replied half under her breath, but there was nothing in his look, in the unfeigned fervency of his words, that made her think he did not speak true. She remembered still more of the words she had in secret read. *"Turn your eyes away from me, for they have overcome me . . ."*

He looked steadily at her. "Whoever has wronged you, Bess, whoever has poisoned your heart against me, please put that behind you. You needn't fear to trust me."

She freed her hand and began walking again, slowly, her eyes on the snowy ground. After a moment he was beside her once more.

"What would you have of me, my lord?" she asked him finally. "Would you have me pretend something I do not feel?"

"No, love, never that. Just do not deny those feelings you *do* have. Let me woo you. Let me woo you as I should have done had it been allowed me before we married. Then if you find still you cannot love me, at least you will have true cause for it."

"There is no need, my lord," she said. "I am your wife and I know it is my place to obey you. All you need do is say. I will do as you ask."

"You were my wife before," he reminded her and she felt her face redden again.

"I was a child then. I have done with childish things."

He smiled a little. "Not all of them, I hope. We all must have at least the faith of children, if ever we're to see heaven."

"Is that in the Scripture, too?"

He nodded. "Would you care to see it?"

"They say you are a Heretic, my lord," she said after a moment. "Are you?"

"I count myself one, yes. I know there are many who do not approve our ways, but the church has fallen away from many of the true things of God, and we mean to go back to them. The church keeps the Scriptures from the people and uses their fear and ignorance as a whip against them. I believe God wants to speak to every man through His Word, not just to the priests, and that we all must know Him in our own hearts, through Jesus Christ, if we are to have redemption. The church may guide, but it cannot save."

She had heard this before, but hearing it spoken so plainly was still rather shocking.

"It is something I must think on awhile, my lord," she said finally. "Do you often read the Scriptures?"

"Yes."

Her eyes got a little rounder. "Does the king know?"

Tom laughed. "Of course. Oh, sweetheart, if only you knew how much I love you and how much more God Himself does, you would want to read it, too."

"Does it say so? That He loves me?"

"Many, many times—with an everlasting, unshakable love that will never change."

She shook her head slightly. "I think I would have to be very, very good before He would love me so. Some of the sisters at the convent I think were so good. Perhaps the queen, too. They say she's done much out of charity and is very devout."

"You cannot earn that love, Bess, no matter how devout you may be. It is His grace that gives it and not our poor deeds. None of us, even those the church calls saints, is worthy of it."

"You *are* a Heretic," she said. "Do you also hold with those who destroy the relics and smash the statues and shatter the great windows? It is being done all through the kingdom, I hear."

"No, I do not hold with that. If some of the peasants worship such objects in the place of God, destroying those things will not alter that belief. We must pray God will change the hearts of those people. We must see they are taught truly to know Him. Then they will see those things for what they are . . . merely monuments to His glory. I've seen some of the destruction that has been done in the name of God by those who claim to be His. There is a better way, Bess. I know there is."

She had no reply to that, and they walked back into the city, saying little more. He stopped when they reached Winterbrooke Cathedral.

"Will you come with me a moment, my lady?"

She looked up at the imposing place, still magnificent despite the ravages of the war, and noticed again the diligent reconstruction it was undergoing. Even since her arrival, there had been marked progress, though it was likely to be many years before the restoration was complete.

"I went to mass already this morning," she replied, and, with a touch of amusement, Tom shook his head.

"I want to show you something, Bess, if you will."

She followed him up the steps, through the nave, and into the chapel set in one side.

"Oh, my lord," she breathed in amazement. "How beautiful."

The chapel was small, almost circular, with a vaulted ceiling supported with incredibly delicate stone arches, all fluted and overlaid with gold. Within each arch was a stained glass window, all of them together presenting a progression of four hundred years of Chastelayne kings, all kneeling at the feet of the King of Kings, who stood in glory in their midst. Looking closer, she could see the intricate detail in the glass, the borders interwoven with the emblem of each king and with the white saint's rose, the symbol of all the Chastelaynes, showing everywhere.

"How beautiful," she whispered again, mesmerized by the jewels of color the sun scattered across the pale marble floor once it passed through the glass.

"They call it the Chapel of the Kings now that it has been redone," Tom told her, grinning. "I cannot fathom why."

She smiled at him. "It is truly glorious, my lord. I thank you for showing it to me."

"I am glad it pleases you, but that is not why I brought you here. I want you to read something."

He summoned her to the altar beneath the center window, and she saw that there was a Bible lying open on it, perhaps the very one the archbishop had stood before when he performed their wedding ceremony. She was fascinated by the illuminated pages, elaborately detailed from border to border and further gilded by the multicolored light.

One by one, from page to page, he showed her the verses he had spoken of, the ones that told of God's abiding love, of the love and pleasure He meant for marriage, of the righteousness that came solely through faith in His Son. It amazed her how well Tom knew this Book, how easily he took her from one place to another to prove he had spoken nothing but truth to her, and how patiently he answered the questions she asked.

The setting sun was adding orange fire to the light that came in through the stained-glass windows before the two of them left the chapel. By then, Elizabeth was worn out with the tumult of thoughts churning inside her.

"It is something I will have to think on, my lord," she told him. "I wonder if . . ."

"What?"

"Might we talk again of this, my lord?"

He smiled at the timidity in her tone.

"When you will, my lady, and it would please me very much."

"Tomorrow?"

"Tomorrow it is."

She asked him a few more things that night at supper and in bed before they fell asleep, and they spent much of the next few days discussing the things they read and the things he told her, reconciling the beliefs she had held from her childhood to the truth in the Scriptures. And, though he did not realize it, she was becoming aware of the nature of Christ that was demonstrated to the world through His followers, through those, like Tom, who knew and served Him.

It was something she had not considered before, the possibility that her husband could be precisely as he presented himself to be *because* of this intimate relationship with his Lord. Perhaps such a man could be trusted with a woman's fragile heart.

She had counted herself to be a good follower of the church, going to mass almost every day, going to confession and doing the penance the priest assigned to her, taking communion and observing the holy days, but what Tom had was different. There was a light inside him, a reflection of the steadfast love that filled the Scripture, a love that was as undeserved as it was freely given. It was not ritual but true relationship that guided his life.

They often walked beside the frozen river during that time, talking sometimes of what they had read, sometimes of other things, and she found herself smiling, even laughing, almost as often as he did. It began to feel less and less strange to walk with her hand in his, to enjoy the tales he told her of this place and of his boyhood home in the north, to see the sweet warmth in his eyes and not suspect it. She did not know it, but gradually her face lost that mistrustful look she had copied from Ellen, and, her skin glowing from the exercise and from the brisk wind, she changed from merely pretty to truly beautiful.

He managed to refrain from telling her so, attempted, with a measure of success, to keep the look of it out of his eyes when he answered her many questions, but by the end of the week he could not resist one question of his own.

"Bess," he asked, looking out toward the river as they walked, "will you answer me something?"

"My lord?"

"Might I say we are friends now?"

"Friends?"

He turned to her, smiling at the pleased surprise in her tone, and she could not resist a smile of her own.

"Why, my lord?"

"Because," he said, squeezing her hand and going faster. "Because there is so much I want to do that's better shared."

He turned to face her, walking backwards and pulling her with him.

"Run with me to the top of the hill," he urged. "Lie with me in the grass when it comes back fresh in the spring and count the evening stars. Catch snowflakes with me in the winters. Tell me what you dream and what your heart says when it speaks to you alone." He caught her other hand in his eagerness. "Tell me what you want most in all the world and how I can get it for you."

"My lord," she said, breathless at the rush of ideas he was laying before her, for now and for their times to come. "My lord—"

"Hear the songs," he said, moving her with him, turning, twirling, as if there were music to their dance. "There are always songs, Bess, if you will hear them."

He pulled her against him, whirling faster and faster, and she couldn't help laughing at the simple pleasure of it, of the brisk air and blue sky and the joy in his brown velvet eyes. She clung more tightly to him and felt her feet leave the ground.

"My lord!" she squealed, clutching him close, and he slowed to a stop, laughing, too.

"Oh, Bess, you do not know how I love having you here."

She caught her breath, all at once aware of the innocent nearness of his lips to hers and the snug warmth of his embrace.

"I—I would like some water, my lord," she said, feeling suddenly shy, but she did not take her hand from his when he led her to the river.

"The ice may be too thick here," he said, "but we should be able to find a place where—"

He stopped abruptly and tried to turn her back toward the forest.

"Bess, please—"

"What?"

Then she saw it. There, staring up through the ice, was one of the soldiers, his pale eyes wide and surprised, his lank blond hair darkened with ice and blood.

"Who is it?" she gasped, unable to tear her eyes away from the gruesome sight.

"He's been missing for some while now," Tom said. "Come, let's go back."

"That is the messenger you told me of. What happened to him, my lord?" she asked as he pulled her away.

"Please, love—"

"His throat was cut," she breathed, her wide eyes fixed on his. She hid her face against him. "Who would do such a thing?"

"Who would do such a thing?" Philip asked when Tom brought him the news.

"My lord, I never knew him to have an enemy," Lord Darlington replied, and then added grimly, "unless it might be a jealous husband."

"Do you think that might be the case here?"

Darlington shrugged. "His fellows claim he had a mistress high up in court, ever since the end of the war, but he would never say who."

"And the papers he carried?"

"I thought it best to bring my lady away from where he was," Tom explained, "and I had nothing I could use to break him out of the ice, so I could not check him over. My lord Darlington, I expect you will send some of your men to bring him back. Have them search for his pouch as well."

"At once, my lord."

"Then see him buried," Philip said. "And God pardon him."

The pouch was still strapped across Mowbray's shoulder when he was chipped out of the ice, and, though the water had turned them into a pulpy, illegible mass, it seemed obvious that all of the papers that had been entrusted to him were still there. Darlington conjectured that he had been killed and thrown into the river weeks ago and that the recent warm spell had caused enough of a thaw to let his body wash downstream before freezing again where Tom and Elizabeth had found it.

Having ruled out any political motive, no one in the council could fathom any reason for the murder save jealousy, as Darlington had suggested. Despite much inquiry, there was no one who could confirm or deny such a theory, and the identity of Mowbray's high-born mistress remained unknown.

CHAPTER

IT WAS TWO DAYS UNTIL CHRISTMAS, AND STILL IT WAS JUST COLD enough to keep the thick snow on the ground and the freshness in the air. What clouds there were were white and fluffy, tossed across the blue sky with careless perfection.

"Are you hungry, my lady?" Tom asked.

"Yes," Elizabeth admitted. Since Mowbray's body had been found, they had begun taking their walks on the other side of the forest, away from the river. They had been out for most of the morning already today, talking of this and that, and she hadn't realized how quickly the time had gone. "Shall we go back to the palace?"

A touch of mystery in his smile, he led her further into the forest, into a small tree-sheltered clearing not far from a shallow stream. There, on a pile of blankets, surrounded by a lavish banquet, sat the king and queen, smiling at the astonishment on Elizabeth's face.

"A picnic? In December?"

"It is lovely out just now," Tom told her. "We thought you might enjoy it."

She made a quick curtsey to the king and queen. "Do you do this often, my lady?"

"Upon occasion." Rosalynde snuggled against her husband's shoulder. "When my lord has a holiday."

"There is little I must do at court this week, my lady," Philip explained. "Tom and I have yet to determine the particulars of the trade agreement we are to have with Grenaver, but, apart from that, I have told my council we will do no work until the new year." He flashed her his brilliant smile and gestured to the other side of the blanket. "Will you sit, Lady Elizabeth?"

Tom settled her in a comfortable spot and began piling beef and cheese and succulent partridge onto a plate for her.

"Are there none of your people to wait on us, my lord?" she asked, and he shook his head.

"Do we not have enough of that at court all day, Bess? We are hardly feeble, you know."

Over the next hour, they talked and laughed and ate, and Elizabeth found herself a trifle less intimidated by the king's presence. Out here, away from court, he seemed to be no more than just a man, one with traces of his brother's gentleness, especially in his tender care of the queen. It was rather strange to see the high lord of all Lynaleigh picking through the beef, finding the most tender morsels for his lady's plate, or asking if she was warm enough, or coaxing her to eat a partridge leg.

Elizabeth saw, too, how she basked in his attentions, how she took unabashed pleasure in the nearness of him, and how comfortable they seemed together. But they had been married as strangers, too. Elizabeth glanced at her own husband, stretched out beside her, and wondered if they would ever be so close, if it were truly possible.

"Have you had enough to eat, Bess?" Tom asked as he popped the last of an almond tart into his mouth.

"You might catch a deer for her, Tom," Philip suggested mischievously, "if she wants more."

Elizabeth laughed. "I should like to see such a thing done."

"You shall then, Bess," Tom told her. "I will bring you one now."

"I am certain, my lord," she said with a doubtful shake of her head, "without your bow and without your dogs."

"I will catch it in my hands for you, love. The park deer are tame and not so wary as those further out in the forest. With a touch of luck, and, provided I've not eaten too much just now—"

"You are boastful, my lord," Elizabeth said with another laugh, and Tom grinned.

"Shall we see, Bess?" He looked at his brother. "Am I boastful?"

Philip glanced at Rosalynde and smothered a smile of his own. "It would hardly be my part to say, Tom, before your lady."

"Shall we see then, Bess?" In spite of his light tone, there was determination in Tom's expression. "I'll not leave this place so long as you have doubt."

"No, my lord," she replied. "It is such a trifle, I will take your word if you say you can do so."

"If you cannot trust me in a trifle, Bess, then I cannot find fault if you doubt me in something of greater weight. But I will prove you that I have dealt plainly with you. Come on."

The four of them took stealthy refuge in the trees. The stream was mostly ice, but the sun was out and the water made a musical trickle through the snow-shrouded rocks. For a while, they waited in motionless silence, until Philip touched Tom's sleeve and pointed across the water.

A young buck stood there, poised and listening, and Tom moved cautiously away from the tree he had been using for cover. He glanced back at Elizabeth, and then, in a sudden explosion, bounded across the stream. The buck sprang away, arrow swift, but Tom was as swiftly after him, his legs pumping almost faster than Elizabeth could follow. The deer crashed into the underbrush and still Tom was right behind, closing ground.

"Come on!" Philip called, and they dashed after him.

The strip of forest on the other side of the water was only about twenty or thirty yards wide, with a down-sloping meadow beyond. The buck tried to veer off to the left, to keep the cover of the trees, but Philip forced him out into the open.

"There, Tom! There!"

Tom was too winded to answer, but he had not lost sight of his quarry. Rosalynde and Elizabeth reached the meadow just as he put on his final burst of speed. Then he was beside the beast and, in another instant, had brought him down.

"Bravo!" Philip shouted, and Rosalynde clapped her hands, both of them laughing and cheering.

Elizabeth watched in amazement as Tom grappled with the struggling, terrified creature.

"Have I—spoke true, Bess?" he gasped, his chest heaving, and the buck kicked both hind legs into his stomach. The air rushed out of him, but he kept his hold.

"Answer him, lady," Philip urged, and, startled, Elizabeth nodded. "Yes! Yes, my lord!"

Tom let go and collapsed into the snow, and the buck shot back into the trees, landing another firm kick as he did. Tom clutched his shoulder, groaning and laughing as best he could with no breath.

Philip hauled him to his feet. "Well run, Tom."

"Did he hurt you, my lord?" Rosalynde asked. Tom shook his head, and leaned over and braced his hands on his thighs, still gasping.

"It was a most wondrous thing, my lord," Elizabeth said, her eyes shining, and he lifted his head and mopped the sweat from his face with his sleeve.

"Anything," he panted, smiling. "Anything—to prove true—to my lady."

"Good afternoon, Lady Elizabeth," Darlington said with a bow. "I pray you, my lady, can you tell me where Lord Tom is just now? The king has sent for him about the proposal the Grenaven ambassadors have brought."

Elizabeth smiled slightly, knowing Tom had gone to have a bath to make himself presentable after the race he had run that noon.

"Shall I bring him the message, my lord?" she asked innocently. "If I should meet him, I mean?"

"I would be most gratified, my lady. I thank you. I will see if he is in the library."

Once Darlington was gone, she went to Tom's chamber. She lifted her hand to knock, but, with sudden boldness, she merely pushed the door open.

A large tub, still half full of soapy water, sat near the hearth. Tom lay on his stomach on the trestle table. He was wearing only his breeches, and she stared at his chiseled body, trained and toned and sculpted by war, sleek and glistening with the scented oils Palmer was rubbing into his skin. His head was turned toward her, pillowed on one arm, but his eyes were closed, his teeth clenched tight as Palmer's large hands kneaded his bruised shoulder.

"Mass, Palmer, have I not been beaten enough for one day?"

"My lord—" Palmer caught sight of Elizabeth, there in the doorway, but she swiftly put one finger to her lips and they shared a conspiratorial smile. "I will use a gentler touch, my lord."

She crept up to the table and, without changing the rhythm of the stroke, put her hands in place of Palmer's.

"Mmm." Tom's taut face slackened. "Excellent."

"Shall I go on, my lord?" Palmer asked and Elizabeth stopped for a moment.

"Mmm, yes." Tom smiled a little, not opening his eyes, and she continued. "Faith, you have a touch as soft as any maid."

Suppressing a laugh, Palmer bowed and made a silent retreat, carefully shutting the door behind him. Elizabeth went on stroking Tom's back and shoulders, sliding her hands over him, admiring his smooth perfection, admiring the ripple of muscle beneath his skin.

"You shall put me to sleep in another minute, Palmer," he murmured, and she leaned down and kissed the back of his neck. He bolted up with his fists doubled and the most surprised expression on his face that she had ever seen. Their eyes met and they both burst out laughing.

"Best be glad I looked before I struck, mischief," he said, shaking his finger at her, his face very red.

She giggled. "I grant you your man holds you in highest esteem, but I think his admiration has its limits."

"And yours?"

Her smile faded and she swept her eyes over him, knowing he could read her thoughts on her flushed face. "My lord, I—"

He offered her his hand and she took it, letting him draw her closer until she was against the edge of the table, his legs on either side of her.

"Did you want something of me, Bess?" he asked, his voice low and intimate.

"You amazed me running down that deer today, my lord. I have never seen anyone so swift." She rubbed his shoulder, her hand as unsteady as her voice. "Does it hurt you?"

"Not so much I would not do it again if it would please you, Bess. As I said before, anything to prove true to you." He slipped his arm around her waist. "Anything."

With a sudden soft quickness in her breathing, she leaned forward to kiss him. She closed her eyes at the touch, a little sigh escaping her. Then she pulled back.

"I should go, my lord. It is wrong for me to be here."

"How can it be wrong, when I am your husband and you are my wife and we love each other?"

His voice was soft and coaxing, and the brush of his lips against hers was like the fragile kiss of a snowflake. She wanted to kiss him again; everything within her was begging for him to kiss her as she knew he wanted to, but she held him away from her.

"I do not know that I love you."

"You do not know that you do not," he breathed, tracing his lips along her cheek. "Let me teach you to love me."

"As you have taught how many others?" she asked, trying to dull the fierce urge to surrender to him.

"None," he murmured in her ear. "I swear it over again. Not one."

His lips moved close to hers, and, unable to stop herself, she kissed him again, leaning into him, clinging to his iron-sinewed arms. He drew her deeper into his embrace, further into the kiss, finally cupping his hand behind her head to bring her closer.

She broke away from him, trembling.

"I am sorry, Bess."

She pressed her hands to her mouth and briefly closed her eyes.

"I am sorry," he said again, and she could hear the hurt in his voice. "Is there so much in me, sweet, that you could not love?"

She looked at him once more. Was there *anything* in him she could not love? Anything any woman would not adore?

"Is there no one else you desire, my lord?" she asked when she could speak steadily. "Someone who would love you as you wish?"

"You want me to—" He took her hand in his and looked deeply into her eyes, the pain in his intensifying, making her ashamed. "You want me to betray my vows to you? My vows to God?"

"I—"

"Do you truly want me to take a mistress when I've given you my heart and all the love that is in it?"

She thought of him in the arms of someone else, giving his kisses, his love to another. She thought of another woman's mouth on his, that light in his eyes burning for this other and not for her.

"No." She put her free hand up to his cheek, then to the dark cluster of hair at the nape of his neck. "No, please, I never meant that. I could never bear it."

"Nor could I," he said softly. He pressed her hand. "But you do not believe me yet, do you?" He leaned forward once more to kiss her cheek. "Believe me," he murmured against her skin, "please believe me."

She held him there, twining her fingers more deeply into his hair, moving closer to him.

"I want to believe you," she said. She touched her mouth to his. "Help me believe you."

He kissed her lips, full and long, his arms around her. In another moment, she had both arms around his neck, pulling him to her as she kissed his mouth, feeling herself melt into him.

He lifted her off her feet as the kiss intensified, and she clung closer, feeling all the resistance seep out of her like grain from a torn sack. In another moment she would be begging him. In another moment—

"No," she moaned, turning her face to one side.

"Bess," he whispered, nuzzling her ear, but she was struggling away from him. With a trembling breath, he set her on her feet.

"Forgive me, love." He swallowed hard and managed a shaky smile, tracing his finger down the curve of her cheek. "You make it difficult sometimes, my lady, to keep my promise to you when you stand there so soft and fair."

"I am sorry, my lord," she said, feeling the choking tears rise in her throat. "I know you say you love me, that you have all this long while, but how can that be? You asked me if there was so much in you I could not love. Is there so much in me you *could* love? How am I to trust a love I've never earned by so much as a sweet look? How can this love of yours be true when it is based on nothing between us?"

"Because I can see it for what it can be, what it will be if we nurture it. And because it was my choice."

"It was never your choice," she said, her tears turning into frustration. "I was chosen for you."

"But it was my choice to love you, being chosen."

His words were enigmatic to her, like a maze with no beginning and no end.

"Then it is all pretense. Nothing but duty."

His expression turned gentle. "No, sweeting, just a stronger, surer love than mere passion and fancy. It does not shift with the wind."

"And when you tire of me?"

"I hope to have you so much a part of me that that could never be." He put the back of his hand to her cheek, stroking the curved softness, his touch as coaxing as his words. "I would take pains to learn more of you every day until I knew what I now only suspect—that I would not want ever to be long without you."

"Why take such pains?" she asked, pulling back from him again, not trusting herself to be so close to him. "Why trouble yourself when neither of us wants this?"

"I want this," he said. She saw a flash of Chastelayne determination in his eyes. "We are married, Bess, and we cannot change that. We can either stand at arm's length and say it was not our choosing, or we can learn to know each other." Again he touched her cheek, and his face softened with entreaty. "Love each other."

She closed her eyes. "My lord—"

"I remember that first night we were together. You were like a little white dove, trembling and afraid, and I wanted to take you and gentle you in my hands and teach you not to fear. I want that still.

Whatever you decide, you are my wife. There will be no other love for me, no other hope for love. Should I not take pains to win you?"

She covered his hand with hers and pressed her face against it. "My lord—"

"I had far rather be your love than your lord, Bess," he said softly. "I had truly."

She began to cry once more. "I am sorry."

"Shh," he soothed, and she let him draw her again into the comfort of his arms. "Please, sweet, there is no need for tears."

"I know I have been unkind to you, and I never meant it so."

"Never cry for that, love. All I ask is that you not close your heart to me, not until you truly know mine, not until you can see me for what I am instead of what you think I must be." He tipped her face up to him. "I may surprise you."

He grinned at her, and she laughed unsteadily and wiped her tears from his bare shoulder.

"You would surprise me if you did not sicken for going about like this without your clothes."

He stood and picked up the shirt Palmer had laid out for him. "You say it as if I were always dressed so. But, at my lady's will." He bowed and then drew himself up in mock offense when she laughed at the incongruity of the formal gesture when he was so incompletely dressed. "I see there's no pleasing you, madame. You'll not have me a rogue, and you'll not have me a gentleman."

"His majesty will have you horsewhipped if you keep him waiting any longer."

"Philip sent for me?"

"That was what I came to tell you, my lord."

"You certainly took a roundabout way in giving your message, my lady," he said, grinning again. "Not that I would have had it any other way, mind, but I likely should make some haste now in getting dressed, if you will pardon me."

She left him to dress and met the queen in the corridor that led back to the great hall.

"Your majesty," she said with a curtsey, and Rosalynde came to walk beside her.

"I hope you enjoyed our picnic today, Lady Elizabeth. I fear my lord and yours do not often have the leisure for such things except at this time of year."

Elizabeth smiled. "It was rather unusual, I must admit, but I have rarely had such a pleasant meal, especially in the snow."

"Our husbands both have a love for the winter I've yet to understand. I used to worry that the king would catch cold from going out in it in his shirt sleeves, but he never has, and that has made it difficult sometimes for me to convince him not to take Robin out with him."

"How old is your little one, my lady?" Elizabeth asked. She had seen the infant prince often when she sat chatting with the other ladies of the court in the sewing room or in the library and had watched him as he played at his mother's feet, brightening the room with his baby coos and squeals. He was a healthy, chubby-legged child with the king's dark hair and blue eyes, easily master of his parents' hearts and of his uncle's as well.

"Robin is almost seven months now," Rosalynde told her. "The nurse says he will be walking early and talking early, too, perhaps. Philip claims he is talking already."

"Truly?"

Rosalynde laughed. "He claims Robin called him Papa last Wednesday, but in three-quarters of an hour trying he could not get him to repeat it, nor has he yet that he's told me. Oh, but he is proud of our boy. You will see, my lady, when you give my lord of Brenden your first child, what pleasure you will take in bringing him such happiness."

"Do you think that would please him?" Elizabeth asked shyly.

"You have seen him and Robin together. What think you?"

Elizabeth had seen Tom tussling with Robin on the floor, both of them so like the king that, except for his dark eyes, Tom might have been the baby's father. She knew he would love a child of his own, but he would never have one if their marriage went on as it had.

"Might I ask you something, Lady Rosalynde?"

The queen gestured to the seat that was set into the wall beneath one of the windows.

"Shall we stop a moment and talk?"

Elizabeth nodded and both of them sat down.

"You had a question for me?" Rosalynde asked when the younger girl was silent.

"Forgive me, my lady, but they say you were not acquainted with the king before you married. Is that so?"

"Almost. I met him when his family came to my father's nearly five years before that." Rosalynde smiled at the memory. "I was fifteen then and smitten with the bluest eyes I had ever seen. During the few days he was there, I found there was honor and gentleness behind those eyes, and steadfastness in every beat of his heart, and I knew I could love no other."

"And of course he loved you," Elizabeth said, disappointed that what she had been told of this marriage was false.

Rosalynde shook her head. "I would I could say he had. For a long while I feared he might never. After five years, we truly were strangers when we married. Since the marriage was not of his choosing, you might imagine he felt little reason to be pleased at it."

"I can imagine," Elizabeth agreed.

"He went through some very difficult times in the year before we married, and afterwards, too. That did not make him very disposed to care for anyone. It was hard sometimes to love him then, but I am so very glad now that God gave me the grace to do it."

"You loved him even when he did not love you? Why?"

"It was God who gave me that power." Rosalynde smiled a little. "Now I merely love him. It is something I could not choose not to do. I would not be whole without him."

"Why? What makes you love him so?"

There was laughter in the queen's green eyes. "Perhaps because he loves the snow and is abominable at writing verse and looks so like an angel when he is asleep. And he still has those heaven-blue eyes."

Elizabeth frowned. "Little reason for you or anyone to love a man."

"A woman's reason, perhaps. Or perhaps the reason of anyone who loves. As I said, I merely love him."

"But why?"

"Because I can love no other and I must love."

Elizabeth felt a combination of frustration and envy churning inside her. How wonderful it would be to merely love without asking why, or to be loved with such steadfastness despite anything else.

"You are very beautiful, my lady," she said slowly. "Forgive me, but do you ever think the king loves you for nothing more than that?"

Rosalynde smiled again. "If anything, it made it more difficult for him to love me, to believe I could love him and be true to him, to believe it was more than desire he felt for me. He could see how much I wanted him, and he could hardly believe my love was any more than desire either."

"My lady, you . . . you do not think it sin, then, in God's eyes, for a woman to desire such things?"

"I do not," Rosalynde replied, her eyes very gentle. "Not when it is your own husband you desire them of. Why else would God have put such longings in us, except that they are a good thing in His sight? Expressed in love, they form a tender bond between man and wife that cannot be easily broken. You will find it so, my lady, and very easily, I think, with my lord of Brenden. He does truly love you."

"Did I hear my name?"

Elizabeth was startled to see Tom coming down the corridor and wondered how much he could have overheard. Nothing, she was fairly certain, but she could not know.

"My lord," she said, standing. "Have you been to the king yet?"

"I was just on my way, Bess. I trust I've not kept him too long, Lady Rosalynde."

"Neither of you would be troubled with any court matters until after the new year, were I to have my way of it," Rosalynde replied, "but he merely wants to talk over the agreement with the Grenaven ambassadors once again. It seems they have a new article they wish added."

"Mass, they were less trouble when we were at war with them! I had best go see what they are asking," Tom said. Then he grinned at Elizabeth. "Of course, only if you think I am properly dressed now, my lady."

Her face felt suddenly warm, but she managed a suitable answer, and, with another grin and a swift bow to the queen, he left them alone again.

Elizabeth watched him walk away, knowing her every emotion was painted on her face for the queen to see.

"My lady, I—" She sat down suddenly, her dark eyes full of uncertainty. "I do not know what I should think, my lady. How is a woman ever to know for certain a man truly loves her?"

Rosalynde squeezed her hand. "He loves you. Now you must choose to believe it."

❧

The addition to the Grenaven treaty was not such a simple thing after all. Its inclusion affected almost all the other articles that had already been agreed upon, and Tom and Philip stayed up late into the night discussing all of its ramifications.

Feeling oddly lonely, Elizabeth went to bed early, but she woke in the middle of the night with a sleepy tingling in one hand. She tried to flex her fingers to ease it, but they would not move, so she opened her eyes. Tom was kneeling beside her, his hands cradling hers, his cheek resting in her palm. She smiled.

Asleep at your prayers again?

This was not the first time she had found him so, but there was something especially sweet about seeing him there now, his face softened with sleep, his long lashes making dark semicircles against his skin. She moved closer to him.

For what do you make such fervent petition?

She reached her other hand over to touch his hair. She looked again at his strong hands clutching hers, protecting, embracing, cherishing it. He sighed her name and held on more tightly, and her eyes spilled tears.

Do you pray for me, my lord?

She stroked his hair again and leaned over to kiss it. He was praying for her. Out of his tender, fervent heart, he was praying for her. How was she ever to resist loving such a man?

CHAPTER

IT WAS TRADITION IN LYNALEIGH THAT CHRISTMAS EVE WAS A DAY of prayer and thanksgiving for the Savior who had been given to the world and that Christmas Day was a celebration of light and music and dancing in joyous proclamation of that same event.

The first dance belonged always to the king and queen, and there was much to admire in their perfectly-matched elegance. Their every motion, even the sweep of her rose-colored gown as he guided her effortlessly across the floor, had a regal grace to it. Elizabeth stood at her husband's side watching them, thinking on what she knew of the love they had learned for each other, wondering if it was possible that she, too, might be schooled.

Tom told her softly how beautiful she looked, and she could see in his eyes he spoke what he truly thought. She felt beautiful. Her dress was a gift from him, the rich velvet as crimson as holly berries and inset with snow white. Her combs, too, were his gift, holding her bountiful hair with pure gold, ornamented at the top with engraved violets. Violets for faithfulness. How sweet he was.

The herald announced the beginning of the volte, and Tom took her hand.

"Will you honor me, my lady?"

She smiled and followed him into the midst of the other dancers. A few seconds later the music started, brisk and lively, and he was tossing her high in the air, whirling her about, lifting her as easily as if she had been thistledown until she was breathless with laughter. The volte was considered scandalous by some of the older courtiers still, but Elizabeth loved it; it was so like flying and Tom did it with such ease.

She had to have a cup of wine when it was over and a moment to catch her breath, but they danced again afterwards. Twice more. Although the king and queen themselves usually flouted the convention, it was considered impolite to dance only with one's spouse at such celebrations, so Elizabeth found herself partnered with several gentlemen of the court: Lord Darlington, the young Duke of Ellison, a man she did not know with a pointy yellow beard, others she could not remember. All of them, young and old, admired her with their eyes, and it made her feel the more desirable, as though she had some power over them they could not resist.

"Dressed in passion's own scarlet," she heard a smooth voice murmur in her ear, and, startled, she turned away from the man she was dancing with to see who it was.

"Baron Taliferro, I did not think you had returned. I beg you to pardon me, my lord of Eastbrook."

The older man bowed, and Taliferro took Elizabeth's arm to lead her back to the table where the wine was kept.

"I must go away more often, Madonna," he said suavely. "Each time I return you are that much more lovely."

She glanced toward Tom as he danced with Lady Marian not twenty feet away. Then she smiled at the baron.

"You flatter me, my lord," she told him, and there was a glint in his black, black eyes.

"How can I help but worship at so fair a shrine?"

"You must not say so, my lord," she reproved, still smiling.

"No, my lord," Tom said, coming to claim her hand, "you must not say so."

"Your highness," Taliferro said with an ingratiating bow. "I was merely complimenting your lady on the exquisiteness of her gown."

"I will get you the name of the dressmaker, my lord," Tom said pleasantly, "should you like to have one made for yourself."

Elizabeth bit her lip to keep from laughing as Tom swept her onto the dance floor.

"He should be terribly angry, you know," she whispered to him after a moment, an excited glow in her cheeks, but he only smiled into her eyes with his deep velvet ones.

"So should I, but that I know he cannot help seeing how beautiful you are. I shall have to keep you close for the rest of the night, I suppose." He pulled her to him. "Very close."

He began the dance, slow and fluid, in time to the swelling music, and before long she forgot about Taliferro, forgot about anyone but Tom and the warm feel of his arms around her. One dance flowed into another and another and another, and they moved closer and closer with each one.

He said something low, and she felt the brief warmth of the words against her skin, felt herself melting into his embrace. In the silent fire of her heart, she begged him not to bring his lips so close to her cheek. She knew too well the ambrosia taste of his kiss, the warm, keen pleasure of his touch. She looked up at him, knowing if he so much as smiled she would be lost to him. She had to look away.

Just then the music changed again. The rhythm slowed; the melody beckoned with low, insinuating tones. He tightened his arms around her, pulling her closer, leaving her breathless. They separated and turned in the figure of the dance, and then came together again, their eyes meeting. This time she did not look away. She could not, not when those velvet eyes held such smoldering intensity that frightened her and drew her all at once.

Again they separated and turned, this time coming to dance next to each other, his arm around her waist. He turned her to face him again, his arm still firmly around her, and led her a little further from the rest of the dancers, where there were fewer eyes to see them.

The music was suddenly very far away, and she realized they were no longer dancing. He drew her out onto the balcony, looking still so deeply into her eyes, and she was drawn irresistibly closer, hungry for the feel of his lips on hers. Doubtless he could see that hunger there in her eyes, feel it in the inexorable pull between them, but she knew, for the sake of his promise, he would not kiss her, not until she asked. Would it be so wrong? Everything he had showed her in the

Scriptures, everything she had seen of his patient, gentle care of her, told her it would not be.

"Kiss me," she whispered, her lips almost touching his already. "Kiss me now."

"Bess," he murmured, and she pressed up to him.

"My lord—"

He kissed her mouth, and she clung to him, savoring the feel of his muscular arms tightly around her, but then he pulled away.

"We will be missed," he said with a breathless smile, and she let him lead her back into the hall, too dazed to protest.

They danced again and again after that, and all the while she tried to press closer to him, to coax him into another kiss, but he seemed strangely reluctant to allow it.

"I am tired, my lord," she finally whispered in his ear, not moving her head from his shoulder as they swayed together in an intimate semblance of a dance.

For a moment he was motionless. Then he took her arms from around him.

"I will take you back to your chamber then, my lady, if you wish it, but there are some other things I must see to before I sleep tonight."

"Tonight, my lord?" she asked, letting pleading and passion color the words. "Will you not come with me?"

"My lady—Bess—"

"Please," she murmured against him, and, drawing a trembling breath, he turned her face up to his.

"Do you love me, Bess?"

She smiled unsteadily and brought her lips close once more to his. "Please."

They made a brief good night to the king and queen, and soon they were alone in her chamber. It had taken Ellen only a moment to remove the scarlet dress, and Elizabeth had dismissed her and the others before she could do more.

"Perhaps you would take down my hair, my lord," she asked, and he felt through the heavy mass until he found her golden combs and pulled them out, letting the dark tresses fall in a coil down her back.

Unable to disentangle her eyes from his, she put her arms around his neck, and he continued to spread her hair out around her shoulders, his hands gentle and caressing. She leaned into him, breathing deeply of his masculine scent, and he drew her even nearer and pressed a kiss into her hair.

"Do you love me?" he asked, his voice breathless and unsteady. "Do you?"

His eyes were dark with passion, but there was something deeper in them, too, something that spoke to the very depths of her heart. She opened her mouth to answer him, but that something drew her to kiss him instead, a long, slow kiss that made him tremble.

She pressed closer and nuzzled his neck, feeling the want in him and a sudden urge to make that want stronger.

"Oh, Bess."

She felt his tenseness, the effort he was making to restrain himself, but his arms tightened just a little around her. Her kisses teased the underside of his jaw. She looked up at him languidly, her parted lips moist and inviting.

"Why do you not kiss me?"

"Do not play with me anymore," he breathed, his eyes dark fire.

She brushed her cheek against his lips. "Will you not kiss me?"

"Were I to kiss you now, Bess, I could not stop."

She brought her mouth close to his, so close she could feel the sweet warmth of his breath. "I would not want you to stop."

For a long moment he did not move. Then the fire that had smoldered so long inside him burst into intense flame. He cupped her face in his hands, answering her ardent lips with his own. He laced his fingers through her hair, tipping her head back for a more powerful kiss. Her arms went around him, straining him closer, and she felt herself drawn deeper and deeper into the passion's haze, frightened but unwilling to turn back.

"Love me," he murmured against her lips.

"My lord—"

"Love me," he breathed, kissing her again. "Love me."

She answered him with her touch, her kisses and, when she could bear no more, all herself.

He kissed her once again and then nestled his head against her shoulder.

"Bess, Bess," he murmured over and over, the words making angel music in her ear. "Sweet, sweet Bess."

She clung to him and remembered how he had looked at her, his dark eyes all flame and passion, yet filled with unreserved, unbounded love.

"I love you," he had whispered, as if he were making a vow. Then he had made them one, so sweetly, so tenderly, she wondered now why she had ever feared him.

He turned to his side, cuddling her against his heart, and she lay there too weary and content to move, but he wanted more.

"Love me, Bess," he said softly, tracing his fingers over her smooth brow, looking deeply into her misty eyes. "Love me."

She responded with a passionate kiss, but he caught her hands and clasped them against his chest.

"More than that," he murmured. "Love *me*, Bess. Love *me*."

He pressed her hands to his cheek, the deep want still in his eyes, a desire that went far beyond mere flesh. How was she to answer that?

He woke with her nestled against him, breathing a little warm place on his chest, one arm flung across his middle, the other buried under him. He smiled and brushed a soft curl out of her face.

"Do you love me now, my Bess?"

He touched her hair again and felt a strong rush of emotion sweep over him. She had given him herself at last. At last he had her love. What might he not do now to please her?

He tightened his arm around her. *One flesh*, he thought. *One love*.

She sighed, a little soft, dove-like sound, and he drew the coverlet higher over them both and snuggled with her deeper into the bed. Untarnished Eden could not have been so sweet.

"Thank You," he whispered, and her eyes fluttered open.

"Good morning, love," he said.

A delicate flush crept up over her cheeks. "Good morning, my lord."

He brushed her lips with his, and, her color deepening, she hid her face against him. He smiled and put his other arm around her and then kissed her temple.

"Did you sleep well, sweetheart?"

His own sleep had been as deep and restful as any he had ever had, and, even in his unaccustomed embrace, she had seemed relaxed and contented.

She looked up at him, shy wonder in her eyes. "Is it always like that?"

"Like what?"

She hid her face again. "So wonderful."

He cuddled her closer and kissed her once more. "I hope so."

She said nothing else, and he decided he did not want to risk losing this sweet closeness by asking her now, but he could not keep the question out of his eyes. *Do you love me now?*

He merely lay still, holding her close, playing his fingers through her hair. After a while, she pulled the sheet around her and sat up.

"I suppose we cannot stay in bed all day."

He grinned. "Not unless we wish to scandalize the whole court. Imagine, two years married and more and spending the morning in bed."

She blushed again and he touched her cheek.

"Are you hungry, Bess?"

She nodded and he smiled.

"I will send for your ladies."

He threw back the bedclothes, and she turned her face away. He pulled the covers back up to his waist.

"Pardon me, my lady. Would you prefer to rise first?"

Her only answer was a quick shake of her head, and he realized he had spoken wrong again.

"Wait a moment," he told her. He rummaged under the covers and fished out her shift from where it had wrapped itself around his foot.

"Here, my lady."

She pulled it under the covers with her, and when she reappeared, she was wearing it. He did not ask her why she was shy with him after last night; to him it was only a sweet reminder of her maidenhood. He had been carefully modest with her until now; he could be still, until she was comfortable with their new intimacy.

She handed him his breeches from off the floor, still not meeting his gaze, and he slipped into them and got up.

"May I help you dress, love?"

"I really should call Ellen back, my lord, rather than trouble you."

He reached down and took her hand. "Let us be nothing but our own for one day. I can do it if you tell me how all the fastenings go."

"But my hair—"

"Your hair is beautiful just as it is."

She put her hand up to the tumbled curls. "Now I know you are teasing, my lord."

"No, faith," he said, snatching up her brush. "Give me a moment, and you shall see how little such beauty needs to be added to."

She smiled, relenting, and he sat down on the bed beside her and brushed her hair one thick handful at a time, making it curl around his fingers, making its auburn highlights shimmer like satin in the morning sun.

"You can make no improvement upon that, Bess," he said after a few minutes, and, looking into her glass, she laughed.

"I look like a mad woman with it falling loose that way."

He gathered it up in both of his hands and pressed his face into it with a low murmur of pleasure. "The only madness is for such loveliness to be bound up and hidden from the world."

She looked again at her reflection and then furtively at his.

"If it please you, my lord," she conceded, apparently satisfied with his sincerity.

"Grant me the day, Bess," he asked, drawing her back against his shoulder and letting his coaxing words caress her ear. "We will give

Ellen and Palmer and all the rest a holiday for once. I know it is not the fashion, but let us play peasants and serve ourselves today."

"My lord—"

"Put on something plain," he said with sudden urgent eagerness. "I will do so, too, and we can spend the day how we choose. We could go to the marketplace and see what amusements they have. There are always musicians and players and any number of things to see this time of year."

"You mean go among the people alone and unguarded?"

He laughed at her astonishment. "There is always too much commotion if we go anywhere openly. Back in Treghatours, my brothers and I would often go down to the village and play with the other boys. There was no harm in it."

She looked at him rather dubiously. "And they did not know you?"

"Not at first," he said, smiling. "Not until Richard told them that he was the Duke of Bradford so that they would have to play what he chose. He had to thrash two or three of the bigger boys to prove his point."

She laughed. "You may have carried it off then, my lord, but now surely you will be known."

"The people see only what they wish to see," he said, and he wrapped his arms around her and teased her ear again with his lips. "They'll hardly notice a pair of sweethearts gone to market."

She could not resist that. Not after last night.

"Well, but you must let me do something with my hair. I cannot go about like some village wanton."

"Allow me," he said, and in a moment her hair was in two somewhat-uneven loose braids, and there was a sweet unaffectedness about it that was very becoming. Under her direction, he laced her into a simple cream-colored dress, and, with appropriate shoes and stockings, the picture was complete.

"A trifle too fine for a peasant," he decided, "but I swear you are the fairest daughter a merchant ever had."

She leaned over and kissed his cheek and then pulled back, wrinkling her nose. He rubbed his stubbled jaw with a rueful grin.

"I suppose, if I am to have the continued pleasure of my lady's company, I must see to that right away." He looked at his own reflection, still barefoot and shirtless. "I suppose there are a few other things to which I must attend as well."

"If you are going to send your man away, my lord, does that mean I am to wait upon you now?"

"Only if it pleases you, sweetheart."

She wrapped her arm around his and pressed against his side. "It does."

He hugged her closer, but only for an instant. Then he led her to the door and opened it for her. It was the work of but a moment to send her astonished ladies away with instructions to dismiss his servants as well.

"May I escort you to my chamber, my lady?" he asked with an exaggerated, low bow, once they were again alone. Giggling, she made curtsey and stepped out of the room.

"Now it will be my turn to do your hair," she teased, and he sprinted down the corridor.

"You must first catch me!"

"That is not fair!"

She dashed after him, trying to keep her heavy skirts from hindering her, but he knew there was no way she could catch up. Just before he reached his chamber, he heard her make a little squeaking yelp.

"Oh, my lord. No! Wait!"

She was bent over, clutching her ankle, and he went to her.

"Poor poppet, have you twisted it?"

"No, no," she said, her expression pained. "I am not hurt."

"Let me see."

He knelt down, and, before he knew it, she had toppled him onto his backside and scampered to his door.

"I am the winner," she proclaimed, giggling at his astonished expression. "Well, I did tell you I was not hurt."

"Cheating minx!"

He leapt to his feet and lunged toward her. Shrieking, she threw open the door and ran inside, but he was on her in an instant, tossing her onto the bed and tickling her mercilessly.

"Oh, no, my lord! No!" she gasped, laughing.

"Admit you cheated," he demanded.

"No, no!"

"Come, admit you cheated."

"No, no! Oh, yes, yes!"

"Yes, what?" he insisted, continuing the assault.

"Yes, I cheated. I cheated!"

The tickling stopped, and she lay there panting for breath, still trapped there with his arms braced on either side of her.

"You did, indeed," he said with mock sternness.

"So did you," she claimed, and he fixed his eyes on hers.

"I did *what?*"

"You cheated."

"I did *what?!*" he asked again, his expression menacing, and she tried to shield herself with her hands.

"You cheated."

He began tickling her again and she squirmed under him, making only a half-hearted attempt at escape.

"You cheated!" she managed between giggles. "You cheated first! I should tickle you!"

She gouged him under the arms and at once he was helpless with laughter.

"Confess!" she demanded, and he collapsed beside her, unable to tickle her anymore.

"Truce! Truce!" he pled, but she would not hear of it.

"I confessed; now you must!"

"Never!" he panted, trying to defend himself. Then he had a better idea. He rolled over with her, pinning her, struggling, under him. He kissed her. Her playful resistance promptly ceased, and she put her arms around his neck.

"Again," she breathed, but there was still mischief dancing in his eyes.

"I forgot, I must shave now."

He jumped up and doused his face in yesterday's wash water.

"My lord," she moaned, laughing again. She got up and went to sit next to his mirror, watching him trying to shave himself.

"I suppose I've let Palmer spoil me," he said when he drew blood the second time.

"Would you trust me to do it, my lord?"

There was a flash of uncertainty in his eyes. "Have you ever shaved anyone before, Bess?"

"I promise I'll be ever so much more careful than you are being," she told him. "I am certain I could be no worse at it than you."

He grinned at her and handed her the razor. "I would like to keep my nose where it is, if you please, my lady."

"Be still, or you shall have none at all."

A few minutes later, Tom rinsed his face and looked into the mirror. There was only a little scrape along his jaw that hadn't been there before. Satisfied, he smiled at her, and she put her hand up to caress his smooth, tingling cheek.

"I fear you shall never pass for a peasant, my lord, no matter how mean the garments you put on."

"I tell you the people will never notice us. I will put on an old shirt and doublet of Palmer's, from before he came to court, and my oldest boots, and some leather wristlets I got from one of the archers, and I swear we'll not be known."

She looked him over when he was done and decided there was nothing about him now to indicate he was a prince, unless it was the unmistakable royalty of his demeanor, and that could hardly be disguised. The boots were very worn. One of them had a split seam that kept it bunched at his knee instead of properly mid-thigh. The sleeveless doublet was of an indefinable rusty-brown color and just as battered as the shirt, but on him they seemed somehow finer than they were. He had tied his hair back at the nape of his neck, and, combined with his peasant clothes, it gave him the look of a romantic forest outlaw. She decided she liked the way he looked with his shirt sleeves pushed to his elbows like that, showing to advantage his strong forearms. She liked the wristlets, too, though they were very common.

"Now, shall I pass?" he asked, and she shook her head, smiling.

"Only for a prince in disguise."

He laughed and wrapped her in her cloak. Then he led her out into the city.

CHAPTER

TOM AND ELIZABETH WENT OUT BEYOND THE AREAS WHERE THE people were likely to recognize them, out into one of the poorer quarters of the city. There it was just as he had promised her: full of jugglers and magicians, singers and poets, and companies of actors.

They stood and watched one of the companies put on a drama that told of the Advent, of the virgin birth of God's only Son as foretold by one of the least angelic-looking angels either of them had ever seen. With the rest, they hissed a bald-pated Herod as he ordered the slaughter of the innocents and cheered at the escape of the Christ-child from right under the noses of the king's addled soldiers.

Tom threw a handful of money up on the makeshift stage at the performance's conclusion. He led Elizabeth through the shops. He enjoyed mingling with the people without them taking special notice of him, but he could see that she was a trifle put out at not being waited on by each merchant the instant she went into his shop.

"It is rather different than having them bring their goods directly to the palace for you to choose from, is it not, love?"

"I suppose that would hardly be practical for so many people," she conceded with a glance back at the potter's shop they had just left. "Though why anyone would bother with such poor merchandise, I cannot tell."

"It is as much as some can afford, I am sure," he told her. "I doubt the gold merchant across the way gets much business in this quarter of town, though he seems determined to raise some today. Some contest or other, it looks."

"Oh, shall we see what it is?" she asked eagerly, and he led her across the street.

"Test your eye and your arm!" the merchant was calling to all those who passed his shop. "One arrow well placed and you can present your lady with a fine prize from my own wares! Deck your lady with jewels!"

"Do, my lord," she urged Tom, clinging to his arm. "Please? For me."

"Win the prize and win her heart!" the merchant called. Then he looked at Tom. "Here is an archer, or I miss my guess. Try your skill, friend. Try your luck, and win your lady's admiration."

Tom shook his head. "Not today, friend."

"For the honor of your lady," the merchant coaxed, and Elizabeth held more tightly to Tom.

"Oh, please, my lord," she whispered, and, unable to resist the excitement in her eyes, he smiled and tossed the man a small coin.

"Well, I will try it."

He handed Elizabeth his tattered doublet and took the bow that was offered him and went to stand with the rest in as ragged a line of men as ever he had seen. Still there were those that showed, by a sinewed arm or the particular calluses that come only from much use of a bow, that there were indeed seasoned archers among them, and he began to look forward to the competition.

The first round trimmed the field to nine, then the nine were culled to three. The more formidable of Tom's opponents was a man of perhaps thirty-five with eagle-keen gray eyes and the hard-worn visage of the professional soldier. The other was a shaggy-haired scarecrow of a boy of nineteen, one Tom would have sworn had never seen a battle but who had not missed yet that day.

"We have our finalists!" the merchant shouted. "Grayson of Riverdon!"

The soldier gave the crowd a grudging nod and they lifted a cheer in his honor.

"Nate, the miller's son!"

The boy grinned and turned several shades of red, and they

cheered him, too, especially one little moonfaced girl with exceptionally bright brown eyes.

"What's your name, boy?" the merchant urged under his breath and Tom turned to him, unprepared.

"My—"

"Your name, boy, your name. You do know your name?"

Elizabeth laughed and Tom did, too. He gave the man a low answer.

"And Tom of Treghatours!" the merchant announced, and Tom made an elaborate bow that was so out of sorts with his peasant garments that the crowd laughed and cheered him, too.

"Ten on the pretty one," Elizabeth heard a rumbling voice behind her offer.

"Twenty-five," another countered and was quickly accepted.

As the target was put further back, she heard wagering all around her, and she held her head higher to hear how much was being bet with Tom to win. And he *would* win. For her.

The three finalists let fly, and all three hit dead center. The target was moved ten yards further and again the three shot, again all dead center. At ten yards more, the soldier struck a quarter inch out of the black and stalked off muttering about ill-made fletches and the questionable parentage of their makers.

"That leaves only us, friend," Tom said to the miller's son while the target was being taken back yet another ten yards. "Luck and favor to you."

Nate took the hand he offered and grinned again. "You have a keen eye, friend, and I have luck and favor enough even if I cannot best you. I have my Elspeth and I could not ask more."

He smiled at the moonfaced girl and she beamed back at him.

"Your sweetheart?" Tom asked, smiling, too.

"My wife!" Nate corrected proudly. "For nearly three weeks."

"It is a sweet thing to have a loving wife," Elizabeth heard Tom say, and Nate nodded.

"You are newly married, too."

It was a statement, not a question, and she saw Tom almost laugh at his own transparency.

"Better than two years now," he assured the miller's son, "but, in faith, it seems only last night."

"Ready!" the merchant interrupted, and, grinning again, Tom took quick aim and shot. Nate did the like, hitting in the black, too, but slightly to the right of Tom's arrow.

"Nate's out!" someone shouted, and there was a sudden squabble among the crowd. The merchant and several others went to the target, examining each arrow's placement, conferring closely with each other.

"We will take the target back ten yards more and they will shoot again!" the merchant announced and the betting escalated. Elizabeth noted with some satisfaction that Tom was still favored.

Nate glanced swiftly at Tom and back at the girl with the bright eyes. Finally, he took careful aim.

"Half out!" was the verdict of the crowd.

"He's lost unless the other cannot hit in the black at all," someone behind Elizabeth murmured, and the rough-voiced man she had heard before doubled his wager.

Tom stepped up and the crowd was silent. Elizabeth hugged his doublet against her breast and watched him with a glow of admiration in her eyes. He would win and she would have the victor's prize.

He glanced at her and drew back his bow, every muscle in his arms and shoulders pressing taut against his shirt. She stepped closer and he looked at her again. Then he fixed his eye on the target and she caught her breath. Without moving his head, he gave her a quick wink and let fly.

"Out!"

The crowd shouted their cheers, and the girl with the bright eyes squealed and ran into Nate's arms.

"Nate wins!" the people cried out. "The miller's son wins!"

"That was great sport," Tom said, reaching for Elizabeth's hand as the peasants swarmed past them toward their champion, "and he is a fine archer. Shall we go see the juggling now?"

"You purposed to do that," she accused, holding her hand away from him. "You deliberately lost."

"Oh, Bess—"

"Now the prize!" the merchant called out, and there was murmuring through the crowd about what it could be.

"See you, good people, a fine bracelet of gold and pearl!"

He held it up amidst a chorus of oohs and ahs before presenting it to the champion of the day.

"You should have won that," Elizabeth insisted, pouting, and Tom slipped his arm around her.

"Now, Bess, what would you want with such a thing? Look at it."

The "fine bracelet" consisted of a nearly invisible seed pearl on a strand of gold chain with little more substance than spider web. It was barely long enough to clasp around the peasant girl's thick wrist.

"Now look at them," Tom added softly.

Elizabeth watched as Nate knelt in the half-frozen mud of the street and presented his prize to his beloved as if she were a royal princess. The girl's eyes managed to shine even more brightly as she looked adoringly upon him.

Tom squeezed Elizabeth a little closer to him. "Faith, I could buy you a thousand such, but it's likely he could never find the means to buy her even one, or give her such another honor so long as they live. Do not begrudge them that. When I win for you, love, it will be for a prize worthy of you and before the admiring eyes of kings and queens."

There was sudden tenderness in her eyes, and she dropped a quick kiss on his cheek. "You are so—"

"What do you mean throwing that match, boy?" demanded a rough, angry voice, and a pair of brawny hands dragged Tom back a step or two. "You've cost me a fair amount of coin by that trick!"

"Release him!" Elizabeth protested. "That is—"

"Bess!" Tom warned, and she snapped her mouth shut. "Now, friend, do we have a quarrel?"

"You threw that match, boy," the gravel-voiced man insisted, "and you'll make good my losses or I'll make them good with my fists."

Tom looked him over good-naturedly. The man was stocky and bull-necked, with a red-blond beard and a nose that had been broken more than once.

"What is your name, friend?"

"Cuthbert, the blacksmith."

"Well, Cuthbert-the-Blacksmith, you should never wager what you cannot afford to lose."

The blacksmith's face turned livid. "Insolent whelp!"

Tom ducked the crushing blow Cuthbert aimed at his face, and the blacksmith's fist landed instead against the sturdy post that supported the thatched overhang of the merchant's shop. There was an ominous cracking sound, but the structure held steady.

Tom smiled once more. "Now, friend—"

Bellowing with rage, the blacksmith ducked his head and rammed his shoulder into Tom's chest, slamming him against the already-damaged post and bringing the overhang crashing down on them both.

"My lord!" Elizabeth cried, and the two opponents struggled out from under the debris, coughing and spitting bits of straw, much to the amusement of the crowd that had gathered for this new spectacle.

Not seeing any humor in the situation, the blacksmith seized Tom by his now-grimy shirt front, tilting him backwards as he drew back his fist.

"Cuthbert, no!" one of the men called from out of the crowd.

"Shut up!" the blacksmith growled.

"Hold your hand, you fool! That is Prince Tom!"

The blacksmith froze in astonishment. Tom flashed him a half-apologetic grin, and the blacksmith abruptly released him, landing him unceremoniously on the seat of his breeches and raising a little puff of protest from the musty straw.

"My—my lord prince—" the blacksmith stammered.

"How dare you!" Elizabeth demanded. "You—"

"Shut your noise, you!" he said, grabbing her arm with a little shake. "Do you want the Princess Elizabeth to hear about you?"

"That *is* the Princess Elizabeth," Tom said with another grin, and the crowd roared with laughter.

The blacksmith sprang back as if she were suddenly red hot; then he fell to his knees.

"Your highness, please—"

"You should be whipped!" Elizabeth scolded, brushing off her sleeve where he had touched it.

"Please, my lord prince," the blacksmith begged. "You cannot mean to punish me for mere ignorance."

"No, faith," Tom agreed, standing up to dust off his breeches. "If that were the law, you should no doubt be punished twice or thrice a day."

The crowd chuckled, and the blacksmith grew even redder in the face but held his peace.

"Your highness," the merchant said, taking a hesitant step forward, "forgive my boldness, but your lordship can see what has become of my shop . . ."

Tom tossed him a few coins. "That should buy what is necessary to mend it for you." He slapped the blacksmith's brawny back. "And Friend Cuthbert here will do the work to pay his part. Agreed?"

The blacksmith nodded grudgingly, and Elizabeth felt a shy tug at her sleeve.

"Pardon me, my lady," the moonfaced girl said, holding out the prize she had just been presented. "I think, by right, this is yours."

Elizabeth looked helplessly at Tom, and he pressed the bracelet back into the girl's hand.

"Nonsense. You heard the ruling. Nate the miller's son is the champion today, and that prize belongs to his lady by right."

"I'll not take it of your charity, my lord," Nate said, and Tom shook his head.

"There was nothing of charity in your aim today, friend. That prize went to the right man. I swear upon my honor."

"My lord—"

"No more on it, Nate. Friend Cuthbert was merely out some money and meant nothing of what he said, is that not so?"

Seeing the cautioning look in Tom's eyes, the blacksmith vouchsafed another grudging nod.

"There. You see." Tom smiled and fastened the bauble around the girl's wrist again. "Keep that, and this, to remember the day."

He dumped all the coins from his pouch and gave Nate more than half, pushing aside his protests.

"A wedding present."

"Oh, my lord prince—"

"Now, no more, Nate. You were a worthy match for me today and seem a good fellow besides. I pray God will bless you and your Elspeth."

"He has, my lord," Nate replied hugging his astonished wife in celebration.

"Now, Friend Cuthbert, for you." Tom studied the money left in his hand and then looked into the blacksmith's coarse face as he knelt still in the debris.

"My lord?" the blacksmith asked, drawing himself up in anticipation.

"Take care in your entertainment of strangers," Tom advised. He dumped his money back into his pouch and drew the string tight to close it. "And never wager what you cannot afford to lose."

With another smile, he took Elizabeth's arm and led her down the street. Behind them, she heard the good-natured jeering of the peasants and, finally, the blacksmith's reluctant laugh. Tom laughed, too.

"Look at you, my lord," she chided. "You are near as filthy as one of them."

"It washes, love, I promise you. Look."

He took her to the well at the center of the square, rinsed his hands and face in the icy water, and used his sleeve to dry them.

"Better?"

She tried to scowl at him but failed miserably, seeing the streaks his dirty sleeve had left behind.

"What?" he questioned, baffled.

Smiling, she shook her head and dampened her handkerchief to scrub his face with it.

"You are such a child."

"You did not think so last night," he whispered. Then he took his doublet from her, grinning at the color that came up in her face. "Come, shall we see what else is to see?"

They went once more into the shops, but, now that their anonymity was lost, there seemed always a crowd of people around them, bestowing their humble blessings upon the royal couple, tossing out a word of good cheer to commemorate the season, a few hoping for another exhibition of Tom's bounty. The merchants, too, were no longer indifferent to them, but swept aside all other customers to give Prince Tom and his lady their full, cloying attention.

"Let's go home, Bess," Tom murmured after a weary hour of this. "The game's spoiled now."

They did not lose their entourage until they reached the palace steps. By then it was near dusk, and all but a few had wandered back to their homes and suppers. The rest Tom sent off with gracious thanks. Then he led Elizabeth inside, amused at the astonishment of the guards when they were recognized.

"Shall we see what we can hunt up in the kitchen, Bess? Just now my belly thinks my throat's cut."

"That would be wonderful, my lord, and—"

"Pardon me, my lady," Palmer interrupted, hurrying up to them. "My lord, I know you wished not to be disturbed today, but the king was not pleased to have you gone from court without his knowledge. I am commanded to send you to him upon your return."

Tom sighed. "Well, I will go." He kissed Elizabeth's hand. "I suppose we may as well sup with the rest of the court tonight, sweetheart. Go and make yourself a princess again, and I will see you then. Palmer, favor me with escorting my lady to her chamber."

"At once, my lord," Palmer said, bowing to Elizabeth. "My lady."

Tom found his brother still in the council room, alone except for the queen.

"I hear I was missed today," he said lightly. He bowed to his sister-in-law. "Good evening, my lady."

She smiled and Philip shook his head, obviously trying not to smile, too.

"It's not like you to be so careless of your duty, Tom, and so reckless. Faith, brawling in the streets and gaming, and wenching, too, and going about the palace looking more like a sweep's boy than a royal prince?"

"Word comes swift, I see," Tom replied. "Well, I must admit guilt in all charges save the wenching. That one's false."

Philip nodded dubiously. "And I suppose you have an excuse for this lapse?"

"None but love, your majesty," Tom replied, one hand melodramatically over his heart, and Rosalynde laughed.

Philip's blue eyes were warm. "Things have changed between you and your lady."

Unaccountably, Tom found himself blushing like a kitchen girl, and Philip laughed outright.

"You hush!" Rosalynde reproved, swatting him on the shoulder, but he only laughed harder and Tom grinned.

"I suppose I must admit guilt in that, as well."

"Well, I'll not grudge you the day, Tom, but, if you've a mind to disappear again, favor me by telling me of it beforehand, especially if I am to speak to the council on a matter you were to look into for me."

Tom pounded his fist against his forehead. "The trade agreement. Philip, what can I say? I've not thought on it once since yesterday."

"Well, think on it again, but tomorrow will be soon enough. I have put off the Grenaven ambassadors until then, but you must tell me your thoughts on it first thing."

"I pledge it."

"One other thing, Tom."

"Yes?"

"Change your clothes before supper."

Supper in the great hall that night was brief. Scarcely had the last course been served before the king and queen rose and bid the court good night, leaving the nobility free to stay or go as pleased themselves.

Tom suspected that was something of the queen's doing and blessed her for it as he escorted Elizabeth to her chamber not so many minutes later. He could hardly bear to sit there at the table with Elizabeth watching him, shy promise in her eyes and the soft pressure of her hand on his arm to confirm it. As Philip had said, things had changed.

"My lord will do that," Elizabeth told her ladies when they came to her to unbind her hair and ready her for bed. "You are dismissed."

Tom shut the door after them and then stood for a moment simply looking at his wife, admiring the lush jade velvet she was wearing and thinking what a fair thing she was, no matter how she was dressed. He was thinking, too, of the night before and how he longed to touch her again.

"Will you, my lord?" she asked softly, coming up to him. "Please."

Feeling a rushing beat in his heart, he freed her hair and buried his face in it as he had just that morning. Then he turned her toward him. "What next?"

She put her hands tentatively on his chest. "Next you undo the lacings." She pulled the one from his shirt, her eyes fixed on his. "All the way down the back."

He reached around her to do as she bade, and she began drawing his shirt out of his belt, touching her lips to his chest as she did it and pressing her face briefly against him.

"Mmm," she breathed, "I love the smell of you."

He half-smiled and kissed her hair and then went on with his task. It was still only partly done when she began pulling at the lacings that, wrist to elbow, secured the narrow sleeves of his black doublet.

"How do these unfasten?"

He stopped what he was doing and shrugged out of the garment altogether, letting it fall to the floor. Then he put his arms around her again. She began tugging at his shirt, trying to draw it off over his head, and he stopped struggling with her laces once more in order to oblige her. The shirt quickly joined the doublet on the floor.

"Oh, my lord, you are hurt," she murmured, pressing a kiss just below and to the left of his heart, and he flinched a little.

"The merest nothing," he told her as he returned to her laces, but his ribs were bruised blue, and he suspected from the way his shoulder ached that that post had left a corresponding mark down his back.

"You should have punished that impertinent brute," she told him, soothing the place with her hand. "He would have killed you."

"I hardly think so, Bess. He was too angry to fight well and by far too slow."

Finally finished with the last of her laces, he slipped his hand against the smooth softness of her back, drawing her closer to him, feeling the brush of velvet against his chest.

"Besides," he added, looking deeply into her eyes, "I have something much finer for you than what I lost in that match today. If you will have it of me."

He reached into the pouch that hung at his belt and took out the bracelet she had refused from him previously, the one with their initials on it intertwined. She made no protest as he fastened it around her wrist.

Do you love me now? he asked with his eloquent eyes, and she ducked her head against him, which made him catch his breath with a slight gasp.

"You *are* hurt," she said, looking up. "Perhaps we should not—"

"Be still," he whispered, and, nudging her gown into a jade velvet sea around her feet, he quieted her with a kiss.

Dawn had barely crept into the east when Elizabeth woke. Tom was trying to slip his arm from under her, but she snuggled against him, draping her arm across his chest and pressing her face into the curve of his shoulder.

"Mmm, where are you going?"

"I have to look over the additions to the trade agreement," he whispered, brushing his lips against her forehead. "I should have done it yesterday."

"It is so nice just like this," she murmured. "You would not really rather do that, would you?"

"I must, sweet."

She wriggled closer, and he grinned at her.

"Is this the same timid little dove that came to court but a few weeks ago?"

Her face turned pink. "You think me wicked now, for all your saying God meant us to be so."

"I think nothing of the sort, love," he said, pulling her even closer. "You know I do not."

"But I never feel afraid with you anymore, and you've been ever so kind." She caressed his face, tracing her fingers over his mouth. Tom swallowed hard.

"I do have responsibilities, you know." He touched his lips to hers. "As well as it would please me, I cannot spend every moment with you."

"Why not?" she breathed into his ear. Then she kissed his mouth, and somehow he could not think of even one reason.

The sun had been long up when Elizabeth woke again. This time Tom was gone, and Ellen was standing at the foot of the bed, shaking the wrinkles out of the jade velvet dress. Elizabeth sat up with the sheet pulled to her throat, a touch of guilty color in her cheeks. She had not seen Ellen alone since before the dancing on Christmas night.

"Ellen."

The older woman shook her head in disgust. "Hardly here a month."

"But, Ellen—"

"No, my lady, I'll not say another word. No doubt you know your own mind, but I will thank you not to come to me with your weeping once the new is worn off and he grows weary of you."

"I know it may be no more than a brief time," Elizabeth said with a childish pout. "No reason I might not have what pleasure of it I can till then."

"Well, there's my shrewd girl," Ellen said as she laid the dress over the back of a chair and picked up Elizabeth's shift from the floor. "He is a pretty thing, there's no denying. Use him as he uses you and no regrets, eh, lamb?"

Elizabeth curled up under the coverlet again, laying her cheek pensively on Tom's pillow. "I see no harm in it."

If she had told Ellen how she felt now about her husband, about the way her heart rushed just at the sight of him, about how much she enjoyed being wooed and pursued by him, and how pleasant it was to wake cuddled in his arms—if she had told her this, surely Ellen would have laughed her to scorn. Surely Ellen would have called her a little goose and warned her of the deceit of all men. Perhaps she would prove right, too, but that reckoning would have to wait.

CHAPTER

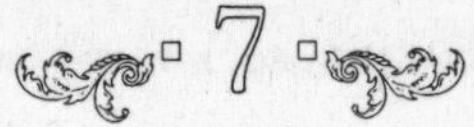

MIGHT I HAVE A WORD WITH YOU, SIR?"

Tom looked up from the sheaf of papers he had scattered on the council table, a harassed expression on his face.

"Mass, Palmer, they've thrown the whole agreement into a coil with their 'one little addition.' I've been two days at this, and still I do not know what I can tell the king to reconcile it all or what he's told the ambassadors to put them off yet again."

"I certainly cannot solve that for you, my lord, but you did wish to hear how the girl Molly is getting along now."

"Yes?"

"They've treated her cruelly, my lord," Palmer told him. "I've had it from Jerome that the laundry girls are at her morning to night for what she was and for what her father did. She bears it well enough, he says, but they can be powerful vicious, forever cutting her with the remembrance that her father was a hanged traitor. Of course they all know the story."

Tom shook his head. "Women can be so cruel to each other." He smiled suddenly and shuffled the papers into a stack. "Put these up, will you, Palmer? Doubtless a short walk will clear my head and make all these trade matters come right. I believe I will pay a visit to Mistress Cooper in the laundry."

"My lord—"

"I think I can find my way there and back."

The chatter in the laundry room immediately ceased when Tom came into it. A dozen startled, heat-reddened faces looked up through the steam. Two dozen chapped hands clutched at wet skirts as the girls curtseyed. Molly stood wide-eyed at the vat of boiling lye and ash she was tending.

"You honor us, my lord," Mistress Cooper said, all aflutter. She had had charge of the laundry and the girls who worked there for much of her long life, and royal visits were always a rarity.

"I see you have a busy place here," Tom said pleasantly, and the old woman smiled.

"My lord, it is," she agreed, "but we're no slackers here."

The girls went quickly back to their tasks, stealing furtive, admiring glances at Tom as they did.

"I came to see if the girl I sent to you is doing well. Molly."

He saw with some satisfaction the impressed looks that a few of the other girls exchanged as Molly made another curtsey.

"She has been a good, quiet girl, my lord," said Mistress Cooper, "and a hard worker."

"Good. I've had charge to look after her and see she's well treated."

Tom went over to the bubbling vat the girl was stirring, and at once his eyes stung from the acrid vapors. Molly's eyes were red, he noticed, but whether that was from the fumes he did not know.

"How kind you are to come, my lord," she said, and he smiled and wrinkled his nose.

"Not the pleasantest of work, is it? Are you sure it is not too hard for you?"

"Oh, no, my lord. It was too good of you to get me a place here in the palace. I can scarce believe it."

He knew the work was grinding, but many girls worked harder and received less. At least she would be sure of food and clothes and shelter and good treatment. With her here, he could see to that himself. He patted her arm.

"Tell me if you want some other work, Molly, or if anyone is unkind to you." He raised his voice a little and scanned the room significantly. "Remember, your friends are my friends, your enemies, mine."

She merely nodded at that, blinking back tears and clutching his arm as he turned to leave.

"My lord, for what my father did—"

"No more of that," he insisted. "I know you were no party to that, and you will anger me truly if you remember it any longer."

She dropped her head and he patted her arm again.

"Let me hear from you how you get on here."

She nodded again, unabashed adoration in her eyes as she watched him and Mistress Cooper walk away. The instant they were gone, one of the girls came to stand near Molly.

"Oh, he's a handsome rascal," she sighed.

"He's no rascal," Molly reproved. "He is a high prince, second only to the king himself."

"I only meant it friendly," the girl said. "Fancy him coming to see one of us. There must be more that you've not told us."

Molly shook her head. "He merely—"

"Girls!" Mistress Cooper cried with a sharp clap of her hands. "You are not employed here to make idle chatter and let the soap boil away!"

"Oh, dear!" Molly prodded the fire to kill it a little. "I am sorry, Mistress Cooper."

"My good report pleased the prince, girl," the old woman said. "Let it remain unchanged."

Molly went back to her work at once, and, in another moment, the other girl made an excuse to work near her.

"Confess," she said under her breath. "You've not told us all."

Molly wiped the sweat from her upper lip and gave the bubbling soap another stir. "He was separated from his men and came to our cottage for shelter. He went the next morning, and I did not see him again until I came to court and then today."

The other girl quickly made her way back to her friends and began wringing steaming water out of some clean sheets.

"She says he stayed the night with her," she told them, careful to keep her voice low.

"What else?" her companions pressed and the girl shook her head.

"Nothing, but I'll get more from her."

"To think, the prince bothering with such a washed-out slut of a girl," one of them crabbed. "How is it he's never taken any notice of any of us?"

Just then, Molly passed by them, carrying the heavy, steaming kettle of soap out to be poured, and the first girl, with a quick wink at the others, followed her into the other room.

"What was it like?"

"What?" Molly asked distractedly, trying not to slosh.

"With Prince Tom. What was it like?" The girl closed her eyes and sighed. "Like holding heaven, I dare say."

"He was very kind to me," Molly said, keeping her eyes on her work. "There was no more to it than that."

"Would he had shown me such kindness," the other girl said with an insinuating smirk. "Oh, just once to have a prince, a real gentleman instead of bragging, ham-handed stable boys and pages. Come, what was it like?"

Molly lifted her head, a touch of anger in her thin face. "I told you, there was nothing between us that way."

"You mean he did not so much as kiss you?"

Molly went back to her work, saying nothing, and the girl crowed in triumph.

"He did! He kissed you! What was it like?"

"I'll not wrong his charity by telling tales of him," Molly said flatly. "Do not ask me again."

❧

At supper that night, Tom met with almost total silence from his wife. It made him remember when they had first married, when, despite his coaxing, she would hardly look at him. She had been afraid of him then, but surely she was not now. She could not be. Not now.

"Will you have more capon, Bess?" Tom asked.

She merely shook her head and did not look up from her plate.

"There will be a play after supper, my lady," he told her. "The company is the best in the city."

"I would like to get some air," she replied, still staring at her plate. "If I may."

"Of course."

He stood up and pulled her chair out for her and escorted her to the balcony.

"I would not want to take you from your supper, my lord," she said with a flash of her eyes, "if you had rather go in."

"No, Bess, I had rather you tell me what has angered you."

She looked out over the city, away from him. "It is nothing. Something has merely disagreed with me."

"I trust it is nothing I've done."

She did not answer, and, from below, he heard the shouts of some of the kitchen boys, playing in the snow after their long day's work. He looked down on them, smiling.

"Did you ever play that, Bess? Taking a snow fortress?"

"No, my lord."

"We always did. Even my father once. I remember it was he and I and John defending, and Richard and Philip laying siege to us. When it was over, the fortress was flat to the ground, and we were all so covered with snow it was hard to say who was who. We never did decide who won it."

She looked a little surprised. "The king played at that with you?"

"You mean my father? Yes. That was long before he was king, of course. He was just the Duke of Afton, and happier for it, too. Mass, he was a fool to give up all that for a crown."

For a moment, he was silent. Then he said, "Perhaps those boys would let me play, too."

"Do you often take sport with commoners, my lord?" she asked with another flash of her eyes.

"There is no harm in it I can see. You enjoyed it when we pretended to be peasants, did you not?"

Her only response was a careless shrug, and he turned her toward him.

"Bess, you are angry with me, I know you are, and I cannot for my life fathom why. What exactly am I to have done?"

"If your conscience does not tell you, I certainly will not."

"Come, now," he coaxed, drawing her a little closer. "What exactly am I to have done? Have you been listening to that old crab's gossip?"

"You mustn't speak so of Ellen."

"Ah, but you knew her by description!"

He laughed and she could not resist a reluctant smile.

"Well, I'll not deny there's been talk."

"There is always talk, love."

"Well—"

What else she might have said turned into a gasp of surprise as an enormous snowball crashed against the side of her head, whitening her dark hair and the shoulder of her ebony gown and leaving a patch of red on her cheek.

"You've hit one of the ladies!" one of the boys cried. "We'll all be hanged sure!"

There was an immediate scrambling of feet and then perfect silence.

"Are you all right, Bess?" Tom asked, trying to keep a straight face.

"Does this amuse you, my lord?" she asked, her eyes blazing.

"No," he managed. Then, in spite of himself he burst out laughing. "I am sorry, sweet, but if you could only see yourself—"

Without another word, she swept back into the great hall and headed for the corridor that led to her chamber. He was right behind her.

"Bess, wait!"

All conversation at the supper table stopped at the sight of them.

"We've had a brief snowfall," Tom explained innocently, and all the nobility laughed as he sprinted after his incensed wife.

When he reached her chamber, he found the door was shut and bolted against him, and there was no answer when he knocked.

"Bess, please, love, do not be vexed with me. Bess?"

Still there was no answer and after a moment he walked away, shaking his head.

"I should have been a monk."

Elizabeth stood on the other side of the door, listening until she was certain he was gone.

"What have you been doing, my lady?" Ellen demanded. "Look at you!"

Elizabeth drew an angry breath and began pulling the clasps out of her hair.

"Well, he's shown his true colors at last, I see," Ellen said, taking over the task. "Whatever he's done, my lamb, I warned you it was but a matter of time. It was bound to be so, after what I told you about him and that little harlot he's put to work in the laundry—"

Keep still, you old crab, Elizabeth thought, a scowl on her stinging face.

"Ready me for bed, Ellen," she said aloud, "Then go away. You weary me."

Ellen did as she was bidden, saying nothing more, but proclaiming her displeasure with every stroke of the brush she ripped through her mistress's thick hair.

"Good," Elizabeth said with a sniff when Ellen finally left the room and she could bolt the door after her.

She got into bed, but she realized after just a few minutes that it was too lonely without Tom. It was cold, too, without him to curl up against.

It was all because of those horrible little boys. They were at the palace to work, not to play, not to make her look foolish before the whole court. As she pulled the coverlet up to her ears, she heard a dull thud against the shuttered window. She paid it no mind until it was repeated, twice, four times.

"Ellen?" she called, but there was no one but herself to see what it was. Wrapped in a blanket against the cold, she went to the window.

Thud. Thud.

She threw open the shutter, and something white streaked in through the window and exploded against her shoulder.

"Beasts!" she shrieked, slapping away the powdery remains of the snowball. "You come up here at once and bring the cook! I'll see he keeps you busy enough that you'll have no time for such foolery! And gives you a switching you'll not forget!"

To her astonishment, she heard a man's deep laughter.

"Must I bring the cook?"

"My lord!"

Tom stepped into the rectangle of light that fell from the window of her tower room onto the snowy top of the castle wall one level below. There was a teasing smile on his face.

"I had rather hoped I might see you alone tonight, Bess, but I will fetch him if you wish."

"My—my lord—"

"I never meant that snowball to hit you, my lady," he said, his expression playful and pleading all at once. "I know you'll hardly believe me, but I never did. I merely could think of no other way to get you to speak to me. Say you forgive me."

She said nothing as she looked down upon him, but she could not deny she was glad he had come back.

"Look, love, there are mounds of snow there on the ledge by you." He spread his arms out wide. "I will stand here and you may pitch all of it down on me if you like. And if that is not enough, I will bring you more still, so long as you forgive me."

"I suppose I did look a sight with all that snow in my hair," she said, her expression softening.

"Only a beautiful sight," he replied. "I would never have laughed, love, but I thought you would laugh, too. I was raised with three rowdy brothers, sweetheart, and do not always remember the delicateness of ladies. But I swear I will learn if you will allow me."

He disappeared into the darkness, and then she heard a rustling in the thick trellis of vines that trained up the side of the tower.

"My lord?"

"Your door is bolted," he said, looking up over her windowsill.

She stared at him in astonishment. "I—I could have unbolted it."

"Say you forgive me," he said softly, moving closer to her. "For all that's been between us these past few days. Because I love you."

"Surely that means little to you."

"Bess, can you say so?" There was gentle reproof in his voice. "Do you know me yet so little?"

She smiled unsteadily. Was she to turn him away for the sake of her pride and the rumor of a year-old kiss? After what had been between them?

"You make it difficult to be angry with you, my lord."

He pulled himself up higher and kissed her, and she sighed and closed her eyes, savoring the taste of him, the warmth of his lips on hers. He kissed the corner of her mouth. Then he nuzzled her cheek and her ear.

"Grant me one thing, Bess," he whispered.

"Mmm?"

"Let me come in before I lose my footing here."

Her eyes flew open and he grinned at her. She could not help but laugh.

"I'll take that as assent," he said as he vaulted over the sill. She flung herself into his arms, making him stumble backwards.

"Careful, love," he said, laughing, too, "or you shall land us both back in the snow."

He shuttered the window again. Then he sat down at the fire and drew her into his lap.

"Tell me now, sweet, why you were cross with me at supper."

"I do not wish to speak of that now," she said, lowering her eyes. "It is of no importance."

"Of course it is." He cuddled her to him. "If it makes you unhappy, it is of every importance to me. Tell me and I will make it right."

She pressed her face against his chest, fighting sudden tears. "Tell me again what was between you and that—that laundry girl."

"Nothing," he said and he kissed her hair. "I swear it. Nothing."

"And tell me what you said to her . . . about me."

She looked up at him suddenly, and he took her face in both his hands, looking steadily into her eyes.

"I told her I belonged to the sweetest lady in Christendom and I could never betray her."

"Never tell me anything more," she murmured. She lifted her mouth to his.

By tradition, the first day of the new year was reserved for the petitions any citizen of Winton wished to bring before the king. These were usually requests for fishing rights or the use of common lands or permission to hunt in restricted areas of the forest. It gave the king an opportunity to show his bounty to his people. The custom had been discontinued during the war, and Philip was pleased to reinstate it this year.

All the nobility was gathered for the event. Rosalynde sat at her husband's side with the baby in her lap for all the people to see. Tom was at his place, too, and Elizabeth was with him, watching the spectacle. Even Lady Margaret who, pleading sickness, had been rarely at court, was in attendance.

There was a long line of petitioners, shopkeepers and laborers, soldiers and peasants, all gathered to speak to the king. More than a few were audacious in what they asked for, but most of the requests were reasonable and easily granted. Some of the people even came with a word of thanks or encouragement or sometimes a small gift. It was one of the few times Philip truly enjoyed being king, and Tom could see it on his face.

"What may I do for you men?" Philip asked late in the afternoon as three freshly scrubbed farmers came before him with awkward bows.

There was a brief murmuring between them. Then they pushed the one in the middle forward.

"We, uh—" He glanced back at his companions and they urged him on. "Your majesty, we grant you felicitations on this new year and ask that you grace us to accept this token of our allegiance to your majesty, and your lady, and to Prince Tom. Oh, and to his lady, too."

One of the others thrust a sack toward him, and he reached into it and pulled out a fat piglet, pink and squirming.

"I thank you," Philip said without a hint of amusement in his smile, and, immediately, Robin fixed his eyes on the animal and began gurgling and reaching for it.

"She's the best of the litter, my lord," the farmer said with a nod, "or we'd not have brought her."

Robin began crowing and bouncing, trying still to reach the piglet, and Philip laughed.

"You have pleased my son more than everyone else today, friends. For that, I truly thank you. Is there nothing you wish from me?"

"Oh, no, my lord," the man said, aghast. "You give us justice and fair rule and we ask nothing more, save God bless you to continue in it."

"I could ask no better answer, nor no finer gift." Philip took the pig from him and showed it to the baby. "See the nice piggy?"

Robin cooed and slapped one slobbery palm against the pig's round belly and it began to squeal. Philip handed it quickly to the lanky blond page that stood attendance there.

"See she's taken care of, Jerome."

"Of course, my lord."

As soon as the pig was out of his sight, Robin began to howl, and no amount of shushing could stop him.

"He should have had a nap hours ago, my lord," Rosalynde said. "I will take him now, if you will pardon me."

She stood and all the courtiers bowed. The three farmers looked very uneasy as they watched her leave.

The one in the middle cleared his throat. "Your majesty, perhaps we should not have—"

"Nonsense," Philip interrupted. "Even a prince must learn he cannot have everything he sees. Even such a fine pig as that one."

All three of the men turned bright red under the praise and almost tripped over each other in bowing out of the great hall.

"You cannot buy such loyalty," Philip murmured, and Tom nodded in agreement.

The next man in line was short and slight, his lank hair sparse and nondescript, his whole person reminding Tom of nothing so much as a weasel. He obviously had never been inside a palace before.

"I am to deliver this into your hands only, my dread lord," the man said, his unaccustomed eyes darting all the while from one courtly splendor to another. Philip grinned and reached out to the man.

"Well, here is my hand, fellow. Give me your message."

The messenger ducked his head and held out the paper, forcing Philip to step down to get it. As he read it, the amusement in his expression vanished, leaving him frozen there in bloodless incredulity. Tom left Elizabeth's side and took his brother's arm.

"Philip?"

"No," Philip murmured, almost pulling the note in half with his vise-like grip. "Oh, God, please, no."

He let it flutter to the floor and Tom snatched it up.

"Philip—"

"Dismiss them, Tom," Philip said, his trembling words hardly coherent. "I—I cannot see them now."

Nobles and commoners alike watched in amazement as the king left the court without even a word to them.

"Go after him, Rafe," Tom ordered, but Rafe was already heading for the corridor that led to Philip's chamber.

Shielding it from the concerned, curious eyes that surrounded him, Tom read the message. It was as brief and deadly as the stroke of a dagger.

Elizabeth tugged at his arm. "My lord—"

"Holy God help us, Bess," he breathed. He read the note again. It was unsigned, written in an undistinguished, neat hand he did not recognize. When he looked up, he noticed that the messenger had disappeared.

"Find the man that brought this," he told Palmer quietly. He raised his voice to speak to the court. "The king will hear no more today. He prays your patience and will see all of you in good time."

The people filtered out of the great hall in murmuring knots of twos and threes, wondering among themselves at their sudden dismissal. Tom read the note over once more, telling himself again and again that there could be no truth to it, but unable to still the goading voice inside him that said it at least was possible.

"What is it?" Elizabeth asked, trying to see the paper.

"Please, my lady—"

"He sent me away, my lord," Rafe interrupted. "He'll not speak to me or allow me near him. No, nor anyone."

"We must send the queen to him," Tom said, wishing he was at liberty to answer the anxious question in the older man's eyes.

Rafe made a hasty bow. "I will fetch her, my lord."

Palmer came back into the court as Rafe was leaving.

"There is no trace of the man, my lord. Shall I send out more men to search?"

"No, and tell no one I sent you after him. This may be nothing, but, true or false, a rumor of it could make things difficult for the king."

"Of course, my lord. Is there nothing else I might do?"

"Yes, hurry up Rafe with the queen."

"I am here, my lord," Rosalynde said, suddenly at Tom's side. "Master Bonnechamp said the king went very pale at something a messenger brought and left the court without explanation. What has happened?"

He knew she could have learned little from Rafe's account, but he knew, too, how well she read his brother. No nuance of Philip's moods ever escaped her. She would know how best to comfort him and strengthen him in this.

He glanced at Elizabeth. "Please, Bess, have patience. Palmer, take my lady to her chamber. We will talk later, sweet."

Palmer took Elizabeth's arm and bowed smoothly to the queen. "If you will pardon me, your majesty."

"Please," Tom said, seeing Elizabeth was about to protest. Aware of the bewildered concern on the queen's face, Elizabeth made no objection.

Tom watched them disappear into the corridor. Clutching the paper more tightly, he turned to Rosalynde, wondering what he was to say, searching for words that would not wound.

"What has happened?" she asked again. "What is in that paper that made my lord lose color so swiftly and that you could not speak of before your lady?"

"Will you sit down?"

She put her hand to her throat. "Is it so bad as that?"

"Please, my lady."

She sank down onto her throne, her eyes fixed on his.

"You must be strong now, my lady. What is in this note may be no more than a brutal jest. Think it no more until we know otherwise."

He put the crumpled paper into her hand and watched disbelief and pain pass over her face as she read it.

Katherine Fletcher did not die in Bakersfield as you were told. She is living in Ivybridge with her father. A righteous king and true knight would do right by her. You know the just claim she has on you.

Tom took Rosalynde's hands, wadding the note between them.

"Oh, it is cruel. It is too cruel," she said, her voice as unsteady as her cold fingers.

"Be strong, my lady. For his sake. Until it is proven, if it can be proven, he will need you with him. He will need your comforting."

"What can I say to him? How can I ever comfort him? If she is alive—"

"Please, my lady, you must show steady in this if he is to bear it at all. Your grief would break him now."

She pressed her lips tightly together and closed her eyes. Then, after a moment, her expression smoothed and she lifted her head.

"I will go to him."

CHAPTER

PHILIP STOOD GAZING INTO THE FIRE, WATCHING THE MOCKING dance of the flames. He had seen his dear wife Katherine taken away, taunted and stoned and spit upon by the vengeful crowds, denied the dignity of anything more than a shift to cover her tender body. That body he had held dear, the one he had exchanged innocence with, had been burned. Long ago, it had been burned. He still was sickened with the remembered smell, but he had not seen the burning.

You said for me to remember your love and forget all the rest.

He had. Almost he had. With Rosalynde, by God's pure grace, he had found love and peace and healing for his deep wounds. Now those wounds were again ripped open and rubbed with salt.

The message said Kate was alive. How he would have rejoiced once at that news. Now it plunged him into torment. If Kate was alive, then Rosalynde—

Rosalynde had loved him beyond what he would have believed was mortal capacity to love. Even at his most extreme cruelty, in the cold, bitter depths of his grief, she had loved him and taught him to love her, taught him to trust his heart to her. Now, if Kate was alive, Rosalynde was not truly his wife. She could not even keep the place and title of queen. They were Kate's, just as he was himself. If Kate was alive, his marriage to Rosalynde was nothing but adultery, their happiness stolen, their child—

He went to the chest that sat at the foot of his bed and began pulling things out of it, piling them one on another until he reached the ornate gold-fitted box that was buried at the very bottom. He took it out and sat down on the bed with it.

It felt heavy in his hands, heavier than its small size and weight warranted, and for a long while he merely held it there. Then, knowing he could not still the tempest inside him, he unlatched it and lifted the lid.

"My lord?"

Rosalynde found him sitting on the bed, surrounded by his scattered possessions, staring at the long braid of golden hair that was wrapped around his hands like a rope to bind him. She knew at once it was Katherine's. He had told her how they had cut off her hair to proclaim her condemnation, the hair he had praised like warm sunshine.

"Philip?"

"They told me she was dead," he said, not looking up. "They said she was burned."

She knelt down before him and squeezed his arm, her eyes filled with compassion and pain for his pain. It had been a long while since she had seen that look on his face, that stunned, sickened look that made her think his heart's blood had suddenly drained away.

"Oh, Rose, if she is alive—"

She gently unwound the braid and laid it in his lap. She took his hands and held them in both of hers.

"Whatever happens, God will make us a way to bear it."

"I cannot—" He drew a tight breath and she could feel him trembling. "I cannot bear it all again."

He looked at her, his eyes pleading; then he pulled her fiercely up into his arms. "Do not lose me, Rose. I cannot go back into the darkness."

"Philip—"

He kissed her hard, desperately. Then he pulled away from her and stood up, his hands shaking as he stuffed the braid back into the box that had held it.

"I—I need—" He put the box back into the chest and began cramming everything else in a jumbled pile on top of it. "I am going riding."

She picked up one of his shirts, folded it, and laid it carefully with the rest of his things only to have him shove it down between some old boots and cover it with a rumpled cloak.

"Philip, it is nearly suppertime. Surely morning would be—"

He closed the chest and a moment later he was gone, leaving behind nothing more than a curt order for Rafe not to follow after him or allow anyone else to. Rosalynde ate little that evening, and, when it grew late, she could not sleep, knowing he was out in the night alone. He was familiar with the roads, she was well aware, but his mind would not be on them. He would be driving his horse recklessly through the cold darkness, trying to outrun the pain.

It was after eleven when she heard a noise in the nursery and crept in to see if the baby had awakened. Philip was there, sweat-stained and disheveled from his ride, his brow furrowed with the deep ache inside him. He was rocking their sleeping child in his arms and whispering against his satin cheek.

"I am sorry, little summer Robin. Sorry, sorry, sorry."

It was a moment before he realized she was there.

"He pulled himself up by the bed curtains this morning and took a step or two," she said softly, trying to smile. "Then he fell onto his little backside. He had such a look on his face when he did it, as if he did not expect—"

"I have to go there."

"He was too surprised even to cry."

"I have to go there, Rosalynde." He touched his lips to the baby's cheek and laid him back in the cradle. "I cannot live this way."

She nodded. "I thought you would need to find out for certain."

His mouth turned up a little at the corners, and he touched her cheek. "How well you know me, Rose. And you always understand. You always—"

His voice caught deep down in his throat, and she put her arms around him.

"Philip, please—"

He kissed her as he had before, hard and fierce and desperate, sinking into the familiar comfort of her embrace, holding her as if the touch of her could soothe his aching soul far more than his body. She responded with as deep a passion, drinking in the feel of him, the scent of him. She needed this. Right now she needed this. Soon he would go to find out the truth, and if Katherine was alive—

He shoved her away with a sob. "You mustn't touch me. I mustn't touch you."

"Please, love," she begged, her arms around his waist, "I know you must go. I'll not ask you not to, but do not leave me this way. Kiss me again. Hold me. If it must be the last—"

He pulled her up against his heart and pressed his cheek against her hair. "Rose, sweet Rose, can you think I want to leave you? You know how I've needed you. How I need you now." He held her tighter. "How I want you."

"Just this once more," she breathed, "if it must be the last."

She could feel the struggle inside him as he held her there. She could feel it in the strained tautness of his body and in the breath that shuddered out of him.

"I mustn't betray her any more than I have, Rose. Help me be strong in this." He held her even closer. Then he set her on her feet and gently took her arms from around him. "Please, help me."

She clutched her hands over her heart, so they would not reach for him anymore, and swallowed hard to keep the tears from her eyes. When he took her back to her chamber and left her alone, just touching her forehead with the most chaste of kisses, she made no protest. It was long hours before she slept, but she filled the time praying that he would find peace, and truth together with it, whatever God meant that peace and truth to be.

"Talk to me, Philip."

Tom was sitting by the fire in Philip's chamber. Rafe had told him of Philip's order that he not be followed, so Tom had determined to wait. He had been there nearly five hours before Philip returned.

"There is nothing I can say." Philip cupped his hands in the wash water that had been hot when Rafe had brought it early that evening. "I must go to Ivybridge."

He splashed his face and set his teeth against the chill.

"Could you not send someone to see to it, Philip?" Tom asked. "I know this wants careful handling. I will go, if you like."

"No." Philip stripped off his soiled shirt and dropped it on the floor. "If she is changed, you might not know her."

Tom knew the questions that would be clawing at his brother's mind now. If Katherine was alive, why hadn't she come back to him, gotten word to him somehow, before now? Unless, thinking her dead on the pyre, her executioners had doused the blaze and somehow, through some miracle, she had been spirited away. But, if she had lived through it, what would be left of her?

"*You* might not know her," Tom said and Philip shook his head.

"I would." Philip splashed the cold water on his bare chest and began scrubbing his skin with the towel. "There is nothing for it, Tom, but I must go. I will take Jerome with me, though."

Tom stood up. "You cannot think to go so far with no more guard than that. Be reasonable. Our enemies would be only too happy to find you unprotected and take you prisoner or take your life."

Philip dipped his hands again into his wash basin and ran them through his hair. "If they do, I leave Lynaleigh to you. You have the next claim."

"But Robin—"

Again Philip shook his head. "So long as there is doubt, so long as there is even a possibility—" He leaned on the table, his arms braced against it and his head bowed. "I wish I could say it was not so, but, if Kate is alive, then Robin cannot be considered in the succession. I realize now what Father meant when he said he had a sacred trust to keep the bloodline pure. God and all heaven knows how deep I love that boy, but, if Kate is alive, he is a bastard."

"Philip, no."

"If I could have known this would happen, I would never have brought him into this world." There was sudden pain in Philip's sensitive face. "At least I do not have to stop loving him."

Tom knew he was thinking of Rosalynde and the love between them that had been so hard won, the love they could no longer call holy if Katherine was alive.

"It may be the report is false. Anyone can write a message."

"I cannot be sure, not until I go there. If she is alive—" There was a tortured look in Philip's eyes. "God forgive me, I do not want her to be alive. Tom, I loved her. I love her still! What kind of monster am I that I wish her dead? But Rosalynde—" His voice broke and he clutched his side as if to still the pain. "Heaven and earth, Tom, how can I leave her?"

"God will make a way for you to do what you must," Tom said, drawing him down into one of the chairs. "He will care for Rosalynde, too. As for Katherine, if she is alive, she'll not hold you to fault for what you could not possibly have known." He leaned down to have his eyes level with his brother's. "She'll not hold you to fault for wanting to keep the peace and happiness you've found. She could not ask more in mourning than you have spent for her already, not if she loved you even the half of what I know she did."

"God will make a way," Philip repeated, looking at the ring he wore on his right hand. It had none of the gleaming magnificence of the ruby ring that marked him as a true-blooded king of Lynaleigh. It was scarred and bent, the lions engraved in it almost mangled out of recognizability, but Philip had forbidden the goldsmiths to repair it. To him, it was a symbol of something more precious than his royalty and every mark on it was a reminder.

He had been given the ring by the Duke of Westered, Rosalynde's father, the day they had married, and Westered had told his new son-in-law to send the ring back to him if ever he was in need of help from him and his army. As the war became more desperate over that summer and fall, Rosalynde had urged Philip to send for her father's help. He had proudly refused, growing more and more adamant until, in a fit of temper, he had thrown the ring out into the snowy night in faraway Treghatours.

Months later, when Winton was surrounded by Stephen of Ellenshaw's men and Philip knew there was no way of escape, he had finally acknowledged his helplessness and called on God for help. That help had come the very next day in the form of a great army, Westered's men, summoned through some miracle by the ring Philip had thought forever lost.

He was never certain how it got from Treghatours all the way to Westered to bring help at just the moment he needed it. He was only certain of the One who had arranged for it to be there.

"I remember and I believe," he said now, turning the battered band of gold that circled his finger, and some of the strength came back into his face. "But I must go to Ivybridge."

Tom noticed the half-conscious gesture and then looked at the ruby that graced Philip's other hand. "You may as well cut your own throat as wear that openly without an army at your back."

"I will leave it here," Philip said. "If I should not return, I want Robin to have it. If I could not give him an unspotted name, I can still acknowledge him mine."

"Let me come with you, Philip," Tom said, suddenly urgent. "The two of us together—"

"No."

"Philip—"

"No. Who will keep the kingdom for me, Tom, if not you? Who else can keep our pack of noble wolves from tearing out each other's throats? Who can best care for the queen in my absence? She trusts you above anyone at court, and I know you would never wrong her trust. Or mine. Please, Tom, give me the assurance that, whatever I face out there, here there will be certain peace."

Tom bowed his head and knelt before his king, one hand over his heart.

"So God make me faithful."

Tom came to bed late, stripping off his clothes and getting into bed without a candle. Elizabeth had been asleep some while, but the gentle motion woke her and she instinctively pressed close to his warmth.

He did not put his arms around her as he usually did, and after a moment, she opened her eyes. In the darkness, she could only see his profile against the pillow, edged with firelight, but she could feel without seeing that there was something troubled about him.

"My lord?"

He drew an unsteady breath. "I did not mean to wake you, love. I am sorry."

"What news did that messenger bring the king today?"

He did not answer for a long time. Then, without warning, he grabbed her hand and held it hard.

"Pray, Bess. Please, for Philip and for his lady, too, pray."

"What am I to pray, my lord?" she asked, startled by his urgency.

"Just pray that God will be merciful. I cannot tell you more."

She could hear the anguish in his voice, and somehow she did not have the heart to press him to explain. Instead, she leaned up and touched her lips to his forehead. He pulled her closer, holding her tightly to his heart.

"I would die if ever I had to be without you, Bess," he said with surprising fierceness, and she merely clung to him, half afraid to know what it was he could not say.

"You wished to see me, my lord?"

Jerome stood hesitantly in the doorway to the king's chamber and wondered what calamity had prompted a royal summons so shortly after dawn. Philip motioned him closer.

"Come in."

Jerome closed the door and went to him, the disquiet in his master's taut face painting concern on his own.

"I've known you not much more than a year, Jerome, but there are not half a dozen, nor hardly the half of that, I would sooner trust."

"I've done no more than duty, my lord."

"And done it better than duty asks. Would you be willing to do yet more?"

"Of course, my lord. You have but to command me."

"Then I must first command your silence. What I tell you must go no further. Not even your confessor is to hear of it."

"Of course, my lord."

"Next, for a time, you must forget I am the king. Not majesty, nor lord, simply Philip." There was a hint of amusement in Philip's expression. "Your elder brother."

"My brother?" Jerome asked incredulously. "If that pleases you." He flashed his lopsided grin. "Philip."

"Good. Do you know of a place, south almost to Grenaver, called Ivybridge?"

Jerome nodded.

"If I am to get there unhindered, it will have to be in secret. No one will look twice at a pair of brothers out to seek their fortunes now the war is over. I will need you to show me places we might stop at along the way, places such men might frequent." A slight smile touched Philip's face. "I have never stayed at an inn."

"No doubt you will find it an education, my lord. Am I to know our errand?"

The smile vanished. "I do not know what gossip you might have heard since you've been at court, Jerome, or if they yet speak of it, but there was a girl once—she, uh—Lady Margaret was married to my elder brother, Richard, until he was killed two years ago. Of course, his death meant Margaret could never be queen, so she quickly shed her mourning and married our enemy, Stephen of Ellenshaw, and backed his bid for the crown. It was no hindrance to her that she was carrying my brother's child at the time, or that that child was true heir to the throne. She merely poisoned it in her womb so it was born dead and she was free of the inconvenience. It was no more to her than that."

"I knew she had betrayed your father and gone to Ellenshaw, my lord. I did not know of the child."

"Back then, when she first married my brother and came to court, she had a waiting woman, in truth little more than a girl, Katherine Fletcher. She was—" Philip shook his head, as if he were searching for words expressive enough. "She was not what most would call beautiful, but I thought her so. She had the gentlest way about her. She was—when she—" He walked to the window and looked down on the garden, on the winter-barren silhouettes of the rose trees. "She knew of Margaret's infanticide and told me of it," he said without emotion. "I went to the king with it, but he twisted her words and mine and had her condemned for the murder and for witchcraft, too."

"Witchcraft? My lord, your own father?"

"I loved her. My father knew it, and knew, too, I would never give her up. He ordered me to marry someone of the nobility in order to strengthen his hold on the throne. He told me I could keep Kate as my mistress so long as the wife I took and her kin knew nothing of it. I told him it could never be so, not with me. So for that trifle, conscience, for that nothing we call honor, because I would not betray her and myself and the wife he wanted for me, he had her killed. He claimed she had by sorcery enslaved me to her will and had killed Margaret's child so I would be next heir and she might, through me, be queen."

"If she was found guilty of witchcraft, that would mean—"

"Burning."

"Oh, my lord."

"I came near to madness when they told me she was dead. I spent, oh, I cannot say how long, in grief for her, but God gave me His mercy and my queen to pull me back from the abyss." Philip turned from the window, his eyes reflecting the torment he had passed through. "I thought I would never have to look into it again."

"You needn't tell me, my lord, if it pains you," Jerome said quietly.

Philip shook his head. "I had word yesterday that Kate is still alive."

"Alive? Oh, my lord! Are you certain of that?"

"I must make certain. The queen—"

"She loves you so, my lord, and she is your wife. Whatever your feelings were for this Katherine, surely—"

"You do not understand. Kate and I were married. I never told my father that. It would have only enraged him more, but she was my wife, never my mistress, and it was only after I thought her dead that I consented to marry again. Now she may be alive. Knowing that—Jerome, you must see—"

Jerome bit his lip, pity in his gray eyes. "The queen. And the little prince, too. I am sorry."

"For their sakes as much as my own, I must know for certain about Kate. She told me once that her father was an armorer and a maker of arrows in Ivybridge. The message said she is there with him now."

"But how did she survive, my lord? Why have you not heard before now?"

"I cannot say. The message said only that she is alive and in Ivybridge."

"Of course I will go with you, my lord."

Philip nodded. "Remember this must be between the two of us alone. The queen knows of it, and my brother, but there is no one else. If the news got out, it might destroy the peace we made out of the divisions of our late war."

"They could not torture it out of me."

"One thing more. If anything should happen to me and you escape it, I want you to promise me you'll bring my ring back to my brother, so he will know. This one," Philip said, indicating the battered gold band. "I am trusting you, Jerome."

"I will bring it though I die the moment after."

"Thank you."

"I will be ready to leave when it pleases you, my lord."

Again Philip nodded and Jerome bowed, the gravity of his trust showing in his young face.

"Jerome?"

He stopped at the doorway. "My lord?"

"Whatever we find in Ivybridge, I have truly loved the queen. She has been life and breath to me. Nothing else could tear me from her side."

Jerome's only answer was an understanding nod.

Philip pulled on his boots, the old ones he rarely wore anymore even into the forest, and stood up. If anyone asked, he was spending the day hunting with his page. The rest of his clothing bore that out and was not fine enough to attract notice when he went among the people. Jerome had secured him even meaner garb that he planned to change into at the first opportunity. No one would see a king when they looked on him then.

"Be wary, Philip," Tom said, taking his brother's hand in a strong clasp. "Keep to the quiet towns and the side roads. Above all, let no one know who you are."

Philip nodded and Tom released his hand, smiling a little.

"I suppose you knew that without my telling you."

Philip took the worn cloak out of the chest and dropped the lid back down, his taut expression unchanging. "When I've been an hour gone, tell the queen and give her my ring. She does not think I am leaving until nightfall." He looked at the floor. "I could not bear the parting."

"Philip—"

"Send for Joan to come to her, will you, Tom? I do not know why I never thought to before. Joan would be a deal more use to her than any number of these light-brained geese that attend her now."

"I'll do it straight," Tom promised.

"Beyond that—"

"Did you mean to leave without a word, my lord?"

They both turned at Rosalynde's gentle voice and Tom bowed.

"I will see if the boy has your horses ready, Philip," Tom said, giving his brother's shoulder a steadying squeeze. "We will meet you in the stable."

Rosalynde waited until she heard the door close. Then she reached out one soft, white hand.

"Without one little word to me, love?"

Philip knelt before her and kissed that hand as if he feared he would profane it with his unworthy touch, and she dared one last time to stroke the dark sleekness of his hair, breathing a blessing upon him as she did. She would not beg him again to kiss her lips or hold her in his arms. She had always loved his principled strength, and she loved it now, even when it hurt. If she had been Katherine, she would have wanted him to be so perfect in his faithfulness.

"You have been too good and true, my lady," he said, not looking up. "I would I could have been so good and true to you."

"You have. These past months—"

"No. I've wanted to. I've wanted to make up for all the hurt I brought you before, but I've repaid you with this instead." His head drooped lower. "You deserved a better fate than to be matched with such a wretched fool."

"Do you truly wish my good?" she asked.

"You know I do."

"And you would not wish to see me hurt?"

"No, never."

"Then do not speak ill of him I love with all my soul."

He touched his lips again to her trembling fingers, holding them there for a long fervent moment, as if he knew once this kiss was broken there would be no more. Then he lifted his head, and she saw that the crystal depths of his eyes were made bluer and deeper with the tears that stood in them. There was such longing in those eyes.

Somehow she did not cry and she was glad. She did not want to burden him with her grief or make worse for him what was already torture, and how much better it would be for him to remember her eyes filled with love rather than tears.

Still clutching her fingers, he stood up. "It has been a sweet thing to walk beside you, my lady. A sweet, sweet thing."

In spite of her resolve, a deep sob tore through her.

"Oh, Rose—"

She clutched him to her as if she would memorize him all over again. Then she pushed him away.

"Go now, my lord, or I can never bear for you to go at all."

"Farewell," he said, his face a mask of kingly dignity. Then he took the ruby ring from his finger and pressed it into her hand. "This is for my son. Tell him I love him."

She clutched it to her heart, and she caught his hand, the one with the other ring still on it.

"Remember, love."

He touched the scarred gold and nodded once. Then he was gone.

❧

Tom knew where he would find Rosalynde once Philip left her. The west tower was set highest in the castle, highest in the whole city, and from there she would be able to make that final sight of her beloved last longest. He stood in silence behind her until Philip was no longer even a speck along the horizon. He put his reassuring hands on her shoulders.

"He will come back, my lady."

"With her, do you think?" she asked, turning to him.

"I cannot say. I can scarce believe such a story true, but I cannot promise you it is not."

"If it is, you know where that leaves Robin."

"Lady Rosalynde—"

"The bastard child of a king's mistress."

"My lady—"

"A king's harlot."

"You were never that to him."

She put one hand on her stomach. "What am I to do now? I could not tell him."

"Tell him what, my lady?"

She lifted her eyes to his, a pleading sadness in her delicate, pale face. Then she let the tears come.

"I am with child again."

CHAPTER

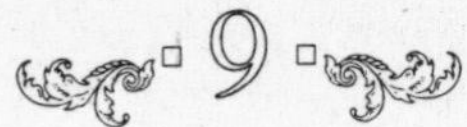

THE WINTER CAME BACK FIERCE AND HARD, MAKING TRAVEL SLOW and uncomfortable. Every day Tom watched for a sign of Palmer returning from the north, from Treghatours, with Joan. Then, late one afternoon, when he and Elizabeth were returning from their walk, he saw a carriage and an unmistakable long-haired rider leading it through the gates.

"Palmer!"

He sprinted down the palace steps into the courtyard.

"Palmer, you did bring her?"

Palmer dismounted, his expression surly, his rough hands and face covered with deep scratches.

"Yes, my lord, and a few others she insisted accompany her."

"Yes?" Tom grinned. "I take it you did not get on well with at least one of them."

Palmer scowled and there was a mournful howl from inside a pouch on his saddle.

"Oh, Palmer, you did not—"

Tom tore open the pouch and pulled out a perturbed-looking gray cat with a white muzzle and white legs and huge gold-green eyes. At first she hissed, but, seeing who it was that held her, she started to purr and butt her head against his chest. Tom took the hint and began scratching her under the chin.

Palmer shook his head in disgust. "It's beyond me and that's flat.

I had as soon face another rebel army as that little hellcat, but hand her to you, my lord, and she is sweet as a new lamb."

"You are the bravest man I know," Tom said, laughing, "I swear."

The carriage slowed to a stop, and, cradling the cat in his arm, Tom reached up to open the door. At once he found himself half-smothered against Joan's ample bosom.

"Tom, my honey-love."

"I am so glad you've come, Joan," he murmured, blinking back unforeseen tears. He straightened and smiled down into her sweetly-lined face. "Come. You must meet my lady."

Elizabeth was still standing at the top of the stairs, watching, and Tom dragged the old woman up to her.

"Bess, Bess, this is Joan. I have told you about her. Joan, this is my lady, the Princess Elizabeth."

"My lady," Joan said with a puffing curtsey. "Please, my lord, you may be two-and-twenty, but it's been some while since I was." She bobbed another quick curtsey. "Your pardon, my lady."

"My lord has spoken of you much, Mistress Joan," Elizabeth said with a shy smile. Tom had told her of his home in the north and of this woman who had been more than a mother to him and his brothers since before he could remember. "And I suppose this is Grace."

Tom smiled again and held the cat out to her, but, taking a quick look at Palmer as he unloaded the baggage, she took a cautious step backwards.

"Yes, I thought it might be."

"Never be afraid of her, love," Tom said. "She'll be used to you soon and you will see what a sweet thing she is. My younger brother, John, raised her by hand. She followed him about like a dog and it near broke his heart to leave her behind in Treghatours." There was a sudden wistfulness in his eyes, reflected in the sparkle of a tear in Joan's. "Since he died, she's been rather particular of the company she keeps, but we are old friends, she and I. Are we not, my Grace?"

He began rubbing behind her soft ears and she purred again, nestling against him.

"And where is the child?" Joan demanded as she unfastened her cloak. "And his little mother?"

"She's been longing to see you since she left Treghatours," Tom said, taking Elizabeth's arm.

"Come along, Nan," Joan called. "We haven't all the day, now."

"Yes, Gran," came a girl's voice from the carriage. Then, laden with a pile of bundles, the girl stepped into the courtyard.

"This cannot be little Nan!" Tom exclaimed, going back down to her. She could not have been above seventeen, but she was nearly as tall as he was, a raw-boned redhead with a plain, friendly face and a handful of freckles scattered across her broad nose. She beamed at him.

"It has been some while, my lord. I am head and shoulders over Gran now."

"So you are," he said with a laugh, seeing small resemblance between her and her little, round grandam. "Well, you must meet my lady, too, Nan."

Shifting Grace into a more secure position, he took some of the girl's bundles, and, Palmer trailing after with the rest of the things, they all went into the palace. Once inside, Tom sent Nan to the kitchen to feed the cat and had Palmer settle the baggage. Then he and Elizabeth took Joan to see the queen.

"She does not know you were sent for," he told Joan as they approached Rosalynde's chamber. "But she will be that glad to see you."

One of the serving women admitted them, and they found Rosalynde sitting in her window with Robin sound asleep against her shoulder. Her emerald eyes brimming with tears, she was looking out into the forest, where she had last seen Philip, Tom was certain, and too wrapped in thought to notice she had visitors.

"The very picture of my Philip," Joan said softly, sitting beside Rosalynde and touching her fingers to the baby's dark curls.

Rosalynde turned from the window, and Joan held out her arms, her weathered face filled with maternal compassion. An instant later, mother and child were enfolded in those arms, and Rosalynde began sobbing out all the grief that was in her broken heart.

"Come, Bess," Tom whispered, and he led his wife from the room.

Within a few days, Joan had brought her particular bustling efficiency into the palace. Sweeping aside all of the queen's high-born attendants, she looked after Rosalynde herself, and, Tom found, she had taken almost complete charge of the baby, too.

"Philip would be glad to see you with his son," he told her when he stopped into the nursery. "He's often said Robin would be none the worse to have you part of his bringing up."

She scooped the last bit of porridge into the baby's mouth and quickly spooned back in the little bit that dribbled out at one side. Grace sat next to her, her white paws tucked under her and her green eyes watching every bite.

"He's sure his father's image, I must say," Joan said, scraping the bowl and setting it on the floor for the cat to finish. "He will have my lord of Afton's dark eyes, though."

Though Tom's father had died a king, to Joan he would always be as she had known him first almost thirty years before: Robert, Duke of Afton. Tom smiled a little at her unchanging ways; then he looked more closely at the baby's eyes.

"That's odd. I swear they were not so even two days ago."

"But that was two days ago," Joan said wisely.

"I had thought sure by now they would stay blue, like Philip's."

Joan tickled the baby and made him crow. "We had thought so of yours, too, when you were this one's size, but one day they were all flecked with brown just like this, and soon there was no blue left to them. This one will look more like his uncle than his father."

"The queen will be disappointed."

Joan laughed. "Faith, no. Disappointed?" She chucked the baby under the chin. "In this bonny little cherub she dotes on just a hair less than the king himself?"

"She has made much of him being like Philip."

"And so he is, no matter his eyes turning dark."

"But she will miss them being blue. Doubtless it would please her to have that much to remind her of Philip." Tom smiled a little. "Not that she would forget."

"No woman in love forgets."

"No," Tom agreed, a sudden sadness in his eyes. "No woman in love."

"Make yourself useful," Joan said briskly, thrusting the baby at him. "I must fix his bath."

She went to fetch the kettle, and he held the wriggling bundle against his shoulder, immediately feeling the sharp tug of a little fist in his hair.

"You will make—ow!—quite the cavalier, Robin, with such hands." He loosened the baby's grip only to feel a yank at the back of his head. "Ow! Mercy, my lord prince, I yield."

Robin crowed again, apparently quite pleased with his victory, and Tom set him on his feet.

"Perhaps a short walk will be safer."

With the baby clinging tightly to his fingers, Tom took a few careful steps across the floor. Robin was wobbly but determined, and soon he needed only one hand to steady himself.

"Look, Bess," Tom called when she came into the room. "He will be walking alone soon."

She came shyly closer. "May I hold him, my lord?"

He grinned. "If you care to risk it. Mind your hair, though."

She took the baby into her arms, cradling him against her, but, clearly in no mood for cuddling, he squirmed and whimpered until she handed him back to his uncle.

"He prefers you, I see."

Tom stood him on the floor. "He merely has an important task to be getting on with." He took Robin by one hand again and guided him for a few more steps before turning back to Elizabeth. "See if he will come to you."

She bent down to hold her hands out to him, but, abruptly, she straightened.

"Ought you to have that cat so near the baby?"

Tom watched as Grace lapped up the last of the milk and porridge with her delicate pink tongue. "She knows well enough to stay out of his reach, Bess, though I know he would love nothing more than to give that tail a fierce yank."

"Surely you know the danger, my lord," she said urgently. "A cat will suck the breath out of a baby given the opportunity."

Tom laughed. "What notions you have, love!" He picked up the cat and the baby, too. "Do you think Robin would lie still for such a thing? Or that a cat's mouth could cover his mouth and nose at once, or that her lungs could hold all the air in his? And if all that were possible, why would she desire to do such a thing?" He let Grace jump back to the floor. "Superstitions, love, and groundless hearsay will always lead you wrong."

"Well, they always say it's so," she replied, feeling a trifle foolish, "but it does not seem too likely as you lay it out."

"*They* are often quite wrong, sweetheart. You should never listen to them." He grinned at her. "Now see if Robin will come to you."

He urged the baby forward, but Robin only clung to his leg and held more tightly to his hand.

"Go on, Robin."

The baby would not be coaxed, and, after a moment, Tom tossed him up into the air and caught him in a big bear hug.

"At least you come by your stubbornness honestly. Faith, if you've taken on half your father's good qualities as you seem to have taken on most of his bad ones, I shall be too proud of you."

Elizabeth came closer to them. "I think you are proud of him already, my lord."

Again Tom smiled. "You've found me out, I see. Well, I fear I could not love him better were he my own."

He pressed his cheek against the baby's, and she was struck again with the resemblance between them, except for—

"His eyes, my lord. They've changed."

"Joan says they will be like my father's."

Robin fixed his plump fist once more in Tom's hair, and, coming up behind him, Joan dislodged it.

"Here, let me have the rascal."

She took him for his bath, leaving Tom and Elizabeth alone.

"She is very devoted to your family, my lord," Elizabeth said. "She even sent her granddaughter to look after me."

"I hope you approve."

"Oh, yes. She is better with my hair and clothes than ever Ellen was, though I must confess Ellen is green over it."

"I am glad you are pleased," Tom said with a laugh. Then his expression sobered. "Philip was wise to send for Joan. It eases my mind to know she will be here for the queen and for the baby, too, now that I've so much to do. I'm due in council right now, in fact."

Elizabeth's mouth turned down slightly. "I had hoped we might have some time together, my lord."

He put his arm around her and kissed her cheek. "Perhaps this afternoon, sweet. I really must go. I only stopped for a moment to see Robin because I hadn't in some while." He smiled ruefully. "I do not take much to this playing king, Bess. I would that Philip would come back and do it for real. But come walk down with me. We can at least have that."

At the council chamber, he kissed her cheek once more and then went inside. The doors were closed and she was left in the corridor alone. She was not alone for long.

"We meet again, Madonna."

"My lord of Warring," she said, her eyes lighting. "You are back again, I see."

"Yes, and to such news!" Taliferro shook his head in amazement. "What's this mysterious business that's taken the king away from court?"

Elizabeth's smile faded. "I do not know. No one does, I think."

"Not his own brother, lady? That *is* odd."

"Oh, he knows. There is nothing between those two kept secret."

Taliferro smiled slyly. "Then you do know, you crafty baggage. Well, I'll not press a confidence between husband and wife."

"But, truly, I do not know."

He looked shocked.

"Surely my lord of Brenden would trust you to—" He smiled sheepishly, and Elizabeth could not have missed the discomfort in his expression. "Well, let me tell you what we've been doing in Warring, my lady."

He led her away, and, though she spent the next hour in his company, afterwards she could remember little of what he had said.

"A room for the night, innkeeper," Philip said in imitation of the swaggering imperiousness he had observed in the soldiers and tradesmen at the other inns they had stopped at. It had astounded him to see how many levels of servant and master were beneath his rulership.

"There's only one left, behind the kitchen," the man told him, not looking up from his tap. "Pay in advance, supper is included, ale is extra."

Philip meekly handed over a few coins and noticed Jerome's poorly-hidden grin.

"The inns down here are busy enough," the boy explained as they sat at one of the rough tables. "Doubtless the innkeeper sees no need to fawn over his guests."

"It has been an education," Philip admitted wryly, "just as you said."

The past few days had taught him to keep close watch on his horse and to show only a small amount of money at a time. He had learned, too, that the beggars who flocked to him when he rode out as king also flocked to the taverns with the alms they were given, often miraculously cured, at least for the night, of the ailments that had driven them to beggary. Thinking on these things, he promised himself that, once this ordeal was over, he would come among the people again and learn more of them.

A blowzy, ill-dressed woman with snarled black hair brought out two plates of watery stew, smiling at Philip as she set them down. "I will show you your room, pretty, once you've eaten."

"I thank you," he said absently, still wrapped in thought.

She leaned down to whisper into his ear, "Send the boy away, and I will show you more."

Her suggestive tone, more than her words, cut through his inattention, and he fixed her with a sharp, withering stare.

Seeing the unmistakable refusal, she snorted in contempt. "Perhaps the young one is man enough—"

"Innkeeper," Philip asked bluntly, "is it not the law that you could be fined or even closed entirely for trading flesh at your inn?"

The man merely laughed. "King's law, in truth, but his fine majesty would find himself closing most all the inns if he were to follow it in good earnest. Celia there is merely kitchen help. What other bargains she strikes are her own business."

"You could pay more and do worse," she said, looking Philip over once more. "Pity you haven't the fire to match your looks."

"Get back to the pudding, Celia," the innkeeper ordered. He brought Philip and Jerome each a cup of ale.

"Have this to soothe your temper, sir," he said, suddenly disposed to talkativeness. "I'll not add it to your reckoning. Celia is long past her day, now, and I expect you'd be wanting something younger and prettier. Though, by the look of you, I'd say you've never had to pay a woman."

"Is the king's law so openly flouted?" Philip asked, now more amazed than angry. He knew the court was not the only place where women were bought and sold, but he had not thought they were peddled so brazenly among the common people.

"The king!" The man laughed again. "Well, the king is a good boy and a good king, I'll wager, but there's hardly a man among the commons could uphold all his laws. He means to have us all saints."

"He would—"

"He would scarce have need to buy a woman's comfort," said one of the men from the next table, a farmer, by his look. "He could command what he wanted."

"No, faith, no!" the innkeeper said good-humoredly. "They say he keeps very true to the queen."

"Oh, and well he would," said another of the men, "and so would I or any man, if I had such a flavorsome wench to warm my bed."

Anger flashed into Philip's eyes and Jerome grabbed his arm. "Remember what we are meant to do, my lord," he said softly. "There is a man near the door I think was at the inn in Lydon, and in the stable I saw—"

"I saw the queen once, lads," the second man said with a leer. "All soft white flesh and the promise of heaven in every curve. If ever there was a woman made—"

The muscle in the arm Jerome held contracted into steel as Philip's fists tightened.

"Let it go," Jerome said, his voice rising. "Please, my—"

Philip's eyes widened in warning and Jerome cleared his throat.

"My brother," he finished lamely. Then he dropped back into an urgent whisper. "Please, my lord, remember who you are meant to be."

"Here, friend. No need for a quarrel," the first man said, seeing the dangerous look in Philip's eyes, knowing neither he nor his companion nor both of them together could take him on. "No offense meant to the queen, eh, Oswald?"

"By the mass, no!" the one called Oswald said cheerfully. "There's not a kingdom in a thousand miles has so fair a queen to grace it."

"The queen is a most lovely and chaste lady," Philip said tightly. "You would do well to remember that, friend, when you dare speak of her."

"Brothers, are you?" the innkeeper asked, seizing the opportunity to break the tension. He looked from Jerome to Philip and back again. "I would never have guessed it. Different mothers?"

Jerome nodded. "But the same Father."

Catching his meaning and the mischief in his eyes, Philip could not hold back a sardonic smile.

"Give my friends there a cup of ale on my score," he said with a nod toward the next table, "and yourself, too, innkeeper. Provided we drink, in all reverence, to the queen."

The offer was met with friendly enthusiasm, and the conversation quickly turned to local matters, giving Philip and Jerome once more an opportunity for private talk.

"You must keep your temper, my lord," Jerome whispered.

"Do all the commoners speak so?" Philip asked, still indignant.

"They mean nothing by it, my lord. It is the way of the peasants to talk of what the great ones do. They can but dream of such life as we have at court."

"I should have struck that loose-mouthed swine for daring to soil my queen with his thoughts!"

"Patience, my lord, or we are undone. As I said, I think we may be followed, and—"

"Near the door?" Philip glanced that way. "Which one?"

"He is gone now, but I am certain I saw him in Lydon, and there was a horse in the stable I know I've seen before somewhere, with trappings all decked out in little bells."

"Then we'll not stay anymore in the towns. Are you game to go by way of the forest?"

Jerome nodded, a little spark of excitement in his eyes. "That should confound them."

"Let us make a good show of settling in for the night. We'll leave when they are all sleeping."

It was all Tom could do to hold the kingdom together in his brother's absence. There were always grumblings from this noble and that over lands and rights to them, over wrongs done one to another, over the grievances of the merchants and the peasants. There was news of unrest among the people over the disruptions of the Heretics, or of those who claimed to be Heretics, or of those who claimed that they claimed to be Heretics. And always there were questions about the king, questions Tom could not answer.

More and more of his time was taken up with his duties. He rarely saw the queen except at supper, he rarely saw Robin except for a few minutes every three or four days, and his walks with Elizabeth ceased altogether.

She was disappointed that he no longer had time for leisure. Even the entertainments and dancing after supper often went on without him, and the moments he stole for her here and there, the nights he gave her, only made her time alone more starkly empty. It was not unusual for him to come to bed long after she was asleep, drop down in exhaustion beside her for a few hours, and leave before she woke. It seemed to her now that there was only one man who had time for her.

Taliferro had all the time in the world.

Philip huddled over the tiny, sheltered fire, trying to draw warmth from the pale flames, but he dared not stoke it to blazing. Since they had taken to the forest paths, he had shared Jerome's suspicions that they were being followed. Two nights earlier, they had heard the clatter of horses and, with it, the jingle of tiny bells, the kind that might ornament a bridle. It could have been coincidence, but Philip and Jerome had concealed themselves in the trees until the sound passed. Then they turned east for a few miles. They had been doubly cautious since.

Philip glanced at the lanky figure sprawled out on the other side of the fire. Jerome had been asleep a long while, needing nothing but a blanket to cushion him from the hard winter ground, but Philip knew it would take more than that to lull his own restlessness. Tomorrow they would reach Ivybridge and he would know for certain. What would he find there? Perhaps Kate, but would she be his Kate?

He thought back once more to the morning he had asked her to marry him. He had caught her as she went to fetch water for Margaret's bath and had drawn her into the cover of the rose trees, convincing her with sweet words and kisses that he would love her and protect her forever. How brief that forever had been.

He remembered her shyness, the fear and love in her eyes, the modest drop of her lashes to her flushed cheeks when she told him she had nothing suitable to wear to be married in.

"You shall, Kate, I swear it. You shall have gowns so fine your Princess Margaret shall pale beside them. Until then—" He had broken off the most perfect of the pink and white blossoms and fashioned them into a garland for her hair. "Until then, what better ornament could you have than God's own artistry?"

He had taken her to the well so she could admire the sweet picture she made, and he could see it still, the reflection of those two young faces in the water, teeming with life and love. He was no longer that boy; too much had happened since. Could she still be that girl? And what of the child she was to have given him?

There were few who knew of that anymore. Rosalynde and Tom were likely the only ones now. He hadn't told Jerome that part of the story, the part he hadn't known of himself until more than a year after Katherine had been taken from him. She was to have had a child. Perhaps she did even now.

He did not know, he could not, but when he had thought of it before, when he had healed enough to be able to think of it at all, he liked to think that the child was a girl, as graceful and gazelle-like as her mother. He called her Tabitha in his heart, there where she had been christened and buried. She would be almost two now, if she had ever been born at all, a bright-eyed toddler with Kate's pretty ways, perhaps with that same warm sunshine in her hair. Or perhaps, in truth, the child was a sturdy little boy with Kate's dark eyes and sweet smile. Perhaps—

He pulled his blanket up around his shoulders and tossed another handful of twigs on the struggling fire. Tomorrow he would know.

The house was dark, hidden in the trees, almost strangled in ivy, standing curiously alone in the twilight. Philip knocked at the door, a soft, hesitant knock, and it was immediately opened by a tall man with sparse, once-blond hair. He looked Philip over for a moment before bowing gravely.

"My lord king."

"You are her father?"

The man nodded. "I knew from what she said of you that you would come."

"Master Fletcher, I pray you understand—"

"Please, my lord, come in. You will want to see her."

Philip drew a hard breath and stepped into the dim room. At once he saw that there was someone sitting on a bench in the corner, out of the filtered sunlight the tiny window admitted. Fletcher cleared his throat.

"There is someone to see you, daughter."

The huddled figure lifted its head, and Philip saw that it was completely swathed in bandages. It had been over two years; surely her burns would no longer require wrapping.

"The scars will not bear looking on, my lord," Fletcher said, reading the question in Philip's eyes. "There's scarcely enough of her left to make up a woman, but she is woman enough still that she cannot endure the thought of anyone seeing her ruined flesh." He turned toward her again. "Daughter?"

"Who?"

Philip winced hearing the rough grating voice, forever mangled by smoke. Katherine's voice had always fallen like music on his ears. Now he could not recognize it.

"I must see her face," he said quietly.

Fletcher shook his head. "You would see nothing there you would recognize."

"I must know for certain."

Fletcher pulled him back toward the door. "My lord, you have been a soldier," he said, his voice low and urgent. "You have seen what is left of one who's been burned alive. Give her that much kindness to leave her some dignity."

Philip squeezed his eyes shut. He had seen. He had seen the blackened limbs with the fingers and toes burned away and the faces that no longer had lips or noses or ears. Is that what lay beneath those wrappings?

"If I could just see into her eyes—"

"She has none! They were burned blind and now they are scarred over."

Philip drew back in horror. "Oh, Kate!"

"Who's there, Father?"

Philip looked again at the poor sightless thing as it strained in the perpetual darkness to hear, and Fletcher stepped from between them. When Philip had crept close enough to her, Fletcher left them alone.

"Who is there? I can feel you."

Philip dropped to his knees beside the bench and reached his trembling hands toward her. He had to touch her. He had to somehow know this was Kate. He remembered still the look and the feel of her satin skin, and now—

He dropped his hands. "Have you much pain?"

His voice sounded stiff and unfamiliar to his own ears, but he knew from her surprised gasp that she recognized it. The silence pressed upon him until he felt certain it would crush him if it were not broken.

"Kate?"

"No. No, I am not."

She tried to turn away, dropping her head just as he remembered she would do when she felt ashamed. He touched one bandaged arm.

"Kate?"

Her breath came in little trembling gasps. "I told them you must not know. I begged them to let you believe I was dead. I *am* dead."

"Oh, Kate, no." He felt the tears choking off his breath, and he held her arm more tightly. "Kate—"

The wrapping came away in his hand, raveling away from her, falling in heaps at his feet, exposing her blackened flesh, and filling the room with the smell of her burning. Her charred, fingerless hands reached toward him and then crumbled into ash as he in terror beat them away.

He scrambled away from her and saw her now-unbandaged face, seared and mutilated, moving closer to him, the lipless mouth speaking now in Kate's silken voice.

"My sweet Philip—"

He woke in a cold sweat, his mouth fixed in a silent scream.

"Oh, God." He tore at his shirt where it constricted his breathing and gulped down the cold, dark air in dry, stabbing gasps. "Oh, Jesus, God."

He wrapped himself in his nerveless arms, feeling the hammer of blood at his pulse points, remembering, remembering.

There on the ground near him, Jerome slept undisturbed, a slack, peaceful smile on his face.

CHAPTER

THE HOUSES IN IVYBRIDGE WERE SMALL, HUDDLED TOGETHER AND leaning over the street, almost touching, as if to confer with each other. What secrets they shared would never be told. The village was empty.

"I suppose there's no one to ask the way," Philip said, looking about uneasily.

"The smithy is there, my lord," Jerome pointed out. "An armorer would likely be close. Perhaps there."

The house he indicated was overshadowed by its neighbors, narrow and sturdily built, abandoned like all the rest. Philip went to the door and, after a moment's hesitation, lifted his hand to knock.

"Wait, my lord," Jerome warned.

Philip turned. Then he heard it. The faint sound of bells.

"A trap." He spun Jerome away from the house. "The horses. Quick!"

"Too late, my lord." A black-bearded man, Philip's height and half again his breadth, stepped out of the side street behind them, backed by five or six armed men. Two others had hold of Philip's horse and Jerome's. "I trust, for the boy's sake and your own, you will come without a quarrel."

"Cafton." His hand still clutching Jerome's shoulder, Philip stepped back until he was almost against the door. "Who are you jackaling for this time? Ellenshaw is dead."

The man's smug expression did not change. "That needn't concern you, my lord."

"Do you mean to cut my throat in the street as you did my father's?"

Jerome's eyes widened.

"Though the stain of another usurper's blood could only ornament my blade," Cafton said, "I have orders to the contrary. If you will come this way, my lord—"

"Now, Jerome!"

Philip crashed backwards through the door, dragging the boy with him.

"Surround the house!" Cafton ordered. "Some of you follow me."

Philip and Jerome bolted to the top of the house, with Cafton after them.

"They're in the back, too!" Jerome said after a swift glance out the window.

"This way."

Philip flung open the window that overlooked the street and leapt the short distance through the window of the house across the way. Jerome was immediately after him, and both of them dashed across the floor and dropped out the rear window to make a desperate sprint for the river. Cafton and his men were hot behind them.

"If they make the river, we've lost them!" Cafton cried. "Stop them!"

One of his men leveled his crossbow and fired. The bolt caught Philip on the right side, just at the waist, tumbling him facedown into the water, with only the tall reeds to keep him from being washed away.

"My lord!" Jerome cried, scrambling down the steep bank after him, the long, wiry grasses tearing at his legs and arms as he did. He had to reach his master before their pursuers did, before he drowned. He dragged Philip up out of the water, struggling with the dead weight, fearing he was already too late.

"Please, my lord!"

Blood and water puddled the ground under Philip's body. There was not even a bubble at his bluing lips to show he still breathed.

"My lord," Jerome begged, lifting Philip's head. "Oh, God, please!"

"The boy's down there!"

Jerome looked up. Cafton was there above him, with his men, all of them bristling with drawn weapons. Raging grief boiling up inside him, Jerome leapt to his feet.

"Murderers!"

"*I am trusting you, Jerome.*"

He could not face them now, as fiercely as he wanted to, as ready as he was to meet death to avenge his king. His king, his friend, had given him a trust. He could not fail him now.

"Take him to You, holy Christ," he whispered as he wrenched the battered ring from Philip's limp hand. Then, with a glance at the men coming toward him, he dove into the icy river.

He heard the hissing thunk of arrows as they hit the water all around him. One grazed the back of his leg, but he swam on, the current sweeping him beyond Cafton's reach.

He bobbed up for a gasp of air and saw them carrying Philip up the bank. Then there was a sudden explosion of pain inside his head and the black water closed over him.

❧

The darkness in Tom's spirit was heavy and oppressive, like the dull clang of mourning bells, and all his prayers could not seem to disperse it. He told himself it was merely weariness, merely uncertainty, but somehow that did not suffice. For a few days he pulled back from work, hoping to ease his impression that something was very wrong, but it did not seem to help. It only left him feeling guilty for neglecting things he knew his brother would have wanted done.

In desperation, he prayed again and again, but still his prayers seemed lifeless, unable to pierce the heavens. He had somehow to break through.

"I am going to spend tonight in the chapel, Bess," he told her as they were finishing supper. "There is something I must have peace on, and I plan to take tonight to pray."

"But, my lord, all night?"

"Sometimes it takes that, love." He embraced her and tried to coax her into a smile. "I know it's not been very pleasant for you, sweetheart, but it is not forever. Philip will come back and then we will have our time."

"And if he never comes back?" she asked bleakly and his mouth turned grim.

"That is in God's hands now, Bess."

When the meal was over, he asked again for his wife's understanding and went to the small chapel that adjoined the king's chamber. After posting Palmer outside the door to guarantee he was not disturbed, he began to pray.

An hour passed, then two, and he felt the heaviness waning. Then doubt stabbed through him and the foreboding overwhelmed him again. Still he prayed, calling on God in His faithfulness to do His perfect will.

"Jesus, Lord, grant him peace where he is. Watch over him and set this all right, according to Your pleasure." He bowed his head lower. "Oh, Lord, out of your mercy—"

He felt something touch his hair and looked up.

"Bess."

"Have you done with your prayers, my lord?" she asked with a shy hint of a smile, and he stood up.

"I had thought you would be long asleep by now, sweetheart. Is there something amiss? Palmer should have called me."

She shook her head and put her hand up to his cheek. "I made him let me in. I could not sleep without you. Can you not come to bed now?"

He took her hand, squeezing it as he moved it from his face. "I told you, love, I've pledged this night to prayer." He kissed her fingers. "Come, let me have Palmer take you back to your chamber."

She traced the fingers of her other hand down the back of his jaw. "I had rather you took me there, my lord," she said. Her voice dropped to a husky whisper, "and stayed there with me."

He took this hand, too, and held it with the other in both of his.

"Not tonight, sweetheart." He touched his lips to her cheek. "As much as that would please me, not tonight."

"Do you pray for the king?" she asked with a little pout.

"He needs all our prayers now."

"Where did he go? Will you not tell me?"

"I cannot."

"You do not trust me," she said pettishly.

He swiftly put his arms around her and kissed her cheek again. "Only with my life and my heart and all my love."

She nestled against him. "Come with me," she whispered, nuzzling his chest. "If you love me, come with me."

"Please, sweet, you know I cannot." He took both her hands again. "Would you have me break a vow?"

"Would you rather break my heart?" she asked, looking up at him, letting her lip tremble. "After all your fair words, my lord, will you tell me religion means more to you than I do?"

"Religion means nothing to me," he said, touching his lips to her hair, "but my God means everything. Would you have me break a vow to Him?"

"He will understand." She began pressing her mouth to his throat. "Pray tomorrow."

"Bess—"

"Tomorrow," she murmured against his lips, and he crushed her to him, taking her offered kiss with sudden fierce passion.

"Yes," she sighed, and he held her abruptly away from him.

"No." He was breathless, but his face was as stern as she had ever seen it. "It is not right, my lady. You know it is not."

"Why?" she asked innocently, toying with his hair. "You said it was God's will we should love each other." She linked her fingers behind his neck. "Enjoy each other."

"It is," he said, something troubled in his expression. "But not before Him, love. Never before Him."

Once again he took both her hands and looked deeply into her eyes. "I have made a vow, Bess. To God Himself. I cannot break it."

"Not even for me?" she asked, lifting her mouth to his with seductive promise.

"My lady, please—"

"Pray tomorrow," she murmured again, trying to draw him closer, but this time he would not yield.

"Do not force me to choose between you," he said, his voice grim and still. "I could not choose you."

Startled tears sprang into her eyes and she stepped back from him.

"Bess, understand—"

"It was all a lie then," she said bleakly. "All those times you said you loved me."

"No." He pulled her back into his arms. "It was never a lie. I love you as much as a man can truly love a woman, not just passionately, but wholly." He turned her face up to him. "I would die for you."

She was still for a moment, transfixed by the quiet certainty in his words. She swallowed down a sob. "That is easily said."

"Not by me."

Shamefaced, she stood tiptoe and kissed his cheek. "I am sorry, my lord. I'll not trouble you again."

He held her closer and surprised her with a deep, meaningful kiss.

"We will have tomorrow, sweetheart."

She swallowed hard once more and stepped back from him, the kiss and the low caress of his voice leaving her almost too weak to stand.

"Good night, my lord."

"Good night, love."

"Now where did you get off to so late, my lamb?" Ellen asked, taking Elizabeth's cloak when Palmer returned her to her chamber.

"I merely went to speak to my husband a moment."

Ellen sniffed. "It's a wonder he did not insist on returning with you."

"I had hoped he would," Elizabeth said with a sigh, crawling between the sheets Ellen had warmed for her. "He said he's pledged tonight to pray for the king and would not be coaxed."

"He told you that?"

Elizabeth nodded.

"And you believed him?"

"Yes."

"A poor excuse, I'd say, my lady," Ellen clucked. "Very poor."

"What do you mean?"

Ellen shook her head, a look of sage foreboding on her pinched face. "I mustn't say what I've no proof of, lambkin. Perhaps it is just as he told you."

"Ellen, what?"

"There is hot, young blood in my lord of Brenden's royal veins, my lady. It's rare a man refuses his own comely wife unless he has some doxy on the side."

Tears filled Elizabeth's eyes. "That is not fair, Ellen."

"Now, my lady-love, do not cry," Ellen soothed, sitting next to her and drawing her head to her shoulder. "There is no proof of any such a thing. Only idle words from idle tongues."

"What words?"

"Doubtless the girl merely means to make a name for herself, and it is nothing more."

"What girl?" Elizabeth demanded.

"The one he's put to work in the laundry, my lady. That Molly."

Elizabeth pressed her lips together. "What has she said?"

"Now, my lady, I told you long time ago that any man is like to behave so. I do not mean to fret you, but I would not have you ignorant either. We women must look out for one another if we're not to be bested at every turn."

"What has she said?"

"That he stayed the night with her."

"He told me so himself already. It was during the war and there was nothing between them. He swore to me."

Ellen looked less than convinced. "Oh, he swore, did he?"

"It is always the worse when they feel they must make an oath on it." Ellen said it all the time, and Tom had sworn.

"Well, if he did, I mean, if they, well, that was a long while ago. Before we, I mean—"

"Of course it was, lovey. I am sure the rest is merely gossip."

"The rest?"

"Well, if they've been seen together here at court, mind you I say *if*, surely that is nothing at all. If you choose to wink at it, my lady, can I do less?"

"Seen? Ellen, tell me all you know and do not torture me one word at a time!"

"Well, my lady, the tattle is that they have been seen late several nights now, very close together and quite alone. What would anyone think and expect to be believed?"

"But he is always with me nights. Do you—"

Ellen held up her hands in resignation. "I am sure it is just as you say, my lady. Come, lie down again and think nothing more of it. Perhaps miracles are not ceased, and you have lighted upon the one constant man left on God's earth."

Elizabeth put her head down on the pillow and watched as Ellen put out the candles, still clucking and muttering to herself.

"Constant or no," Ellen said, coming back to draw the coverlet around Elizabeth's shoulders, "no man's worth losing a moment's sleep for."

Elizabeth let her tears well up again once she was alone.

"I love you as much as a man can truly love a woman. I would die for you."

Liar, she thought. *Liar, liar, liar!*

Mary and Joseph, how could he say such things, such deep, sweet, beautiful things, and lie the whole while? Could any man look so and still lie?

She took an unsteady breath and rubbed her eyes with her fists. Ellen was always suspicious of men. Perhaps it was the court wag-tongues who did not speak true. Rumor was a notorious liar. She knew she was herself spoken of, her name illicitly linked with Simon Taliferro's, and that was pure falsehood.

We will have tomorrow, sweetheart.

She smiled a little at that, remembering Tom's last kiss, thinking what a pity it would be if she were to be angry with him and he did not kiss her that way again.

Ellen is an old crab, she told herself as she snuggled into the downy bedding, thinking what tomorrow would be.

"We *will* have tomorrow," she murmured. Then she fell asleep.

CHAPTER

ELIZABETH WAITED UNTIL WELL PAST MIDNIGHT THE NEXT NIGHT before Tom came to her chamber.

"You shouldn't have stayed up, love," he said, bending down to kiss her cheek as she sat up in bed. "I did not know or I would have sent you word the council would be meeting late."

"Is there something wrong, my lord?"

"No," he said on a weary breath. "But there is so much Philip would know better how to deal with than I do. Would there was some word from him."

She watched as he pulled his shirt off over his head and stretched his sleek shoulders. Her heart began to quicken in anticipation.

"Perhaps there will be something soon," she said. She drew back the coverlet for him, making invitation with her dark eyes.

He smiled at her and sat down on the bed.

"Perhaps. Perhaps he will return soon and I can turn my attentions elsewhere."

"To what?" she asked, nestling against his back as he took off one boot and struggled with an obstinate strap on the other.

He smiled at her again, a little ruefully, and eased the boot off. "To things as they were before he left. When I had time to spend with you."

"You have time now," she murmured against the back of his neck as he slipped out of his breeches and crawled into bed.

"Now," he murmured as he snuggled up against her. "Now is nice."

For a moment she merely sat there, stroking his hair, waiting. When he did not move, she turned his face up to hers and kissed his slack mouth.

"My lord?"

"Mmm?" he mumbled, already half asleep.

"Do you not—"

He managed to open one eye. "What?"

"Do you not want me?"

He smiled and nestled against her again. "Always."

"Now."

He groaned. "Oh, Bess, I've not slept in two days—"

"There *is* someone else," she said plaintively. "Some doxy you keep."

He laughed softly and cuddled closer, still not opening his eyes. "And to whom have you been listening now?"

"My lord—"

"Whoever it is, love, there is no truth in it. Let me have a little sleep and I will prove it to you, I swear."

"It is always the worse when they feel they must make an oath on it."

When she was certain he was soundly asleep, she shifted his head onto the pillows and got out of bed. A few minutes later, wrapped snugly in her cloak, she was walking in the garden, avoiding the curious glances of the sentries, trying to imagine the trees covered with blossoms and leaves, the ground lush with grass and strewn with flowers.

It was deep winter now. When she had been here before, it had been mid-September and this garden had been falling asleep, shedding its summer abundance. It would be months still before she would see it bursting with new spring. Perhaps it was never spring here. Perhaps this garden was always dead or dying.

I would die for you, Tom had told her.

"Ha!" she said half under her breath. "You cannot even stay awake for me."

She paced further, chilled by the icy bite of the wind, thinking how pleasant it was back in bed with him, even when he was asleep, nestled against her. Perhaps she had been unfair. Perhaps—

"You must be near frozen out here, Madonna."

She turned with a startled gasp. Taliferro was standing in the shadow of a barren tree, scarcely three feet from her.

"My lord, I did not know I was observed."

He smiled at her, a quick twist of his thin lips. "I saw you from my window, princess, and thought you must be troubled to walk in the cold so late alone. Is there some way I may be of service?"

She shook her head. "I merely wished to think."

"A fair young lady rarely has cause to think such deep thoughts, Madonna, unless it is upon some matter of the heart. Surely, my lord of Brenden—"

Without warning, the tears flooded from her. "I think he is—he has—there is a girl in the laundry—"

"You mustn't listen to gossip, my lady," Taliferro soothed, putting his arm around her waist, "no matter how well evidenced. There are always explanations."

"You have heard it, too."

"Scandal is easily brewed and quickly spread. Sometimes it is the duty of a princess to affect a touch of deafness."

"Then you believe it?"

"I, Madonna? I am scarcely one to judge."

"But I asked him about it, just now. He told me there is no truth to it."

"There. You see? He would best know, whatever else anyone has seen."

"He told me so, but then he laughed." She sobbed and made a little moan at the stabbing pain it brought. "He dared laugh at such a thing."

"He laughs, Madonna, because he's never known what it is like to be betrayed. He'd not be so merry were he to suffer the same."

"But—"

"But, no, my lady, I would never suggest you pay him in his own coin. You are his wife and subject to him. You dare not and he knows it so. That is why, behind his pious facade, he has such insolent disregard of you and your poor feelings. I would not have my own lady served so." He took her hand with the utmost tenderness. "Not if she were possessed of the depth of beauty that has been so graciously bestowed upon your fair head, Madonna."

He kissed her fingertips. Then he turned her palm up and slowly, sensuously pressed his warm mouth upon it. For a long while she was still. Then she drew her hand away.

"My lord—"

The devotion in his expression deepened. "How he could be false to you, I do not know. Yet know, sweet lady, that there is a heart that beats as true for you as you could wish, a heart that weeps blood for your pain and would gladly comfort you should you ever find need of comfort."

Self-pity filled her eyes with tears, and he gently dabbed them away with his silken handkerchief.

"My lady, my lady," he crooned and she found herself in his soothing embrace. He was covering her hair and forehead with light kisses, murmuring her name, holding her closer and closer. Then he lifted her chin with one cool finger and looked deeply into her eyes.

"Come to my love, Madonna," he said, his voice as mesmerizing as his black eyes.

Her face was flushed with weeping, and her full lips trembled as she looked up at him for a long moment. She pushed her hands against his chest.

"I will be looked for, my lord."

She broke free from him and ran back down the path and straight into Tom's arms.

"There you are." He smiled and pulled her close. "When I woke—"

Taliferro came sauntering out of the trees, and Tom's eyes narrowed.

"Good evening, my lord of Warring. I see you have been looking after my lady for me again. I shall have to find a way to repay you."

Taliferro bowed. "Your highness. We were both suffering from a touch of restlessness, and I was amusing the princess with a few tales of my travels."

Tom glanced at Elizabeth and saw the guilty roundness in her averted eyes. Taliferro saw it, too.

"I think her highness is eager to learn about the things of the world, and there is much I could teach her." There was a slight smile on his thin lips. "You've never been outside the kingdom, have you, my lord?"

Tom felt his face burn. He had been given a man's responsibilities since he was fifteen, and he did not often feel like a boy anymore, but next to Taliferro he did. He felt young and foolish and woefully inexperienced. He could see the mocking light in Taliferro's eyes, the look of contempt for his innocence. He could imagine Elizabeth's fascination with the thoughts this man of the world had brought to her, thoughts of the practiced pleasures he could give her that her young husband would have no knowledge of.

"Lynaleigh has a sweet charm all her own, my lord," Tom said coolly. "A man might gain nothing in traveling outside her but the knowledge that everywhere else falls far short of what she has to offer and that he was a fool ever to leave her."

Taliferro shrugged negligently. "Possibly, my lord. Well, I will bid you good night. And you, Madonna. Perhaps we will speak of this again."

Tom watched him stroll back into the palace. He took Elizabeth's arm.

"My lady, I would not have you deceived by such a one."

She turned to face him, her shame expressing itself in anger. "I suppose if there is deceit to be brewed, you had rather do it yourself."

"Bess, hear me now. Before you came to court, he tried his devices on the queen. She has eyes for no one but Philip and never even noticed his attempts, so now he's turned to you. Faith, if Philip had ever caught him at it, he'd for certain not be troubling you now. A man like Taliferro—"

"You have always hated him! Well, do not think to play tyrant to me, my lord. I will speak to whom I please when I please, just as you do."

He shook his head, baffled. "To whom have I spoken, Bess, that displeases you?"

"What you do is of no concern to me, my lord," she replied. "I am merely your wife, and if you choose to make me a fool before the whole court, I must suppose that to be the prerogative of princes."

"What? Oh, surely you cannot mean Molly again."

"You told me, swore to me, there was nothing between you," she accused. "Will you tell me again that's so?"

"Of course."

"Do you think me a fool?"

His eyes flashed in answer to hers. "Only if you call me a liar."

"You did not so much as touch her, my lord?"

"No." He thought for a moment, perplexed. Had he? Certainly there was nothing in his conduct when he was in the laundry that would convey he felt anything but kindness toward the girl. "If I did, it was such a slight thing that I cannot remember it."

"Well, I see now what a 'slight thing' women are to you, my lord."

"There was nothing! The girls in the laundry were unkind to her, because of her father, so I went to tell her, in their hearing, that she had a friend in me. I told you what she lost for my sake. I cannot let her suffer for it still, but there is no more in it than that. Mass, even had I wished to, what do you think I could do there before Mistress Cooper and all her girls?"

"I do not mean then. What was between you when you stayed the night with her?"

"I told you before," he said, exasperated. "There was nothing between us. What more can I say to you?"

"Nothing?"

"No."

"You never kissed her?"

He exhaled heavily. "Yes. Yes, Bess, I did."

"Liar!" she spat. "How dare you say there was nothing between you!"

"It *was* nothing. I swear it! Please, Bess, sweetheart—"

"Never swear now! Not to me!"

"Please, Bess. It was not as you think. I told you I'd been separated from my men back then. They died all around me that day, by the hundreds, and I thought Palmer had been killed, too, in defending my escape. I had been alone on foot in the forest two days without anything to eat when I came to Molly's house. They had nothing to eat either, nothing to drink except the sourest beer I've ever tasted, but I drank it for lack of anything else, to get the cold rain out of my bones. As I said, her father had told her to keep me there the night. She—" He shook his head, regretting the memory. "I let it all sway me for a moment, the drink and the weariness and the grief, and, before I realized it, I was kissing her. Bess, I knew it was wrong, believe me I knew, and I stopped it there. I asked her pardon, and there was no more to it."

"Why did you not tell me so when I asked you before?" she asked, her voice as hard as her eyes.

"It was nothing, I tell you still and truly." He rubbed his eyes. "Perhaps we should speak of this tomorrow. It is late, and we both would do well to have some rest and time for consideration before we go on. I am worn near to raveling."

"I would prefer you went to your own chamber now, my lord."

He stared at her as she stood there pursing her lips in that way he was certain she had learned from Ellen.

"If that is what pleases you, my lady," he said after a stunned moment. "I am sorry, truly, that I have offended you. I wish it were somehow in my power to change the past, but it is not, and I can do nothing for it now but ask your forgiveness." He kissed her hand, adding softly, "I will miss you."

She pulled away from him, and her rigid expression did not change.

"There are any number of women who might fill my place in your bed, my lord. They say all cats look gray in the dark."

"That is not so, Bess. Not with me. What we have shared—" His brow furrowed. "I'll not lie to you and say I take no pleasure in it, but it is not just sport to me. Do me the grace to remember the times I have lain with you, asking no more than a gentle kiss and to hold you as we slept."

"Because you have that slut in the laundry to satisfy you!"

"Bess—"

"Do you deny you often meet with her alone?"

"No, but, Bess—"

"Why is that, if she is not your lover?"

He dropped his eyes. "I cannot say why just now."

"No," she spat, "you can never say why about anything!"

"Trust me. Please, Bess, if you love me—"

"I never said I love you."

She flung the words at him like a slap, and then there was a moment of painful silence.

"No," he said finally. "Whatever else has been between us, you never have."

"Just because we have, uh, become intimate, my lord, in truth changes nothing."

"I see."

"We have done no more than duty," she said weakly, and something like shame colored her cheeks at the look on his face. "If it is pleasure to us both, then that simply makes it easier."

"I see."

"Pleasure is not the same thing as love," she added, suddenly feeling very foolish.

"No," he said, and his voice was grave and soft. "I am very well aware of that."

Again there was that painful silence and the hurt in his eyes.

"I will bid you good night, my lady, before I say something I will regret."

"My lord—"

He stopped mid-stride and wheeled to face her.

"You told me once you had no wish to be anyone's harlot," he said, his rare anger tightening his jaw. "Neither, my lady, do I."

She heard his step, light and swift on the path, and then there was silence.

CHAPTER

ELIZABETH FORBADE HERSELF TO CRY THAT NIGHT, ESPECIALLY since she was sure Ellen was just waiting for the opportunity to tell her that she had known all along this would happen, but it took everything in her to do it. The bed was so wide and empty without Tom, and she shivered all night without him to curl up against. How was it that the nights before could make this night alone so miserable?

She was cross that morning with Ellen and all her other ladies as they dressed her. Even Nan could not please her today. The weather had turned truly cold again, and new snow had fallen in the night, and she was reluctant to go out into it to go to mass.

"Why do they not better clear these paths?" she complained as she followed Ellen to the cathedral. "I've snow all in my shoes."

Tom had always accompanied her to mass before, making sure each morning that she got there warm and dry, but now, of course—

"I beg your pardon, my lady."

Elizabeth turned to see a slight, dark-haired peasant girl curtseying before her, someone from the kitchen, she supposed.

"Yes?"

"Forgive me being so bold, lady, but I must set something right with you."

"That is the girl, that Molly," Ellen said disdainfully. "How dare you even show your eyes to a lady of quality! Go back to the stews where you belong!"

Molly did not shrink from her. There was nothing but grim determination in her thin face, a face that held a great deal of sadness for being hardly sixteen. "Please, Lady Elizabeth, I ask only a word. For Lord Tom's sake."

"Go on ahead, Ellen," Elizabeth said after a condescending moment of consideration. "I will be along."

"My lady!"

"Go on. I'll be but a moment."

Making her reluctance well known, Ellen walked on and Elizabeth looked again at the girl.

"Well?"

"My lady, I know there has been gossip since I came here to Winton, gossip touching Prince Tom, and I thought you ought have the truth of it from me."

"The truth?" Elizabeth asked, holding herself a little more stiffly. "The truth that you have been my husband's mistress since you came to Winton? Is that the truth you mean?"

"You mistake, my lady," Molly replied, looking steadily at her. "For me, I do not care that all the court thinks so, but I tell you true he never touched me."

"Even when he stayed the night with you?" Elizabeth demanded.

"No, my lady, not then either. I would have gladly given myself to him for the kindness he showed me, but he is a man of honor, truly, and would not."

"He sent you to say so," Elizabeth accused, but the girl's solemn expression did not change.

"No, lady, he did not. I have no need to lie. Why should he want me when he has you with him? Even back the first time I saw him, I knew I had no hope of him. He told me then and there he belonged to you." There was a sudden longing in her expression. "Would there was someone who loved me so."

"He told me he kissed you. Do you deny that?"

"No, my lady, that much is true, though he never had any plan to do it and never would have without the help of the liquor I gave him. Believe me, lady, I know the look of a man with such designs, and there was none such in him that night. He was merely tired and grieved and needing some comforting. Even you might have pitied him."

"Well," Elizabeth faltered, "of course—"

"I have been a harlot," Molly said bluntly. "He knew I was, but he begged my pardon as if I were a lady born." There were sudden tears in her eyes, but she held her head a little higher. "He begged my pardon for a mere kiss that I pushed him to, and I'll not leave him to suffer for my fault now."

"And what of your clandestine meetings with him? Do you deny those as well?"

"No, my lady," Molly replied. "But you have no cause for offense in those."

"Of course not," Elizabeth said coldly. "And I suppose you cannot say what you meet with him about."

Molly shook her head. "I swear it is not what you think." She clutched Elizabeth's hand, sudden anguish on her face. "Please, my lady, they say you've turned him out of your bed because of it, and that's hardly right. He's done you no wrong."

Elizabeth's face turned hot. How quickly that news had spread. "You of all people should know better than to believe gossip, girl."

Suddenly flustered, Molly drew back her hand. "Forgive me, lady. I've said too much, but it would be a sad thing indeed if you were to break so fine a heart as his and toss it underfoot for no cause."

"That is hardly your concern," Elizabeth told her, but, hearing the touch of softness behind the words, the girl smiled.

"I'll not trouble you again, my lady."

She dropped a quick curtsey and then ran down the path and was gone.

Elizabeth was oblivious to the holy words of the mass, to the music and the candles and the incense. Instead, in her place at her husband's side, she went over the conversation she had had with the girl from the laundry. *"Would there was someone who loved me so."*

She glanced at Tom as he knelt beside her, his eyes closed and his gentle mouth moving in prayer. It strained credulity to think there was only innocence in his meetings with this wench, yet everything she had heard of him, everything she knew of him herself, spoke of his steadfast integrity and of his dedication to the Christ he loved.

"Good morning, my lady," he whispered as they filed out of the cathedral with everyone else. He smiled tentatively, but he looked tired, as if he had slept no better than she.

"My lord," she said evenly, too aware of Ellen's watchful eyes boring into the back of her skull.

He said nothing else until they were standing in the snowy path again. It was almost the spot where she had talked to Molly; she could still see the small print of the girl's rough shoes and her own velvet ones.

"Bess, will you hear me a moment?"

"The weather's turning foul, my lady," Ellen interrupted. "I dare say you will want to go in now."

"Of course, Ellen." Elizabeth looked at her husband for a moment. She began walking again. "I am too cold to stand here and talk, my lord."

"I beg your pardon," Tom said, and, with a sigh, he followed her back to the palace. When they reached the door, she turned to him again with a touch of a smile on her face.

"It is much warmer in the library, if you would care to talk there."

She sent Ellen away with her cloak and prayer book and a look that warned the older woman not to say a word in protest. She went into the library with Tom and shut the door.

She was always impressed when she came into this room. The royal library was the largest and most valuable in the kingdom, and Tom had read all of the books. That always impressed her, too.

"You wished to say something, my lord?" she asked when he held his silence for a few minutes. He turned from his pacing and came to sit beside her.

"Only that it was wrong of me to lose my patience with you last night." He shrugged repentantly. "I can only plead weariness and stupidity by way of excuse."

She sat there twisting her fingers together in her lap, her head bowed but her eyes turned up to him. "I suppose I might not have quite such a temper, my lord. And I might keep better watch over my tongue."

He let his breath out slowly and used one arm to pull her against him.

"What are we to do now, Bess? I can say no more than I have already. You have every bit of love and faithfulness that is in me, but all that is useless if you do not believe me."

She laid her head on his shoulder. "You make me want to believe you." She laughed hesitantly. "I've been told it would be a pity to break so fine a heart as yours, my lord."

Surprised, he laughed, too. "I should think so."

She looked up at him again, suddenly serious. "It is just that sometimes I cannot help hearing what they say about you and remembering what I've heard of other men, and I can hardly—"

"Tell me one word I have said, a single look in my eye, that tells you I am not just as I have claimed. Tell me that, by your own witness, and I will never deny your suspicions again."

Tears filled her eyes, and she hid her face against him.

"Judge me by myself, sweetheart," he pled softly, "not by anyone else. I ask nothing more of you."

For a few minutes he merely held her there. Then she lifted her head again.

"You make me ashamed, my lord."

"I never meant to do that, love. I only want you to be happy." He kissed her forehead. "I can never be unless you are."

They talked until past noon. Then, after they had eaten alone, they spent the afternoon in his chamber playing chess. Elizabeth proved to be a good player.

"That is excellent, my lady!" Tom told her after she came subtly close to besting him. "I shall be very pleased to have someone to match me again. Philip is brilliant at it, but he'll not play anymore. He says he's had enough of war, even in sport, to last his lifetime."

There was a sudden tinge of pain in his smile, and she came to his side of the table and put her arm around him.

"I suppose you've had no word yet," she said and he shook his head. "Nothing."

She stroked his hair, feeling a sudden pity for him, realizing that perhaps he needed something more from her than just the comfort of her bed.

"Is there nothing I might do, my lord?"

Just love me, his eyes pled, but again he shook his head.

"We can only wait." He exhaled heavily. "Wait and wait and wait."

"You've had a lot of waiting in your life, have you not, my lord?" she asked with a wry smile, and he smiled, too, and pulled her into his lap.

"You would think with so much practice I would be better at it."

She put her other arm around him and turned his face up to hers.

"You needn't wait for everything," she said and he kissed her tenderly.

"I am so glad you are with me now, love," he whispered. "I could not bear all this alone."

She kissed him again and he held her closer, closing his eyes and losing himself in her gentle touch. She covered every bit of his face with kisses, sweet and caressing, giving and not demanding.

"Bess—"

There was a sharp knocking at the door, and she held him where he was.

"Do not answer," she whispered. "They will go away."

Again there was a sharp knocking followed by Palmer's urgent voice. "My lord, are you there?"

Tom sighed and set Elizabeth on her feet. He went to the door. "What is it now, Palmer?"

"Forgive me, my lord, but the lords of the council sent me for you. They're at each other's throats over a matter they cannot agree upon, and they will have no one but you to settle it."

"Tell them I will be there," he said with a touch of impatience. Then he went back to Elizabeth. "I feared I would not escape them long. That's my punishment for shirking my duty all day. I am sorry, love."

"Must you?" she asked, tears in her dark eyes, and he cupped her cheek in his hand.

"I suppose I must." He kissed her lightly and then said with sudden intensity, "But I promise you we will have supper together, and I will keep the night for you alone."

❧

She put on her finest gown for supper that night, the white velvet she knew he favored. He had told her once it made her look as pure and fresh as a saint's rose, and she had not forgotten. When she came into the room, she saw him sitting at the table holding Grace in his lap, feeding her bits of mutton and kissing her as he did.

"That cat's a beggar, my lord," she scolded lightly. "You should not waste that on her."

"There's plenty more in the kitchen," he said absently, and, bending down, she turned his face up to her.

"I was not talking about the mutton."

A flame of passion leapt into his eyes, and he snatched a quick kiss as she sat beside him, certain that, apart from the cat, no one had seen. Grace herself, taking offense at being superseded, disappeared under the table.

Tom smiled and briefly touched his fingers to the white shoulder Elizabeth's gown left invitingly bare.

"What an intoxicating thing you are, my lady."

"And you," she replied, seeing how especially fine he looked. He wore a sleeveless doublet of forest green, belted at his lean waist. His shirt sleeves were of the new style, long and full, but open from the shoulder down and laced just at the wrist to display the well-made arm beneath. No one, she noted, wore the style so well.

There might have been no one else in the great hall that night for all they knew. The food and wine seemed to appear by magic, and, though they spoke of nothing, they needed no one's help to keep the conversation flowing. By the final course, they were sitting hand in hand, eating little and drinking only of each other's looks of love. Both of them made little sounds of impatience when Palmer interrupted them.

"I beg your pardon, sir, but I must have a word with you."

"Well?"

Palmer lowered his voice. "Lord Darlington asks that you come at once to the guard room."

"The guard room?"

Palmer glanced around and spoke so low even Elizabeth could not hear him. "They've found the boy, my lord, the one his majesty took with him."

"Jerome?" Tom leaned closer to him. "What do you mean they've found him? Is he dead?"

"No, my lord, but very nearly."

"What happened to the king?"

"I do not know, sir. Will you come? My lord Darlington was most urgent in sending for you."

Tom stood up. "I pray you excuse me, Bess. There is a matter I must see to."

"You've not finished your supper, my lord," she protested. "Where are you going?"

"I cannot tell you now, my lady." He forced an easy tone and a smile for the benefit of the onlookers. "It is but a trifle, love. Nothing to worry you."

"My lord—"

He leaned down and kissed her ear, whispering as he did, "I must go, love. Forgive me."

He found the door to the guard room was heavily secured, though it was clear that the soldiers did not know why. Answering nothing to their inquiring glances, he went inside. Jerome was sprawled out on the heavy table the armorers used, his peasant clothes now little more than rags, his whole body scraped and bruised. The physician was leaning down with his ear to the boy's battered chest, and Rafe was washing the grime from his face. Darlington was pacing at the foot of the table, his patrician countenance grim.

"Will he live, Master Livrette?" Tom asked.

The physician held up his hand for another moment of silence and then straightened.

"Your pardon, my lord. I do not think he is as bad as first we thought. He is weak, but he breathes clear and has a steady heartbeat.

"Has he said anything? About Philip?"

"Nothing, my lord. He's taken a heavy blow to the back of the head, or perhaps he has an arrow wound left untended a few days." Livrette felt down the length of Jerome's left arm, searching for broken bones and finding nothing. "Otherwise he seems whole enough."

"When do you think I might speak with him?"

"I cannot say, my lord," Livrette replied, starting on the boy's right arm. "He may be hours or days in waking, and even then he may not remember. Hold—what is this?"

Jerome's right hand was clenched in a tight fist.

"What?" Tom reached over and pried the boy's fingers open.

There in his palm, dulled with dirt and sweat, lay a battered gold ring, the lions engraved on it almost worn away.

"Dear God," Tom murmured, taking it and turning it over in his hand. "Oh, Philip, no."

"It is the king's," Rafe said bleakly.

"Rafe," Tom began, seeing the older man's sturdy vigor suddenly vanish, but he could not continue. What could he say of comfort and assurance when they all knew the ring's most likely significance?

"We must wait until the boy can tell what he knows," Livrette said finally.

Tom nodded. "We mustn't make any conclusion until then, but I will send out men to search, too. Perhaps Philip is merely hurt or captive. We cannot presume—"

"Let me make one of the party, my lord," Rafe said.

Tom put one hand on his brawny shoulder. "Rafe, I know you did not want to be left behind when he went. I know you do not want to be left behind now. But he commanded you especially to watch over Robin in his absence. Would you leave that undone?"

"I have lived a long time, my lord," Rafe said keenly, "but not so long that I am too feeble to look after the charge your father gave me almost twenty years ago."

"Rafe, I never said—"

"There is a whole squad of soldiers set to keep the princeling safe. I dare say I could do no more than they in that, but, if you think I will stay behind when my boy is missing or perhaps dead, you will find yourself mistaken." Rafe gave Tom a defiant look. "My lord."

"Well, you shall make one, then," Tom conceded. "My lord Darlington, take four or five of your men—you know the ones you can most trust—and see what you can learn of the king's whereabouts."

Darlington made a brief bow. "I will, my lord, and will send you word the moment I know anything."

"For now, not a breath of this to anyone," Tom said. "We cannot have this among the people. It can only stir trouble. Who was it found him?"

"Two of my men," Darlington said. "Both of them proven silent and loyal."

"Good. Make certain of it."

"I will. You will tell the queen, of course."

Tom shook his head. "Especially not the queen."

"My lord—"

"She grieves for him already, just having him away from her. What would such news do to her now?"

Again Darlington bowed. "Very well, my lord. We will go in the morning, before dawn."

He left the room and Tom went back to Jerome's side.

"Master Livrette, I will trust you to inform me the moment he wakes."

"Of course, my lord. I will do everything that I may to make that soon."

Tom thanked him and turned to go, but Rafe stopped him.

"I thank you, my lord. I could not stay behind, not knowing."

"I know, Rafe. Would I could go, too."

Rafe squeezed one arm around Tom's shoulders. "Be strong, boy. His lady will need you more than ever now."

Tom nodded. "I know."

He walked back toward the great hall wondering how he was to keep this latest news from Rosalynde. He trusted those who knew already to keep silent, but how could he keep the truth of it off his own face under her perceptive eyes? He could not even ease his grief by telling it to Elizabeth. There were those at court to whom she was too close, to whom she might let slip one or two innocent words that could bring Philip's whole kingdom down around them.

He turned a corner, and his heart made a sudden thud against his ribs. The queen was coming toward him, and he saw in her face that she had read already the anguish in his.

"My lord," she began, but he responded with only a polite bow, and, grasping the ring more tightly, he moved on toward the great hall.

"You've had word from him," she insisted, and he stopped, reluctant to face her.

"My lady—"

"He's found alive. It must be so, or you would have told me."

"Please, my lady, I've had no such news."

"I know you too well, my lord. You would not lie to me, but you might not tell all, thinking to spare me pain."

Still he could not look at her, lest she read the truth in his eyes. "I know nothing for certain yet, my lady. You mustn't—"

"Please," she begged, her voice breaking, "please, please! Whatever it is, I must know it."

She clutched his hand, the one that held the ring, and he tried to pull away from her.

"What is that you hold? It is from him!" Using both hands, she struggled to pry his fingers open, tears welling up from inside her as she did. "Please, for pity, do not torture me."

Their eyes met and he relaxed his grip. Seeing the ring, she could not hold back a low cry, a piercing echo of the one inside his own heart.

"I did not want you to know of it, my lady, until we are certain of its meaning."

She pressed her hands over her mouth, sobbing. "Oh, my beautiful, sweet Philip."

"Let me take you to your chamber, lady. There are too many ears and eyes here in the open."

She leaned heavily on him as they walked, following him blindly, pressing the ring to her heart as the tears slipped unbidden down her cheeks. In low whispers, he told her everything he knew so far, but he could not even convey the comfort of certainty.

"Please, my lady, not a word to anyone," he said, meaning to leave her at her door. "One breath of this could destroy all he's fought for, all he wants for your son. All he wants for you."

"You will make a fine king, my lord," she said, making an effort at serenity. "He will be proud of you."

"No, my lady. If he is dead, his son—"

She leaned up and kissed his cheek. "That cannot be now. Robin will never miss what he did not know, and I have no wish to be queen without my king."

She broke down again, and he put his arms around her, forcing his own tears back. "Please, my lady, trust God for him. You've done so before. But, if truly he is dead—"

She clung more tightly to him. "Sweet Jesus—"

"Shh. If truly he is dead, Robin shall reign after him. I'll not be another King Edward and take a place that is not rightly mine."

"Oh, God, my God, please," she mourned, and he opened her door and led her inside.

When he left the queen's chamber much later, Tom's eyes were tired and there was a sharp pain between his shoulder blades. He had tried to calm and comfort her, but he knew he had done it badly, being himself comfortless. There was little either of them could say or do until there was some certain news of Philip.

He paused when he reached Elizabeth's door and hoped, despite their spoiled plans, that he would find her in a gentle mood. He wanted just to lie in her arms and rest his aching head against her soft breast, to have just a touch of tenderness to soothe the pain in his heart and a touch of solace to help him bear his grief.

She was sitting at the hearth, edging the kerchief she had been working on, still fully dressed. She did not look up when he came into the room.

"Hello, love," he said, leaning down to her, but she jerked her face to one side, her lips pursed but not for kissing. He stepped back, bewildered. Then he smiled a little in weary apology.

"I did promise you the evening, Bess, but it's not half past eleven yet, I'll wager, and that makes it this evening still."

She continued with her sewing, saying nothing as she stabbed her needle through the unresisting linen. He pulled up a chair beside her and straddled it backwards.

"Oh, now, Bess, forgive my leaving you so long."

"Perhaps it should not strike me odd, my lord, that you find me stale company now." Anger colored her face. "I suppose it was bound to be so, once you had won me."

He sighed. "I know it must sometimes seem so to you, Bess, but I swear it is not. If it were left to my choice, I should be with you day and night. As it is, I simply have very little time to give you." He touched her hand, the one not armed with the needle. "There is so much I must look to now, love. Bear with me awhile."

"You have time enough for our good queen," she observed, throwing his hand off hers as she knotted the end of the thread and snapped it off.

"She is part of my charge, Bess. God knows I've seen little enough of her as it is. Come, sweet, do not be cross with me. I have that enough from everyone else in the court. I had hoped for a gentle word from her I love best in all this world."

He reached again for her hand, but again she jerked away from him.

"And what did she say, my lord, this best-loved one?"

"What?"

"What gentle words did her majesty have for you all this while tonight?"

"That is hardly kind, my lady. Surely you cannot grudge me the moment or two she's taken up. Have some charity for her."

She said nothing and he rubbed his forehead, trying to ease the throbbing tension there. He wished he could tell her what had kept him so long, wished she had chosen some other night to pick a quarrel, wished she cared for him enough to sense his pain and want to soothe it.

"Please, Bess, you know she is grieving for Philip and worried for Robin and ill with the child she is carrying."

"Perhaps she is merely unsure whom this child will favor. I always considered it something of a wonder that her eyes are green and the king's blue, yet their child has eyes as brown as—" She paused in a sarcastic show of surprise. "Why, as brown as yours, my lord."

He pressed his lips into a tight line and closed his eyes. "Not this again. Not now."

"And why not now?" she demanded.

"Her father's eyes are brown, my lady," he told her, forcing his voice into calm evenness, "and my father, Philip's father, had such eyes as well."

"You must count yourself fortunate in that, my lord," she observed, and she jabbed her needle back into the fabric to begin once more her deft, brutal assault. He clenched his jaw.

"You wrong me, lady, and the queen. As for the child, you well know he is Philip's image."

"As you are, my lord." She smiled fiercely. "Again, how fortunate for you, fortunate she can claim a Chastelayne husband to explain her Chastelayne child."

"By heaven, Bess, you do me wrong!" He stood up, doubling his fists. "By your reckoning, I must have fathered every brown-eyed child in the kingdom!"

"Oh, poor, wronged Lord Tom, who never strayed by so much as a thought unborn!" she mocked. "Do you think I am still to be pacified with a lie and a smile? I *saw* you with her! I went to find you and I *saw* you holding her in your arms, whispering to her, kissing her! With my own eyes, by my own witness, I *saw* you! What justification can you make now?"

"Is that it? What you saw was nothing more than comfort, Bess. We've had news of Philip that—"

"Pretty excuses! Pretty excuses!"

"My lady, if you will hear me—"

"Save your honey words for your mistresses, my lord. I've had a surfeit of them."

"Have plain truth, then," he shot back, "if you've an appetite for it."

Laying her needlework aside, she set her mouth in a hard, defiant line and stood to face him, her expression daring him to make further denial.

"I do love another woman," he said, no trace in his eyes of the velvet gentleness she was used to seeing there. "Not the queen, nor Molly, nor any of those you've so readily accused me with, but yet a sweet-tongued, gentle-spirited woman who believes me when I tell her what is in my heart and wants the love I have for her." He laughed from deep in his throat. "Would I not love such a one over a sharp-clawed, railing scold who holds my every breath suspect?"

"Have her then!" Her hand flashed up and struck him hard across the mouth. "Have your honey-tongued strumpet!"

He looked every inch proud Chastelayne as he stood there drawing hard, trembling breath through clenched teeth, with his head tossed up and white-hot fury in his dark eyes and his whole stance a warning.

"My lady—"

"Keep silent," she hissed. "You've said quite enough."

He laughed again, shaking his head in exasperated disbelief. Then he stalked out of the room, leaving behind him only a rattling slam of the door.

"Have her then!" she shrieked once more. She stripped the bracelet from her wrist and flung it out into the corridor, slamming the door again afterwards.

The blood beat in her temples. "*I do love another woman.*" Perhaps she had misinterpreted what she had seen with him and the queen earlier. If so, she had expected him to swear his fidelity, to plead for her love and understanding, as he had always done before. Or, if her fears were true, she had at worst expected him to confess a meaningless dalliance and beg her forgiveness. But, no, he had proudly proclaimed his love for this other, unashamed and unchastened.

She felt doubly a fool for believing any of his words, for imagining that there had been no falsehood in his kisses and no deception in his embrace. His eyes, his touch, everything about him had whispered his deep love for her, but now she knew it was not so, that he was no better than the rest of his breed for faithlessness.

"*I do love another woman.*" Dare he say so to her, with that cavalier flash of his eyes and that arrogant laugh? She cursed him to the blackest pit of hell for that, cursed him with every foul oath she knew. He was just as Ellen had warned her, and worse. There were no men to be trusted.

"*Yet know, my sweet lady, that there is a heart that beats as true for you as you could wish, a heart that weeps blood for your pain and would gladly comfort you should you ever find need of comfort.*"

She drew a shaky breath to keep back the angry tears that seethed inside her. Taliferro would understand her. He would appreciate her and not laugh. And Tom would be sorry, so sorry.

She looked into her glass, pleased to see wild daring in the eyes that blazed back at her.

"If you care to play at infidelity, my lord, I can give you as good as you send."

CHAPTER

13

BY THE TIME HE REACHED THE END OF THE CORRIDOR, THE LOUD, angry thud of Tom's boots had slowed and softened.

"Dear God, what did I say to her?"

He turned and pounded the wall with his fist. Then he pressed his burning face against the cool stone. He wanted to go to his own chamber, to be alone with his grief and his wounded pride, but he knew he could not, not until he had made things right with Elizabeth, and then there would be no need to be alone.

"What a great return a little investment of love will bring." He had told Philip this once and not so long ago, but that was before Elizabeth had come back to court, before he had realized what a complex business this being married was.

"Oh, Philip, where are you now?"

He knew it was unfair to expect Elizabeth to read his mind, to know somehow, without being told, of the grief in his heart and to somehow comfort it. What had possessed him to tell her he loved another? That was no way to win her love or prove his own. Little wonder she had struck him. What was she to think, left in the dark as she so often was, not knowing how much he wanted to confide in her, left to draw her own conclusions about his silences and his absences from her?

He wiped his hand across his still-stinging mouth and walked a little further, cooling the wrath that rose up in him at her remembered accusations, determined still to prove that love brought its own rewards, determined still to love her as Christ loved His church. By the time he turned and went back to her door a few minutes later, he was prepared to ask pardon for his ill-chosen words and take patiently whatever reproof she had for him.

"My lady has gone to her bed, my lord," Ellen told him before he could even speak. "You would do as well to go to your own."

"Please, Mistress Ellen, tell her that, as humbly I am able, I beg a word with her. I swear I'll not keep her long."

"I have my orders, my lord."

"Please, mistress, just give her my message. At the least, let her know I am here."

Her lips pursed, Ellen made a terse curtsey and shut the chamber door. A moment later, she opened it again.

"My lady is asleep."

Tom frowned in impatience. "Did you tell her I was here?"

"I did, my lord. She says to tell you she is asleep."

"Please, Bess," he called into the darkness of the chamber, "give me just a moment."

"She is asleep, my lord," Ellen told him forcefully. "Good night."

Before he could say another word, she shut the door again, and this time he heard the unmistakable clank of the bolt being shot home. For an incredulous moment, he merely stood there. Then, turning to go, he noticed something shiny at his feet, catching the flickering torchlight. It was the bracelet with Elizabeth's initial and his own, tossed in a forlorn heap against the wall. He picked it up and rubbed his finger over the nick in one of the scripted *T*'s.

Cradling it in his hand, he carried it with him to bed.

How like him to come back again, smooth tongued and all honey, to lie once more and say he loves me, Elizabeth thought, watching from her place of concealment in one of the alcoves as Tom walked away. With a rebellious jerk of her chin, she drew her cloak around her and crept down the corridor in the opposite direction. When she reached Taliferro's door, she stood for a moment before it, suddenly not so certain as she had been.

"I do love another woman."

She heard the words again and the careless laugh that had accompanied them, saw again the proud anger in Tom's tautly lined face, and felt the hot, suffocating fury rush through her once again.

"Would I not love such a one over a sharp-clawed, railing scold?"

She rapped on the door, three quick blows that seemed to echo in the empty corridor, and one of Taliferro's serving men opened to her.

"My lady?"

"Who is it, Wat?" she heard Taliferro call from inside, and the servant bowed to her.

"Will you come in, your highness? It is the Princess Elizabeth, my lord."

"Yes, pray you come in, lady," came the silken answer. The man opened the door wider, and Taliferro stood up from his table, deftly sliding a blank sheet over the one upon which he had been writing. He was dressed still, at least to his shirt, despite the lateness of the hour.

She stepped just over the threshold, and Taliferro came to her, reaching for her hand.

"You grace my humble quarters with your beauty, dear princess."

"My lord—" Her heart was pounding so loudly in her ears she could hardly hear herself speak, but she forced her lips into a thin smile. "I wish merely a word with you, my lord."

He smiled and dismissed his servant. Then he bent to kiss her hand, drawing her further into the room as he did.

"Surely I can afford you more than just one word, Madonna. I have long hoped you would come some night to me . . . to talk." He led her to the bench before the hearth and sat down close beside her, still holding her hand captive. "What would you speak to me of? I am here only to please you."

"You were telling me of your travels, my lord," she said, looking up at him with that coy invitation that she had used on Tom, but her voice sounded feeble even in her own ears. "You said we would speak of them again."

"So I did," Taliferro said, a hint of a knowing smile on his face, his black eyes fixed at first on hers, then moving to her trembling lips and then to the inviting curves of her body. The pounding in her ears grew louder as he began massaging her hand, sliding his fingers higher and higher up her arm with each stroke. "Where would you have me begin, Madonna? And how far would you have me go?"

There was an unflattering wolfishness in the way he looked at her, but she only brought her mouth nearer to his.

"Begin where you please, my lord, and stop where you will."

"I have learned much in my travels, lady, much it would please me to share with you." His hand was at her shoulder. Then he slipped it up to her throat and turned her face up to his. "If you would learn of me."

She closed her eyes and felt his mouth on hers in a searching, expert kiss, a kiss that left her cold.

"I do love another woman."

She sighed as if he had pleased her, and he kissed her again, harder and deeper, slipping his cool hands down her body with a wanton familiarity that made her shiver, but not with passion.

"Would I not love such a one over a sharp-clawed, railing scold?"

Fear rushed through her when she felt him tugging at the lacings down her back, but she forced it away and sighed again. Tom would be sorry. So sorry.

Taliferro's hands were at her bodice now, and she caught sight of herself in his glass. She was letting this man, this man she did not even want, she was letting him take her . . .

"Like any harlot—"

She tried to pull away from him, but he only clasped her more tightly, his hold on her suddenly painful.

"Please, my lord," she cried, panicking, and he looked up at her, a sly look of triumph on his angular face. She squirmed away from him and stood up.

"I must go, my lord. I never meant—"

"Oh, you meant, Madonna, indeed you did. And I meant, for quite some while." He stood, too, his soulless black eyes fixed on hers, hypnotizing in their power to draw her and to hold her. "Why struggle against what you truly wish for?"

She tried to pull her clothing into some semblance of order, some pretense of modesty, feeling the sting of tears in her eyes. "I only wish to go."

She went to the door, had her hand on the latch, but he caught her there and spun her to face him again.

"You may tease Brenden so, Madonna, but I am not so easily trifled with."

He pushed her against the door, shoving himself against her to hold her there. She could feel the latch stabbing painfully against her spine.

"I will have what you promised me, lady."

She was crying now. "Please, my lord, I never promised—"

"Your eyes promised." He kissed her cruelly. "Your lips promised." He slid his hands over her again. "You came here alone at night of your own volition. For what, Madonna, if not this?"

"I will scream," she whimpered. "Someone will come."

"You needn't play the innocent with me, lady. You are hardly a maid that you might claim you did not know what you were doing. Scream, if you dare, if you wish the whole court to hear of your visit to my chamber. If you wish that pretty fool, Brenden, to know of it."

She had, oh, God, she had wanted Tom to know, to weep and bleed and writhe at the knowledge of it. He had told her triumphantly of his love for another, but all she could think of now was his gentle eyes and the tenderness of his touch.

"I would never force you."

"No, my lord, I beg you. He mustn't know. Please—"

"Then buy my silence."

He forced another kiss, his hands bruising in their rough intimacy. Then he swung her up against him. She made no more struggle.

Not half an hour after she had left it, Elizabeth returned to her chamber.

"I want a bath, Ellen," she said dully, letting her cloak drop to the floor behind her.

"At this time of night, lamb?" Ellen clucked. "I told my lord of Brenden you were already abed. What if he comes again asking for you?"

Elizabeth's lip trembled. "Ellen—"

"You needn't worry, my sweeting. I told him you were not to be disturbed."

"I want a bath, Ellen," Elizabeth repeated, almost choking on the words.

"My lady—"

"Now!" Elizabeth cried, tearing at her dress, snapping the laces in her haste. "Do it now!"

"Yes, yes, of course, lamb," Ellen said, trying to soothe her. "Let me do that and Nan will make you a lovely bath."

The rest of the women scurried to do as they had been told, and Ellen more hindered than helped Elizabeth out of her clothes.

"Take that away," Elizabeth said, kicking free of the torn white velvet. "I do not want to see it again."

"Of course, my lady," Ellen said, gathering it up.

"And this."

Elizabeth wriggled out of her shift, worsening the rip at the neckline. Then she tore the combs from her hair and flung them onto the floor.

"Those as well," she commanded, and Ellen scooped up her hair to smooth it.

"Don't!" Elizabeth cried, jerking away from her.

"Now never you worry, my lamb. Hasn't your Ellen always looked after you? My lord of Brenden will never know—"

"Go away, Ellen."

"My lady—"

"Leave me! All of you, go! Except Nan."

With a snort of displeasure and a black look at Nan, Ellen swept out of the room, taking her mistress's discarded clothing and the rest of the women with her. Nan said nothing as she filled the tub and settled Elizabeth into it. For several minutes there was nothing but taut silence.

"Make the water hotter," Elizabeth ordered, scrubbing her skin with a rough sponge, immersed to the neck in suds.

"You'll blister sure, my lady," Nan protested and Elizabeth threw the sponge at her.

"I said hotter!"

Nan fetched the steaming kettle from the hearth, murmuring her disapproval as she emptied it into the bath. "All that fine white skin."

Elizabeth bit her lip against the pain and scrubbed harder.

"Rub yourself raw, lady," Nan said almost under her breath. "You will never make yourself clean inside."

Elizabeth's face turned white, despite the heat. "What?"

"Forgive me, my lady—"

Elizabeth wrapped her arms around her knees and laid her head down on them, sobbing.

"He did not even trouble to remove his boots."

Nan knelt beside the bath and stroked her wet hair. "Oh, my lady, my lady."

Elizabeth could not look at the openhearted girl, not when she knew that degradation was blazoned in every line of her own guilty face. How different it was to merely lie with a man, to be used by a man rather than be made love to by him. Taliferro had been a brusque and selfish partner. She would not say lover. There had been no love in what they had done—only shame, eternal shame.

She was an adulteress. She who had once not allowed her own husband to touch her in holy marriage had given herself to another, had forever soiled her body and her soul in committing mortal sin. The contempt she had had for her father's infidelities, for Tom's, for all the inconstancies of male-kind, she heaped now a hundredfold upon herself. There was not enough water in the wide ocean to cleanse her now.

Nan merely allowed her to cry, and for a long while her tears added to the already brimming tub. Finally she lifted her head, swallowing hard in determination.

"Well, it is over and not to be undone." She cupped her hands and brought them up full to rinse her face. "Bring me another shift."

Nan did as she was bidden, saying nothing as she helped her mistress dry herself. She put the clean white garment on her.

Elizabeth studied herself in the mirror. Except for her unsettled expression, she looked no different than before. Tom had other women, at the very least the one he had admitted to, and still slept soundly at night. Why should she be any different herself? If she did not think too much about what had happened, she would soon forget, and it would be as if it had never been. And Tom—and Tom—

"Oh, God, what have I done?" she sobbed, the pain knifing through her again. "Oh, Tom."

She sat down on the bed, and Nan sat beside her, comforting her in her arms.

"You must tell him, my lady. Lord Tom loves you. Tell him and ask his pardon and he will forgive you."

"No, no, I cannot. He would never forgive me. He would only use it against me, remind me of it again and again, just as I have done him."

"If you do not tell him, it will be always between you, corrupting whatever else you might have with him. Tell him plain and have it over. It will hurt, but it will also heal."

Elizabeth shook her head against Nan's shoulder, her voice choked off by tears.

"You must at least make it right with God, my lady," Nan said softly. "Do not leave this sin unpardoned. Surely you know He will forgive you."

Elizabeth slipped down to kneel on the floor, drawing Nan with her.

"Pray for me, Nan. I cannot bring myself to do it."

"You must, my lady."

"Please, Nan, please."

The servant girl took both her hands and prayed the long night through that her mistress would come to a place of reconciliation with God and with her husband. Elizabeth said nothing, but clung to her and wept.

The next day, Tom came several times to Elizabeth's chamber, but each time he was turned away. For two days more it was the same. He tried to attend to his ever-increasing responsibilities, but he could not keep his mind on them much. There was no word yet from Darlington's party—he knew he could not rationally expect it so soon—but it would have been some comfort whatever it was. The only thing that brought him any satisfaction was Taliferro's departure from Winton to take more of the promised supplies to his people.

Jerome still had not regained consciousness despite the many prayers lifted up on his behalf, especially by Lady Marian. Tom had decided it would be too cruel to make her wonder anymore about the boy's whereabouts, and, certain of her trustworthiness, he had told her of his return and granted her request that she be allowed to help in nursing him. He wished he could give the queen such comfort.

Shattered by the silent testimony of Philip's ring, Rosalynde rarely left her chambers and rarely let Robin from her side. The court was a grim, quiet place. Tom spent much of the little free time he had in the midst of the reconstruction at the cathedral. There was much yet to be done, but it pleased him to see it going up stronger and finer than before. It pleased him to know there would one day be no trace of the destruction that marred it now.

He liked best to go there at night, when the sounds of construction were stilled and the workers, spiritual and temporal, had gone to their beds, leaving him alone in the quiet with God, to find comfort for his griefs, answers to his problems, and trust for those that had no answers yet. But for this sweet communion, he felt intensely alone, grieved for the loss of his lover and friend, disheartened that she refused still to see him, that she returned his notes unopened.

"Oh, God, my Father," he prayed, kneeling in the Chapel of the Kings, "tell me what to do. I must tell her. I must make this right with her, but she will not let me. Lord God, for sweet Jesus' sake, let me speak just a word to her, just to tell her the truth. Please, Lord."

He dropped his head down, not knowing what else to say. Then he heard a noise behind him in the darkness. He froze and put his hand on his dagger. Again he heard the sound, the tiniest bit clearer than before, and he stood up. It was weeping, a woman's soft weeping, at the back of the chapel.

Noiselessly, he went toward it, wondering what woman would be bold enough or desperate enough to come here at night alone. He was only a few feet away when he realized who was kneeling there.

"Bess?"

She jerked her head up and her weeping abruptly stopped.

"I did not think anyone would be here, my lord. I will leave you to your devotions."

She gathered up her skirts, but before she could stand, he dropped to his knees beside her.

"Will you not hear my confession, my lady, before you go?"

"Confession, my lord?" she asked, haughty-eyed. "That is a task better suited to your priest. But, no, I suppose you Heretics have little use for them."

"Do you not think husbands and wives should confess their faults one to another, Bess?" He took her cold hands. "Would you not tell me if you had wronged me and ask my pardon?"

Her lip trembled. "My lord?"

He bowed his head. "I have wronged your heart and my vows, my lady, and I beg you to forgive me that."

"You've admitted your infidelities to me already," she said, her voice stiff. "Is there something more you have to reveal?"

"That was wrong of me, Bess. I ought never have told you such a thing."

"You said we should confess our faults."

"That is what I mean to do now, love, what I have tried to do all this while. When I told you I loved another woman, I deceived you. That other I spoke of is only your fair self, when you've a temper as sweet as your beauty and a touch of tenderness in your heart for me." He caressed her cheek and tried to get her to smile. "You were something of a shrew that day. Nothing like the Bess I love."

"Then you never—"

"I was never false to you." He held up one hand and put the other over his heart. "I swear before God Himself, here before His own altar, I have never touched any woman but you. May God remember all my sins if I have sinned against you in that."

"You told me—" Tears streamed down her face. "You made me believe—"

"That was wrong of me, sweet, I know. I would scarcely be a Chastelayne without my share of pride, but I should never have lost hold of my temper and for that I crave your pardon." He stood up and tried to coax her into his arms. "Can we not make it right between us now?"

"Let me go," she sobbed, struggling away from him.

"Bess, please. Wait!"

She ran from the chapel, and, bewildered, he took one swift stride after her. Then he stopped himself. Head and shoulders drooping, he breathed out a long, wistful sigh.

"Bess."

"Get out!" Elizabeth commanded her startled servants when she reached her chamber. She staggered inside, swinging the door shut behind her, blinded with burning tears but still able to see Tom's repentant face as he told her there was no other woman. "*I was never false to you.*"

"Oh, God, God, God! What have I done?"

Choked by tears, she stumbled to her knees at the side of the bed, burying her face in the bedclothes, bunching them up around her to hide her face and muffle her cries. Tom had been faithful. Always. How was it that she knew that was true now and had never let herself believe it before?

"*I was never false to you.*"

"Then why did you tell me you were?" she wailed. "How could you tell me such a thing and drive me to—"

No, she could not lay the blame on him. Whatever he had said or done, her actions were her own and she alone would reap their fruit.

"Oh, God, help me. Please, please, holy Jesus, comfort."

But she could find no comfort in the cry. All she could hear was the shrill voice of her own conscience.

Adulteress. Adulteress! And behind that, a mocking laugh. *Fool.*

Groping for words, she repeated the prayer of confession she had been taught in her childhood, the one she had tried to say in the chapel, the one she had sobbed again and again here alone, but there was no meaning behind any of it, nothing in it that could take away the shame and the stain.

Oblivious to the silent comings and goings of her waiting women, she lay there for the rest of the night and for the whole next day, feeling numb and empty of everything but the suffocating weight that pressed down upon her.

"I was never false to you. Never false. Never false."

There was a rhythm to the words, a constant pounding that would not stop, but she could not weep anymore. The burning in her heart had consumed all the tears she had not already cried. She lifted her head and caught sight of herself in her looking glass. Her face was swollen, her hair snarled, her clothes wadded and creased. Now, as Tom had said, her temper was indeed as sweet as her beauty. Every bit as sweet.

Roses were rare and costly this time of year, but he had sent her one this morning when still she would not see him. She reached toward the single white blossom, remembering the message attached: "Forgive me, love."

"Oh, Tom, what have I done?" she moaned again, not daring to touch the pristine petals.

By her own choice she had gone to Taliferro and had refused Tom any chance to explain.

"Please, Bess, give me just a moment . . ."

She had heard the remorse in his voice as he had stood outside her door, just moments after he had told her there was someone else. Doubtless he had meant then to explain, but her vengeful heart would not hear him, had never heard him, had wanted him to prove false. Now she knew he had been faithful and she had not, and if there was a child—

She dropped her head back down to the rumpled bedding, forcing back the tears that still threatened. She could not weep any more, not if she was to go to him that night. She took a cloth from beside her basin, soaked it with cold water, and pressed it against her tear-blotched face. With her eyes closed, she lay back on the bed, still and calm, thinking of mild, pleasant things and not of mortal sin.

When the sun no longer lit her chamber, she sat up and lit a taper to peer once more into her glass. Her head still ached, but her eyes were no longer red. There was really nothing left to bear witness to her weeping save a little heightened color in her cheeks and an occasional shakiness in her breathing. Tom would not know anything but that she had realized how foolish she was to be cross with him and that she wanted to make up.

She had to go to him. She had to go now. She had barred him her bed for too long. If she had conceived a child and did not go to him now, he would know it was not his. She could scarcely bear the thought of touching him, of soiling him with her faithlessness, but she had no other way. She was hardly a maid, as Taliferro had said. Tom would have no way of knowing she had been false.

She called her women into the room, ordering them to take away her ruined clothes and dress her for bed. When they had finished and she was again alone, she studied the demure-looking girl reflected in her mirror. The pearl-colored silk of the robe she had chosen made her skin glow and the low neckline only enhanced the delicate satin fullness of her bosom, but she could find no beauty there. Her hair shimmered in the firelight, the auburn highlights making the heavy knot at the nape of her neck look rich and lush, but to her it was no more than a snare. She had made sure that Nan secured it with only a single clasp, a clasp that could be removed easily so her hair would fall over his eager hands and entice him to make love to her.

She had thought it all out. Down to the exquisite fineness of her shift, she had planned each detail of the seduction. He would not want to resist her. He would have no reason even to consider it. He would be no more than a trusting husband taking his wife into a lover's embrace, an embrace God and man called holy. Not like Taliferro's.

She tried to turn her thoughts from Tom, fearing she would spoil her beauty with another torrent of tears, but she could not escape the memory of the pure truth in the velvet depths of his eyes. She cringed at the thought of seeing those eyes filled with pain.

You have wronged him, but you needn't break his heart. He need never know.

She took one final look at herself before carrying her taper to his chamber.

CHAPTER 14

SHE FOUND HIM ASLEEP, LOOKING EVERY BIT THE INNOCENT ANGEL of her fancy. There was something poignant and very vulnerable about him as he lay there, his arms clutched around his pillow, his gentle mouth drooping with sadness even in sleep.

He had kicked the sheet almost off, exposing most of his back and shoulders and one long leg to her admiring, remorseful eyes. That fine, strong beauty had been hers, along with the steadfast heart within it, and she had tossed it all away. For Taliferro. No, for her own rebellious vengeance. The remembrance sickened her, but she drew closer. Then she hesitated again, reluctant to wake him from his ignorant bliss.

But if there is a child—

Be still, she told herself sternly, feeling the tears rise again in her breast. She removed her robe in a quick deliberate motion, laid it across a chair, and leaned down to breathe warm words in his ear.

"My lord."

He stirred but did not wake. Bending closer, she touched her lips to his skin.

"My lord."

"Mmm?" He opened his eyes. Then, with a look of drowsy surprise, he smiled. "Bess."

He leaned up on his elbow, all tousled and flushed with sleep, and she bent close to him again, closing her eyes, unable to look at him and do what she knew she must.

"Shall we have a truce, my lord?" she breathed.

"Oh, Bess." He turned to kiss her, taking her into his arms as he did. "I am sorry, love. I was cruel, and I never really—"

"No," she said quickly, before the tears could well into her eyes and sound in her voice. "I do not want you to tell me. I want you to show me."

He took her eagerly at her word, pulling her into the warmth of his bed, against the warmth of his body. She kissed him fiercely, trying to blot out the memory of Taliferro's touch, but she could tell already that everything had changed.

His hands were on her, expressing the fiery passion she had loved, but now they only reminded her of other hands and brought back an urgent desire to escape. He was kissing her intensely, almost desperately, with all that was in him, but she took no pleasure in it, not with the memory of Taliferro still pressing down upon her and her conscience crying out, "*Adulteress!*"

He paused, and she knew he could feel the hesitation in her. Then he kissed her again, twice more, clearly trying to spark some response and finding none. With a bewildered sigh, he touched his lips to her cheek, just a tiny wisp of a kiss, and then rolled to his back.

"Bess," he whispered, trying to hold her closer, but she lay rigid in his embrace, only a dull, empty pang of loneliness to prove she was yet capable of feeling.

"Do not doubt me, love," he pled. "Do not doubt me anymore. Do you think I would go to anyone else when I have found such pure sweetness here with you? When I need nothing more than that you love me?"

She shivered, and he held her tighter.

"I love you, Bess."

She did not answer him for the tears that almost choked her, and he turned her face tenderly up to his.

"You are still cross with me," he said, a little worried wrinkle in his brow. "But I swear our love is still pure. I've not been false to you; I would never be."

She pushed his gentle hands away and sat up, her chest heaving as she fought for air. "I have!"

A surprised gasp of incredulous laughter escaped him and he shook his head. "Bess, you—"

"I have been false to you, my lord."

He sat up, too, and cupped her face in his hands, searching her eyes, imploring for even a semblance of hope. She could hear the strain of his breathing.

"Bess, you—" He drew another hard breath and looked up, as if he were pleading with heaven. "It was—it was Taliferro, was it not?"

She nodded, unable to hold her tears, not at the sight of his pain. If she had slashed through his heart with a razor, she could not have cut him more deeply.

"Taliferro." He squeezed his eyes shut and dropped his hands. "Oh, Bess."

"I wanted to hurt you." She forced her voice into steadiness. "I wanted to make you agonize over my infidelities, just as I did over yours, but it was nothing like I thought. It was—then I found you had never betrayed me, that I'd been a fool . . ."

"I see we've both been fools," he said after a time, his voice very low. "I suppose it was because of what I said to you, because I hurt you."

"I drove you to say what you did, my lord, and would not let you make it right. Now it can never be made right again."

There was another long silence. His eyes once more met hers.

"Why did you come to me now?"

"He told me I must, in case there was—" She looked down. "In case there was a child." The words faded into an unsteady sob. "My lord, I never meant for it to happen, not truly. I was so angry at you, and I wanted to hurt you, but when it came to it, I could not—I tried to stop him."

"He forced you?"

She saw a flash of fury in his eyes and ducked her head.

"No. Yes. Oh, I do not know. I went to him, I let him kiss me, I let him touch me, but it was not the same. It was not what I thought. I—I tried to make him stop." She swallowed down more tears. "I told him I would tell you if he did not let me go; I told him I would scream, but he said you would never believe me; no one would, not when it was I who had come to him." She hugged her arms around herself, shaking and sobbing again. "He held me so hard, and I was so afraid and he would not let me go. I was so afraid of what he would do. I did not—"

Tears choked off the rest of her words, and she sat there with her face turned away, waiting for him to shove her away from him, out of his bed, and denounce her for the harlot she was. She wept harder at the thought of never again kissing his mouth or bringing the loving light to his eyes, of never again having the strong feel of his arms around her, never—

"Bess," he murmured against her cheek, pulling her close again. "Do not cry. I beg you. I cannot bear for you to cry."

She held fast to him, sobbing while he rocked her against him, feeling his tears burn her skin as he clung to her just as tightly.

"What am I to do, my lord?" she pled brokenly, tortured by his grief and by the unrelenting scourge of her own conscience. "What am I to do?"

He pressed his cheek against the still-bound mass of her hair.

"God forgive me, Bess," he said, his low voice almost choked into unintelligibility. "God forgive me, I do not know."

She pulled back from him and looked at him for a very long time, her breath coming in dry, painful little gasps. She had expected any answer but that. He had always been so certain before. There was such profound anguish in his eyes that she wondered vaguely, beneath her own pain, how she had ever thought herself eager for such a sight. Finally he turned away from her, and she swallowed down one last dry sob.

"Can you tell me that you love me now, my lord?"

For what seemed eternity, he said nothing. Then he wiped his face with the back of his hand.

"Yes, Bess." His voice dropped to a whisper. "I love you."

"My lord—"

"Please—" He caught his breath and began again. "I love you, Bess." He looked at her once more, a determined set to his jaw and insupportable pain in every haggard line of his face. "Let us leave it at that for now."

He leaned back on the pillows again, drawing her head to his shoulder, and she lay there against him, listening to the hard pounding of his heart. Tears burned in her chest, in her throat, behind her eyes, but she could not weep. There were some pains too deep for tears.

"It can never be the same anymore, can it?" she asked finally.

He held her a little closer and the dawn was a long time coming.

The snow came again, blanketing the city in purest white, concealing the bare ugliness beneath. For the next few days, Elizabeth forced herself through the motions of living, of eating and drinking and showing the court only smiles and gaiety. The effort wore on her, and she could see the strain of it in Tom's face, too, as much as he tried to act as though nothing had changed between them.

"I love you, Bess," he would say each night when they went to bed, always with a smile and a gentle kiss. Every morning began the same way, but the smiles were tinged with pain, the kisses cool, and she wondered why he did not sleep in his own chamber. He may as well have.

There was a particular desolation in this loneliness of the marriage bed. Side by side in the darkness, they could not seem to reach across the breach that was expanding between them, and each night brought back her pained realization.

"It can never be the same anymore, can it?"

She could feel him there beside her now, lying straight and still, close to the edge of the bed, not sprawled all over it as he used to be. His breathing was too quick and shallow for him to be asleep.

He is counting the hours until dawn.

She found his hand in the darkness, and his fingers went lightly around hers, but he made no other response. She rolled over against him and kissed his shoulder.

"I am sorry."

"I know."

She knit her brow. There was a strange tone to his voice, not anger or regret or even sadness—only a sort of inescapable, weary hollowness. He was remembering what she had done, remembering again and again and again. She knew he was, and she wanted to hide herself, but she could not let her shame keep this distance between them any longer.

She moved closer and kissed his chest, just over his heart, stroking his shoulders as she did. He put his arms around her waist, but that was all. She wriggled up a little higher and nuzzled the underside of his jaw and breathed a little path of kisses along his throat, back down to his heart, pressing closer with each one. Then she felt him catch his breath, and she lifted her mouth to his.

He turned his face away.

"I cannot. Forgive me, Bess. I am sorry, but I cannot."

"Please, my lord," she murmured against his lips, and then she kissed him. He closed his eyes and held her close, strengthening the kiss as he did, but the response was forced and without passion.

"Please," she whispered once more. "Please, please, do not hate me. Love me again. You told me you would."

"I do." His voice was urgent, pleading as hers was. "I swear I do. I love you, I forgive you, but I cannot stop thinking—"

The breath shuddered out of him and she clung to him.

"Please, my lord."

He pressed her back against the pillows, kissing her once more, but still there was no passion in him. All his efforts could not disguise that.

He broke from her and sat up. "I cannot. Not now."

"Not now," she repeated, thinking that it sounded more like *not ever*. She watched him for a while, sitting with his back to her. She touched his drooping shoulder.

"My lord?"

He glanced back at her, and he began to dress himself, hurriedly, fumbling with the straps on his boots, not bothering to put on his doublet or even lace his shirt. He glanced at her again when it was done, helpless remorse in his dark eyes.

"I am sorry, Bess," he said, his voice half-choked, and she stretched her hands out to him, tears coursing down her cheeks.

"Please, my lord, no."

"Bess, I—" He reached toward her before he drew back once more, shaking his head. "I am sorry."

"Please," she begged, but he only shook his head again, and in another moment even the sound of his step was gone.

"Please," she whispered. "I love you."

Elizabeth did not go to supper in the great hall anymore after that, and Tom did not come to her to ask why. He did not come to her at all. The words she had long ago read in secret came back once again to torment her. "*By night on my bed, I sought the one my soul loves; I sought him but I found him not.*"

"Tom," she sobbed again and again. She had found that jealousy was as cruel as the grave. But was love truly as strong as death? She believed now that he loved her, at least that he *had* loved her. She knew now that she loved him, beyond mere desire, but was it too late?

Seeing her pain, Nan advised her to be patient, to give him time for grief and forgiveness, to go to God with her sorrow, but Elizabeth could foresee nothing accomplished by the passage of time save a widening of the gulf that was between them. It was Ellen who offered a more tangible solution.

"Give him this, my lady," she said when Nan had gone, "and he'll not long stay cold to you."

She held up a vial filled with something thick and viscidly red, and Elizabeth stared at it, as drawn as she was repelled.

"What is it?"

"Nothing harmful," Ellen assured her, "merely something an old wise woman taught my grandam, and it has been in my family since."

"He would never drink that!"

"Of course not," Ellen said with a scornful laugh. "Not as it is. Put it in his wine first. They say it always works and the man none the wiser."

"But, Ellen, I want his love, not just—"

"It's all one with men, girl. Trust me."

Elizabeth came uninvited into Tom's chamber, carrying the wine in a crystal flask. Silver would have shown the taint of the potion, so she dared not use their wedding goblets. Instead she brought two crystal chalices, of the set with the flask, and poured the pungent red liquid into them.

"Is Palmer idling somewhere that he could not serve me himself?" Tom asked when he saw her. He tried to smile as he said it, but his mouth seemed to have forgotten how.

"I asked if I might not bring it, my lord," she said. "I thought we might talk awhile, as we used to."

This time he managed the smile, but her heart broke at the hollowness of it.

"Certainly, my lady."

She shut the door and sat down close to him, watching as he took the first drink. He grimaced a little but did not comment, and certain he thought it nothing but a variation in the vintage, she smiled.

They talked for a while of trivialities, of congenial, empty nothings that did not hurt, and, with each sip of wine he took, it seemed the barrier between them weakened.

"Let me stay with you," she urged when it grew late, her confidence in the potion making her bold, and there was an odd unsteadiness in his expression that had not been there a moment before. She stroked the hair back from his temple. "Let me make you forget the past, at least for tonight."

"That is not so easy," he said thickly, but his eyes were focused on her full, inviting lips, and she felt sure the wine was performing as promised.

She moved closer to him, and he pulled her up into his arms and kissed her with that slow intensity she knew was only the beginning.

"Oh, my lord," she sighed. Then she felt his body convulse, and he pulled back from her, trembling. His hands clutched at the arms of his chair, and there was a clammy film of sweat on his suddenly-pale face.

"My lord!"

She leapt to her feet and fetched a cup of water, wiping his face with her handkerchief as she urged him to drink. He gritted his teeth, groaning at the fierce, intermittent pains.

"Send for Livrette," he gasped. "Oh, merciful God—"

She grabbed his wash basin and held his head over it, tears welling up in her eyes as she did.

Palmer could not find Livrette until it was nearly dawn. By then Tom was sleeping leadenly, looking haggard but out of danger. Elizabeth was herself little better.

"Something he ate or drank," the physician diagnosed. "He seems to need nothing now but rest. Try to keep him quiet a day or so, my lady. I do not think you need worry."

"I will look after him, my lady," Palmer said once Livrette was gone. Then he took Elizabeth back to her own chamber. Watching him walk away, she could not decide if the faint contempt she had seen on his stoic face was real or merely a reflection of her own.

"You look as if you did not rest well, my lady," Nan said when her mistress came into the room, and Ellen looked up from the shift she was mending.

"As I told you," the older woman said, an insinuating look on her pinched face, and Elizabeth yanked the shift out of her hands and hurled it to the floor.

"You hateful old witch! What poison did you give me last night?"

"Poison?"

"What poison have you been feeding me all along?"

"My—my lady—" Ellen sputtered, and the rest of the serving women looked round-eyed at each other.

"And I've been fool enough to drink it in. Every word! Mary and Joseph, just because you know nothing of love, does that mean I must never? Are you so bitter you cannot bear to see anyone else happy? My husband might have died last night thanks to your cursed witchcraft! You should be put to the flames for it!"

Ellen fell to her knees in terror.

"My lady, I beg you—"

"And I've hurt him again and again because I've listened to your groundless suspicions!"

"But, my lady—"

"Never speak to me again, Ellen," Elizabeth said, anger staining her face. "Never let me *see* you again. Take what is yours and go."

Nan touched her mistress's arm. "My lady, you'd not send her out with nothing."

Elizabeth pressed her trembling lips together, cooling a little at the girl's calm voice. She snatched up a handful of coins from her jewel chest and threw them where the older woman knelt.

"You have the time it takes to pick those up to be gone from here."

As soon as Jerome regained consciousness, Lady Marian had sent word to Tom, and now she stood near her beloved, tears streaming down her face as he told of the king who had showed them both only kindness.

"He was not breathing when I pulled him out, my lord," Jerome told Tom wearily. "I saw them carry him off, and that was the last I knew until now. I am sorry, my lady."

Rosalynde was kneeling beside the bed, clutching the boy's thin hand and Tom's, too, her face buried in the bedclothes. Tom swallowed hard, the blow of this news only adding emphasis to the pale sickness that was still on his face from the night before.

"Then he is dead."

Jerome licked his dry lips, and Marian lifted his head to give him a sip of water.

"I tried, my lord," he said, and there was a mournful quaver in his raspy voice. "I would have stayed there with him, no matter all their men, but I had sworn to bring back his ring. I . . . would have . . ."

His head fell limply against the girl's breast, and Tom knew Jerome would say no more for a while yet. He coaxed Rosalynde to her feet and led her from the room.

"Come, my lady," he murmured. "Some hard things we must simply bear."

She walked numbly beside him, saying nothing as the tears coursed down her face, all the while twisting the battered ring she wore in a gesture so like Philip's that Tom wanted to scream at her to stop. When they reached her door, she pulled away from him.

"It is not so," she said, looking up at him, her mouth held firm and defiant. Then she showed him the ring. "He sent me this, rather, God sent me this, to remind me not to despair. He made a miracle with it before, in spite of the circumstances, and He can again."

Tom bit his lip, feeling the searing pain crashing inside him again and again. "Please, my lady, the boy saw—"

"He saw them taking Philip away. Nothing more. If he were dead, would they have merely buried him? Would it not have more suited them to bring his body back as proof of their triumph? Would we not have heard of it?" She pressed her small fist against her heart. "Would I not feel it here if he were truly gone from me?"

God! he cried out in silent desperation. *Make her face the truth! He is dead! Oh, holy Jesus, I cannot bear more.*

Unable to say anything else, he left her for Joan to comfort. He went to his own chamber and wept alone.

It was dusk when Elizabeth came into Tom's chamber. She had tried to see him at noon, but Palmer had informed her that he was sleeping. He had made a disapproving-but-dutiful offer to wake him if she wished, but she had told him she would wait. Now, when he told her his master was awake, she was hardly able to make herself enter the room. Tom was sitting on the bed, and she was surprised to see him fully dressed.

"Are you feeling better, my lord?"

He managed a nod, though, in truth, he looked far worse than he had the night before. Guilt stabbed through her and she fell to her knees before him.

"It was my fault, my lord. I've sent Ellen away because of it, but it was my fault. I beg you, forgive me."

"What?" he asked distractedly.

"It was the wine I gave you. Ellen said it would make you—" Shame washed over her and she struggled not to cry. "She said it would make you want me again, that it would make you love me."

"Another of your games, Bess?" He shook his head, a weary half-smile on his trembling lips. "I haven't the heart for it anymore, Bess. I am too worn to try."

"I am sorry," she whispered helplessly, and there was a sudden tightness in his mouth.

"I have loved you as truly as I know how. Sweet heavens, do you think it was easy waiting for you so long—before we were married and after? Do you think it was easy, with the women of the court offering with their eyes and smiles what I must not have and all my flesh shrieking to answer them? And nothing but God's pure grace and the promise of you to keep me sane?" He scrubbed his face with both hands. "Forgive me, my lady. That is hardly of any moment now."

"No," she pled. "It means a great deal to me. If I could change what I've done—I never wanted Taliferro."

"You should have come to me, Bess, instead of letting him bully you into doing as he wished. You should have let him make what claims he pleased to make and told me the truth of it. I would have believed you."

Though you *never believe* me, *my lady,* she added for him.

"You have said that you wanted to hurt me," he continued. "It should please you to know that you have."

"It does not please me," she said dully. "I hurt myself by what I did far more than ever I hurt anyone else."

"Then it is a wonder you could survive the pain." He drew a hard breath and shook his head. "Forgive me that, too, Bess. I needn't have said it."

"It is no more than I deserve."

"I want to hurt you the way you have hurt me," he said, fierce pain in his eyes, "but I cannot bear to do it. I love you too much." He scrubbed his face again with his hands. "It might not hurt so badly if you had gone to him for love or even lust. But you did it to spite me. After the tenderness we've shared, have you hated me so much that you would go so far just to cause me hurt?" He swallowed hard and his voice broke. "God witness with me here, I cannot tell still what I have done to earn that."

He cupped her face in his hands and looked at her with the most profound sorrow she had ever seen.

"I only ever wanted you to love me."

She could not help the tears that welled up in her again. "My lord," she whispered, "please—"

"Let me speak a moment, my lady." He released her, and only the tightness around his mouth betrayed the emotions he was fighting. "I have but a few things to say, one question to ask. Then you may say whatever pleases you."

"Yes, my lord."

"I have told you I love you. I do love you, my lady. I will love you. But just now—" He pressed his lips together and turned his face away for a moment. "Just now this wound is too raw to bear touching with even the gentlest of hands."

"Please, my lord, when the king returns—"

"Philip is dead," he said starkly, and she lifted her head with a jerk. "That night I had to leave you at dinner, it was because they had found Jerome, who attended the king. He's been unconscious since. Until today. He told us this morning he saw Philip go down. He had Philip's ring as proof."

"That night I had to leave you at dinner . . ."

That was the night she had accused him, the night she had seen him comforting Rosalynde, the night he had tried to tell her about his loss, the night she had gone to Taliferro. He had come to her that night with his grief, and she had given him nothing but betrayal.

"Oh, my lord, I am so very sorry."

Weeping, she reached up and took him into her arms, but his rigid body did not relax against her.

"Please, my lord," she begged, clinging to him, "do not forever be angry with me. Please."

He merely stared at her, as if he did not understand the words, and she sank back to the floor.

"Just two years ago, I had my mother and my father and all three of my brothers," he said. "Now they are gone, all of them. Now I have no one but you, and you—" Tears came into his eyes and he bit his lip, trying to keep them from spilling over.

"*And you do not love me*," she knew he would have said.

"I am weary of playing this fool's game with you, Bess," he said instead. "Faith, I am merely a man. As much as I love you, there is only so much I can bear."

"Why did you never tell me the reason you had to leave me that night?" she asked thinly. "I would have understood."

"I could not. If the news had got into the wrong hands, there is no knowing what may have happened. You and Taliferro were too close. I could not risk it, knowing you had him for your confidant."

She wanted to hold him again, to weep with him, to carry some small part of his grief, to tell him she would never betray him again, but she dared not risk another rebuff. She merely sat there blinking the tears away, keeping silence as he had requested.

"We have a lifetime ahead of us as man and wife," he said, "and I see no need for the news of this to go beyond the two of us. I know you do not love me. Perhaps I was wrong to ever hope for that, but I will try as best I can never to wrong you again, or ask of you anything that is against your heart. That granted, do you want to go on with me? Can you believe in me enough for that?"

"My lord, I—"

She faltered there. *My lord, I love you*, she wanted to say. *My lord, I believe in you*. But she could see in his eyes, hear in his voice that he would think she was only trying to make amends or, at best, that she was speaking out of gratitude or guilt and not out of love. It did not matter that she knew now that she loved him. Just now he could not believe her.

"My lord, I know I have hurt you—I cannot say how that knowledge grieves me—but I am your wife. Forever, as you have said. I would not have it otherwise."

He nodded. "Very well."

She touched his arm. "Might I ask one thing of you?"

"Of course."

"I would like to make a pilgrimage."

"Yes?"

"The sisters at the convent where I was brought up have a most holy shrine. Might I have your leave to go there in penance?"

He opened his mouth as if he would protest, but then he only nodded again. "Perhaps that would be best now. I will arrange it for you."

He helped her to her feet and escorted her to the door. Then, catching sight of the dull pain in her eyes, he lifted her hand to his lips.

"We both need this, Bess."

Before he could release her, she pressed his hand fervently to her cheek.

"I am sorry about the king, my lord. I—I am sorry."

Tears blurred her sight, and she could hardly see to make her way down the corridor.

"Safe journey," Tom said, and he lightly kissed her cheek. Nothing more.

Elizabeth merely nodded, wondering if, however far away it might be, there would be this vast emptiness inside her, this strained nothingness, to carry to her grave. She wondered, too, in the distant part of her that still felt pain, if it would be the same for her gentle, heart-wounded young husband.

"I only ever wanted you to love me."

He stood there and watched the carriage pull away, his body stiff, his face blank. She remembered that first time he had watched her going, when they had been married just a week, when she had been all innocence and he had thought her worth his love. She knew he would not run this time to tell her he loved her. Not this time.

CHAPTER

15

SHE'S GONE ON A PILGRIMAGE," TOM SAID, AVERTING HIS EYES. Joan had caught him as he came back into the palace and went into his chamber with him. She was unable to stand idle any longer in the face of his obvious grief.

"Tell me of it, honey-love."

"Oh, nothing, Joan. She's merely doing her duty to the church. She is—"

His voice broke and she put her arms around him.

"Now I know there is more in it than that. Would I not know my own Tom?"

"Joan," he sobbed, laying his head on her shoulder and holding tight to her thick waist. "Oh, sweet heavens, Joan, it hurts."

She drew him down to the bench with her, still holding him, wisely saying nothing except with her soothing comfort.

"I am sorry, Joan," he murmured once the worst had passed. "I only . . . only . . ."

"Tell me," she urged gently. "What has taken the heart from my brave boy?"

"I know this will never go beyond us," he said. He squeezed his eyes shut, trembling again. "Dear God, I fear I will die if I cannot speak of it to someone. Joan, I've done a terrible thing."

He told her what had happened, the bleak words that had passed between him and Elizabeth, the anger and pain and shame he felt.

"I am as much to blame as she," he said, "and I know Taliferro deceived her. I've seen how truly sorry she is, yet when I spoke to her of it—" He shook his head. "She wanted comforting and assurance from me, and, God forgive me, I had none to give. I cannot see it ever being right between us again. Everything has come out from under me all at once, Joan. I have nothing left."

"There is God still," she reminded him gently. "Will you be faithful to Him though she's not been faithful to you?"

"I cannot seem to find Him anymore." He swallowed down a sob, and it was a moment before he could speak again. "I've prayed and prayed, and all I can feel is pain. Would to God I had been the one to die and Philip had stayed here with his lady. She loves him. Mine would be glad I was gone."

"Perhaps the queen is right and Philip is not dead."

"I wish I could believe that," he said, his voice hardly a whisper.

"We will pray about it, love. Is not our God able to do much, much more than we can ask or even think to ask of Him? Can He not make everything right, even now, if we believe in Him to do it?"

"Oh, Joan, I need Him," he murmured. "Why will He not hear me any longer?"

She kissed his temple. "He hears, my Tom. He always hears. And He knows what we need."

"I can see nothing in any of this to fill anyone's need," he said, with more despondency in his voice than Joan had ever before heard, and she kissed him again.

"You are strong, boy. You've always been strong. Perhaps, knowing her weaknesses, the Lord gave you to Lady Elizabeth because He knew you could help her bear up under it and show her His love, too. A lesser man would have destroyed her over this."

"And who's to help *me* bear up under it?" he asked in desperation.

"There are everlasting arms to bear you up, my love," she said softly. Then, holding him closer, she began to pray.

Philip's first conscious thought was gratitude, profound thankfulness for the soft, cool hands that touched his face and held water to his parched lips. He had been aware of pain, of hot torment, for a long, long time, but it was something that belonged to the solid, inescapable darkness, not like these gentle hands.

"Rose?"

"Shh. Lie still."

The voice was not Rosalynde's, but he knew she had hands like these, loving, healing hands. Perhaps his ears had deceived him.

"Rose?" he murmured again, and he managed to open his eyes a crack.

The brightness was blurred, piercing agony after so long in the dark. What it showed him was deeper torture. The cruel light was behind her, this angel of comfort, leaving her face in shadow, making a halo of her hair, her long fair hair.

"Kate?"

Tears filled his eyes and he tried to blink them away, to bring her into focus.

"Sleep now," she said, and once again he felt the soothing touch of hands on his face, pressing his eyes closed, blocking out the sharp-edged light.

He made a feeble attempt to pull those hands away, but she would not allow it.

"Sleep."

He tightened his grip on her wrists, now holding her there.

"Kate, I did not—I never would—" He clung to her, his breathing coming hard and fast. "They told me you were dead. They . . . told me . . ."

The breath faded out of him, and once again there was only darkness.

Tom lay awake a long while that night, nothing but the dark silence between him and his thoughts. Grace was curled up, warm and purring, on his chest as she had been doing since he had begun sleeping alone, but tonight even that small consolation did not touch him.

He remembered how desolate he had been when as a boy he had first become aware of his mother's faithlessness. He had wept bitterly, shame flooding his heart, making it a lump of lead that swelled in his chest and blocked off his breath. He had felt somehow sullied by her lasciviousness. She had wronged him and his brothers as surely as she had wronged their father. Her wrong to her youngest, John, was most of all.

John, bright, golden John, had not been their father's son, but the son of their mother's lover, and she had died leaving John to face her husband's wrath until the boy, too, died, trying to atone for a fault that was not his. Tom had seen this, had vowed he would not let such a thing happen in his own marriage. Now it had and he—

He shifted the cat, still sleeping, onto the pillow. He got out of bed and dressed himself carelessly, just boots and breeches and a shirt he did not lace. The snow was swirling around the castle walls. He could hear it beating against the shutters, but he took no cloak with him when he went out into the street.

"He hears, my Tom. He always hears."

He could not keep Joan's words out of his mind. This was what he believed, what he had always believed. Was he to abandon it now? Just because he could not see the design, did that mean there was none?

He trudged through the frozen street, hardly feeling the knife-bladed winds that whipped against him.

"He hears, my Tom. He always hears."

He slipped on the steps that led to the cathedral, bloodying both knees on the ice, but he struggled up again, scraping his unprotected hands, leaving a faint red smear on the heavy door when he opened it. He was trembling when he finally reached the altar and stood before the marble statue of Christ that stood with outstretched arms behind it.

"He hears, my Tom. He always hears."

He did. He always had. Tom looked into the eyes that seemed to know his pain and remain untroubled.

"Believe in Me," they seemed to say. *"Trust in Me. I have never wronged you."*

"Oh, sweet Jesus," he sobbed, falling to his battered knees. He had asked that very thing so often of Elizabeth, the one he loved with such depth and such tenacity. He knew the pain it had caused when she doubted him. Did not his Savior deserve better? Yet in the very face of Tom's own doubt, did not that Savior love still?

Tom lifted his head and looked at the statue once more. The artist had captured that in the gentle face—the hurt love that somehow still loved. Tom counted himself as wholly belonging to this same Christ, acknowledging his part in that hurt and accepting the grace of His love. Was it not his part now to extend such love to one who hurt him? But Christ was God Himself, His love and forgiveness not bounded by mere humanity, His mercy flowing from His divine nature. Could a mere man—

He had been man, mere man, as He suffered the ultimate of betrayal and humiliation and pain on the cross, yet He had forgiven, had asked God's forgiveness for those who wronged Him and had loved still. Even now, He loved His church, though she was unfaithful.

"Dear God," Tom murmured, "I can forgive her. I have. I swear I love her still. But how do I forget? How do I get free of this pain?" He looked once more into the serene face, and again the tears came. "Oh, God, my sweet Christ, forgive me; I can never forget. It is past what I am able."

He sank to the floor and wrapped his arms around the statue's legs, pressing his face against the nail-pierced feet, sobs tearing through him.

"Help me. Oh, God, help me."

He prayed long and hard, crying out his grief to the only One who could ease it, and his desolate cries rose above the howling of the storm.

In the gray light of the winter dawn, two monks came into the cathedral to begin their daily duties. Both genuflected before the altar. The older of the two put one thin finger to his lips to silence the novice that accompanied him.

The young monk looked at him, questioning, and the elder gestured. There at the foot of the statue of Christ, Tom lay asleep, one arm still around the base of the statue, the other pillowing his head, melted snow soaked into his clothes and puddled beneath him.

"That's the prince!" the boy exclaimed, and the other shushed him again.

"He often walks here nights. The king's absence has left him a heavy burden." The old monk laid his hand lightly on Tom's damp hair. "And doubtless he has other cares not ours to know, God grant him grace to bear them."

"Do you think he would have us pray for him?" the novice asked, his voice scarcely a whisper. "They say he is a Heretic, against the church."

"Against the church? By my faith, no," the older monk said. "Against the hypocrisy, perhaps, against the form of religion without the Spirit, but not against the church. I cannot speak for another man's heart, but I have seen him here, faithful in prayer, honest in his devotion to Christ. He is no enemy of the true church."

"Is he so given to God as they say?" the novice asked. "That would be a rare thing in nobility, not to say royalty."

"If fruit proclaims the tree, I dare say he is. Doubtless some struggle between flesh and spirit brings him here now." The old monk laid his hand on Tom's head once more, praying peace upon him as he did. "Something he's not yet resolved."

As if by consent, the two churchmen knelt on either side of Tom, and, for a long while, there was only the low, fervent sound of prayer.

The light was gentle when Philip again opened his eyes, just firelight, moonlight, and the particular stillness of deep night.

"Kate?" he whispered, but there was no answer. Had she been nothing but a fevered dream? No, she had been there. Someone had.

He rubbed one shaky hand across his eyes and searched the dimness for any sign of her. The room was decked with heavy tapestries, carved paneling, and other rich appointments. The bed he lay in was deep, downy softness. This was a house of wealth. Even the king's chamber in Winton was no finer.

He followed the moonlight that spilled across the bed to the tall windows at the end of the room. There *was* someone. She was sitting there combing her pale hair, silvered by the moon, looking more shade than substance as she watched the night. He dragged himself up a little.

"Kate?"

She turned from the window and, smiling, came to him.

"You've returned at last."

He dropped back against the pillows. "Who are you?"

"Whoever it pleases you I should be." She put her hand on his cheek. "Your Kate, if you like."

The firelight fell more fully on her face, and he saw that, though she carried it well, she was older than he had first thought. Perhaps twice Kate's fresh nineteen.

"Where is this and who are you?" he asked, pulling away from her.

She had Kate's tall slenderness and her lush, fair hair, but there was no resemblance beyond that.

"You were not so particular of my touch before. It seemed to bring you ease in your pain. Am I not due your thanks, at the least, for that?"

He nodded, remembering the searing torment she had soothed. "I do thank you, indeed. Do me the further kindness to tell me where I am and why you have gone to such lengths for a poor stranger."

She laughed, and the sound was as silvery as the moonlight. "You are not poor. Nor are you a stranger, my lord king."

"You know me, then." There was something in the long, angular line of her face that made him think he must have seen her before. Her fair hair made such contrast to her black, black eyes; surely he would remember. He was too worn to puzzle it out just now.

"I know you, my lord, though we've never before met. I could not let them take your life until I had seen you for myself." Again she stroked his cheek. "The reports I've had of you fall far short of truth."

He pushed her hand away. "Who are you? Who sent those men to kill me?"

"I am called Elandria."

The name suited her face—unusual and oddly beautiful.

"You are mistress of this place?"

She smiled and smoothed the silken sheet.

"Do not weary yourself with questions now, my lord. Everything in time."

"Those men—"

"They cannot harm you here."

"I must—" He looked swiftly around the room, suddenly remembering. "There was a boy with me. Where is he?"

"Everything in time," she assured him. She leaned down and pressed a cool kiss onto his forehead. "Rest now."

He seized her arms with all the force he had.

"Where is he?"

She smiled, unthreatened by his powerless ferocity. "It may not go well with him were you to forget the gratitude you owe me, my lord."

Instantly, he released her. "I would like to see him."

"In time. If, as I said, you remember you owe me your life."

"You have treated me most kindly, my lady, and I am grateful—"

"I see you do not understand, your majesty. Ivybridge was abandoned during the war. It was planned for you to be lured there to be killed, but I commanded that you be brought to me instead. I had heard much of you, the fairest of the Chastelaynes, and thought it a poor waste to mar such beauty and let it rot in the earth."

"But Kate—"

"Burned at Bakersfield more than two years ago, as you had been told. I know those who witnessed it." She smiled as if she were pleased to tell him so, and he looked away.

"All lies," he murmured. "Cruel lies." He lifted his eyes to hers. "Why?"

"My brother knew you would not leave the safety of Winton alone and unguarded for a light cause."

"Your brother?" He searched her face again. Where had he seen its like?

"I am Elandria of Warring."

"Taliferro!"

"Now you see," she said with another smile. "He ordered your death, but I have outwitted him." She stroked his hair. "He shall have the kingdom, but I shall have the king."

He shoved her away and sat up, shaken with the effort. "Never touch me again."

"Speak me fair, my lord," she said pleasantly, "or I cannot answer for what may happen to the boy."

"Let me see him," he demanded and still she smiled.

"My lord?"

He clenched his jaw. "Please."

She laughed softly. "Everything in time."

"Lady Elandria—"

"We will speak of him," she said. "First let me see to your wound."

She threw the bedclothes back, but he held the sheet at his waist, daring her with a hard look to do more.

"Come, my lord, no need for your modesty. You were not so circumspect before."

He glared at her, incensed at the thought of her shameless eyes and bold hands upon him as he lay helpless, but his resistance seemed only to make him more desirable to her.

"You are most exquisitely fashioned, my lord," she said huskily as she stroked her hand down his bare chest.

"I told you never to touch me." He gripped her wrist but she merely laughed, freeing herself without effort.

"I must change this bandage."

He tried to get out of the bed, but she held him there just as effortlessly.

"For your ease, my lord."

He leaned back against the pillows, knowing, if he tried, he might take half a dozen steps before he collapsed. Surely no more.

"If you mean to do it for the sake of charity, I thank you, lady, but if it is to any other end, I can tell you now you will find all your pains wasted."

"All mine, perhaps," she said, tracing her hand down his arm, "but not yours."

Without warning, she jabbed his wounded side with her fingers. He sucked in a loud, startled lungful of air as the pain jolted through him and rolled over him in black, nauseating waves.

"There are many kinds of persuasion, my lord," she observed as he lay there gasping and trembling. "We may have to explore a few of them." He was vaguely aware of her hand once more at his side just as the darkness took him. "You seem to be bleeding again. Pity."

Elizabeth had made her way slowly, wearily on the winter roads toward the convent on the outskirts of Aberwain, south almost to the Grenaven border. She was to stop at the homes of various nobles on her journey and had already spent the past two nights that way. This night she would be staying at the Duke of Ellison's home, just north of Brookton.

The duke was still at court in Winton, but his young wife greeted her royal guest most kindly, and Elizabeth managed the appropriate words of thanks for her hospitality. Her first impulse was to ask to be taken to her rooms at once, but seeing the eager hopefulness in Lady Ellison's eyes as she described the impromptu entertainments that had been arranged in her honor, Elizabeth decided to attend. She knew Tom would have wanted her to show appreciation for the pains that had been taken for her sake.

She endured the company with all the grace she could muster and was relieved when at last she was able to go to her chamber, to grapple once more with her guilty thoughts. The slow passage of her carriage from town to town had given her many hours for reflection and repentance, and without Ellen's acrid influence, she saw more clearly than ever how much she had wronged Tom and wronged herself in throwing away his love.

Nan had urged her again and again to turn to God for comfort, and she had tried. She had confessed her sins and asked His mercy, but she realized she had used Him as she had Tom, as someone to fill her needs and care for her without giving anything in return. She knew Him no better than she had known Tom when first she came to court, and now she had driven Tom away and God was still as far off as before.

She had prayed for His forgiveness, but somehow, without Tom's, it did not seem enough; she could not feel forgiven. Nan told her she must let go of her guilt and self-condemnation and trust God's faithfulness more than her feelings, but she could not. Not until she could make it right with Tom. Why should the great, righteous Judge of all mankind love and forgive her when even her own husband could not? Yet the Scripture had told her plainly of a God from whose love she could not be separated, of a merciful forgiveness in the face of brazen unfaithfulness.

"Oh, my Lord, truly," she pled silently as she lay that night in bed, "can You love me so? Can anyone? Please, Lord, love me still."

When Nan came back from the kitchen and hurried all the other women from the room, taking herself with them, Elizabeth did not even think to wonder why or to ask what had become of the warm milk the girl had been sent to fetch. She was glad when she was finally left to herself, but she found no more sleep when alone than she had in the midst of her chattering women. She merely lay there, wishing for strong arms to hold her, for strong love to warm her, but all of that was back in Winton with Tom. She thought of his lovemaking, all fire and passion, his whole thought on how he might please her.

"I only ever wanted you to love me."

"Tom," she whispered, wondering if he might not hear her faint cry even from where he was. "Tom."

There was a soft knock at her door and she buried her face in her pillows.

"Go away!"

"Please, my lady, give me just a moment."

It was he! She flew to the door, intending to fling it open and throw herself into his arms, but she stopped there with the latch in her hand. He did not want that from her, not anymore.

She opened the door slowly and made a slight curtsey.

"My lord."

"Might I come in, my lady?" he asked, his expression unreadable, and she gestured him inside and closed the door.

"I did not expect you here, my lord," she said, managing to keep her voice steady. "Is there something wrong?"

"Yes, my lady, there is." He hesitated for a moment. Then he took her hand. "You are not with me."

She could not disentangle her eyes from the infinite tenderness in his, even when she felt him fastening something around her wrist. She knew without looking that it was the bracelet. His bracelet.

"Come home with me, Bess."

"Oh, my lord," she breathed, tears filling her eyes, and she laughed faintly and touched her hands to his face. "You came for me."

He said nothing, but his eyes spoke eloquently for him, pleading for forgiveness, for a chance to begin again. Pleading his love. The tears spilled down her cheeks and he took her into his arms.

"I knew before you left I could not bear to be without you," he murmured. "Can you ever forgive me?"

"Forgive you?" She tucked her head under his chin and squeezed her eyes shut. "My lord—Tom—"

She felt him draw a startled breath at that, and she looked up at him, looked deeply into his eyes.

"Tom," she said softly, reaching up again to caress his face. "Tom, I love you."

"You do?" he asked in an astonished little gasp. "Oh, Bess, you do?"

He folded her in his arms, and she could feel the silent sobs shake him.

"Oh, Bess, Bess, love," he murmured, and then he laughed a little. "Do you know, I was in the chapel before I left Winton, trying to make some sense out of all this, trying to find some comfort in God, and He reminded me, just as clearly as I am speaking to you, He reminded me how often I've come to Him, hurting and ashamed and repentant, and how, in the face of every wrong I've done, He's never turned me away. He reminded me how much that kindness, that love, has bred love in me. Then He told me it would be the same for you, if I would love you just so truly. I was almost afraid to believe it, to hope—"

He stopped there and she held him more tightly. How good it was to be there, against the warmth of his heart, shielded in his strength, buried in his love, knowing she had at last given him what he wanted most. And God Himself had sent him back to her.

"I've missed you," she whispered after a moment. "I've missed having your love."

"You've never been without it," he told her, the dark depths of his eyes pledging his truth. "Never."

Again she felt the sting of tears. "You can truly forgive what I've done? And forget it as well?"

"You had my forgiveness long ago. As for the memories—" He pushed an unruly curl back behind her ear. "We will have sweet memories enough in time to take the place of the bitter ones."

She covered his hand with hers and held it against her cheek and then pressed her lips to his wrist. "Dear gentle, sweet Tom," she whispered and the hot tears flooded from her.

"Bess, love," he murmured, pulling her closer and swinging her up into his arms. "Weep as long as you have need."

He sat down on the bed with her, and she clung to him, crying until she could no more. All the while he held her, soothing her with soft words and gentle caresses until she lay limply against him.

"Never let me away from you again," she whispered, touching the bracelet that circled her wrist, and he kissed her forehead.

"Never."

In another moment her trembling breath grew regular with sleep. He kissed her again.

"Never."

It was still dark when she awoke. She was still cuddled in his arms, with her face pressed to his shoulder. Likely no more than an hour had passed.

"My lord?"

She lifted her head, and his hand fell from it. He was soundly asleep, propped against the pillows. She kissed his throat and traced her fingers over his parted lips, wishing him awake. His arm went around her, and he pulled her up against him, kissing her with deep feeling.

"How I've missed you, Bess."

He teased her ear with his lips and kissed his way down the side of her neck. She tried not to tremble.

"Nan will be back," she whispered, remembering the last time they had touched, the barren emptiness of it. If this was the same—

He tilted her chin up to him and kissed her mouth again, as if some inexorable force compelled him to it. "Not tonight."

"She will," she told him, suddenly unable to catch her breath. "She does not know you are here."

He pushed her hindering hand away and his lips found hers once more.

"She knows."

"She does?"

There was a mischievous tug at the corner of his mouth. He kissed her throat high up. "Why do you think . . ." He kissed her a little lower. ". . . they all left you . . ." And lower. ". . . here alone?"

"Oh, Tom."

Again he kissed her, and the taste of him was sweet. His lips traveled back down to the hollow of her throat.

"Tom—"

He stopped her with another kiss.

"Tom," she breathed. "Are you sure, Tom?"

"Shh." He put his mouth over hers, pulling her down with him onto the pillows, but she tried to keep herself from responding.

"We mustn't."

"Be mine again, Bess," he murmured, and he began kissing her once more, slowly, deliberately, not demanding as Taliferro had done, but gently, softly, passionately wooing. "Be mine again."

She felt herself melting into him, her fears dissolving with every intoxicating touch. "But if there is a child, we might never know who—"

He stopped her with another kiss, drawing her closer as he did. "I never want to know."

She lay there listening to his still-rapid breathing and to the sweet words that came to her mind as he rested, warm and languid, against her.

"I found the one my soul loves; I held him and would not let him go."

She kissed his damp brow, tasting the faint saltiness of his sweat. She cradled him closer, stroking her fingers through his hair and down the back of his neck.

"Sweet, sweet Bess," he murmured, not opening his eyes, and she moved her hand to his cheek, wondering how it could be that, in striving to please him, to truly love him, her own pleasure had been intensified.

She felt whole and clean again, as if God had, through this sweet closeness, shown her beyond doubting that she had His forgiveness, His acceptance, His love. Truly, He had given this precious love back to her, and, as Tom drifted to sleep there in her embrace, she whispered a prayer of thanks to the God who loved her so deeply.

CHAPTER

16

FREE ME, MY LADY," PHILIP SAID. "I HAVE TOLD YOU THIS CAN NEVER BE." His captivity had been as luxurious and gracious as the room in which he was held. He had but to ask, and, other than release, his slightest whim was instantly answered. Elandria had arranged for him to be waited upon by several of her menservants, but, all this while, he had seen no woman but her and no means of escape.

Now that he was stronger, she took more and more time from her other amusements to spend with him, sometimes to talk, sometimes to share music or a fanciful tale, but always coming back to her original purpose in having him there. It had become a battle of wills between them, one each was fiercely determined to win. She had given him a life of ease, but he had found no ease in it, longing for home and family, worrying over Jerome, uncertain when his opposition would earn him a caress or a blow, never knowing in his resistance how far was too far.

Just now, she was feeling lazy and indulgent, content to merely talk across a cup of wine, letting her new gown use its influence on him. It was fashioned out of deep violet brocade, cut low and tight in the bodice. He allowed his eyes no lower than her chin.

"It will be," she said and she smiled. "Have I not proven to you I mean only your good? All these weeks, have I not cared for you, seen to your recovery, fed and clothed you with the finest the kingdom can offer? What more could you ask?"

"My freedom." He got up from the table, planting his hands on it and leaning down to her, frowning. "We have spoken on this again and again, lady. There is no more to say."

"Oh, much more," she assured him, and her mouth turned up in a sly, knowing smile. "In time, you will beg for the pleasure you so foolishly refuse."

"Time will change nothing. Do not deceive yourself."

"Time changes everything, my lord. Were our positions reversed, you could force me to your will. As it is, being but a weak woman, I must woo and coax and seduce." Her eyes raked over him and again as she smiled her sly smile. "It takes longer, but it will be much more satisfying."

He shoved himself away from the table with an exclamation of frustrated impatience and strode to the sun-flooded windows. "It is almost spring, lady, and you have had but one answer from me all this while. Keep me here another year or ten or ten thousand. It will not change."

"I can wait. I know your flesh hungers for the touch of a woman. Despite your denials, I've seen you struggle to keep mastery over it. In time, it will doubtless prove traitor to your fine, pious strictness and be a strong ally with me against yourself. I can wait." She laughed her silver-tinged laugh. "How long do you think your precious Rosalynde will wait before she seeks another man's comfort? In another year, in ten, in ten thousand, believing you dead, do you imagine she will not?"

He turned back to her, his eyes cold fury. "Never. She's sworn to me—"

"As you were sworn to your Kate?"

She laughed, and, in another instant, his hands were at her throat.

"As you say, you have seen to my recovery. I am not so weak yet that I could not snap your virago neck and call it justice."

She smiled still, her breath coming in little gasps, her eyes blacker for the sudden blaze of desire in them, her lips fuller and redder, but she did not resist.

"I do not jest with you," he growled, increasing the pressure.

At her half-strangled cry, her guards burst into the room and threw him to his knees at her feet.

"Free me or kill me!" he panted.

"Not yet," she said, rubbing her skin where his fingers had marked it. "I want you. I want the pleasure of breaking you. But, if you push me too far, I will cut your pretty throat."

She signalled her men, and they forced his arms behind his back and dragged him to his feet.

"You forget the boy," she reminded him with another silken smile. "Will you let him die for your pride?"

"That threat has lost its edge, my lady. If you hadn't already killed him, you would have let me see him by now."

"Give in to me, my fair, and you shall see him."

"Let me see him first."

"Then you will—" There was a flash of triumph in her eyes. "I can be very sweet when I have my own way," she purred close to his ear. "You'll find it pleasant to belong to me."

Her lips were on his in a tingling, warm kiss, but his only response was a cold look of disdain.

"I hate a strumpet as I hate hell."

He felt the sting of her palm across his mouth, but he merely stood there, looking all ice and fire, until, once more, she smiled.

"Your pride becomes you too well, my lord. It seems a pity to have to break you of it."

"You cannot take my pride, lady, and I'll not give it you."

"Do you appreciate things of beauty, my lord?" she asked. "Works of art?"

He nodded guardedly.

"It would be a sin to see them destroyed. No?"

Again he nodded, not quailing under the genteel menace in her voice, and she drew a golden, gem-encrusted dagger from the sheath at her waist.

"Beautiful, is it not?" she said softly, making it flash in the sunlight. "Amazing how one thing of beauty can destroy another."

She curled her fingers around his chin and pressed the flat of the blade to his cheek, just opposite the fine scar on the other side. "I should hate to have to mar this flawless creation."

"Cut me into a thousand pieces, lady," he said coldly. "None of them will bow to your will."

One of her men pulled Philip's arm up tighter behind him, wrenching a groan from him.

"I'll not have you injure him," she ordered, returning the dagger to its sheath. "I would hate to damage such perfection with force."

Philip felt the hold on him slacken, and he shrugged free of it, suddenly realizing the power she had given him over her.

"Why do you not beat me? starve me? torture me?" he taunted.

"I shall," she hissed. "I will destroy you, if I must, but I shall have you."

He smiled wickedly and brought his mouth close to hers, his voice an almost tangible caress. "Will you? Will you truly?"

He grabbed her hand and made it stroke his cheek.

"Will you disfigure this?"

He drew her fingers across his mouth.

"Bruise this?"

He slipped her hand down his shoulder to feel the hard muscle there.

"Will you let this be seared with irons?" he asked. Then he traced the long curve of her throat and felt her tremble at the light, tantalizing touch of his hand. "Could you have this broken, knowing you could never hope for another caress?"

She caught his hand and brought it to her mouth, but he snatched it away.

"Do what you will. My flesh means far more to you than to me. Destroy it and you destroy what you most want and give to me what I most want—my freedom."

For a long moment she was white-lipped and speechless. Then she looked him over coolly.

"I keep hawks and falcons, my lord. They are proud birds, not easily tamed, and often I must keep them hooded and hungry until they learn obedience. We will see if such methods prove as effective with kings. Put him in the cell below the guard room," she instructed her men. "Given time there, he will come to me—and willingly."

"Bury me there!" he spat as they seized hold of him once more. "It changes nothing."

"The boy dies," she told him, taking rough hold of his jaw. "Think of that in your dark solitude." She released him abruptly, shoving his head backwards as she did. "Take him away."

Tom had felt something taut and uneasy about the court when he and Elizabeth returned to it, and the slow passage of time did nothing to dispel it. Everything seemed to be as orderly as could be expected under such circumstances, but the calm was like the smoothness of a deep-running river that had murderous currents beneath it.

If he had been one to shirk his responsibilities, he would have taken Elizabeth somewhere sweet and peaceful, to Treghatours, perhaps, to bask in the fresh wonder of her love and lavish her with his, but he knew he could never have done that, not with Philip still gone and Rosalynde left alone to bear it.

Since the night he had fallen on his bruised knees and lifted his ice-scraped hands to heaven, he had begun to have a glimmer of hope that perhaps his sister-in-law was right, that perhaps Philip was still alive. He knew God had made a miracle in him that night, taking the unbearable pain out of his memories and allowing him once more to hope for Elizabeth's love.

"*Trust in Me,*" He had whispered to Tom's heart, and somehow the dread had lifted. Tom was certain that somehow God would make a way.

Tom had told Elizabeth this as they journeyed back to Winton, and, since their return, he had seen that Rosalynde was clinging to that trust as well. She always wore the tarnished ring Jerome had brought back to her, and sometimes, when there was a tinge of doubtful fear in her eyes, Tom would see her touch that ring, rub her hand over it or twist it on her finger until her faith returned. Despite the empty chair beside her at supper and the empty bed she went to every night, it always returned.

"How are you this evening, my lady?" Tom asked her. In the weeks since he had come back to court he had, with Elizabeth's blessing, watched over his sister-in-law. He knew she was struggling with worry and loneliness, and that she continued to battle the sickness of early pregnancy.

"Better," she replied with a wan smile. If she had not told him of it, he probably would not have noticed the slight roundness in her stomach beneath the loosened lacings of her bodice. She could easily have concealed the news for several weeks more, but they had agreed it would be best for the people to know that, even in this uncertainty, the royal line still continued.

"I suppose Joan is seeing you have everything you need?"

Rosalynde smiled again, this time with a little more conviction. "I think she would insist on carrying this child herself if she could devise how to do it."

Tom grinned at her. Then, his expression sobering, he gave her sister a polite nod.

"Good evening, Lady Margaret. I trust you are well."

"Very well, I thank you," Margaret replied, shifting in her chair and fluffing out her voluminous velvet skirt.

"You have been so often ill this winter; I know the queen has been concerned for you."

Margaret brushed an imaginary speck of dust from her heavily embroidered sleeve. "I think that is all past now, my lord, and my sister has worries enough without adding mine to them."

"I cannot help but be concerned for you, Meg," Rosalynde said.

Margaret briskly patted her cheek. "Save your pity for yourself, sister. You may one day have need of it."

With a curtsey, Margaret turned and swept out of the great hall.

"My lord, I will never understand," Rosalynde said, and Tom could see the pain that was in her expression. They talked for a few minutes more as he tried to console her. Then he went back to his place next to Elizabeth.

"The queen has everything her sister has always wanted, Bess," Tom replied when she asked about Margaret, "despite all Margaret's striving to get it for herself. I fear she has not learned yet to be content with her place."

"It must be difficult for her," Elizabeth said. Tom knew she had learned, through her own painful stumbling, to have some charity for the faults of others, and it pleased him to see the growing softness of her heart. He squeezed her hand.

"She has rarely been happy. I think Richard loved her no more than she loved him, and Stephen never loved anyone at all. It is hard to walk this life alone, Bess."

There were sudden tears in Elizabeth's eyes.

"Thank you," she whispered.

Surprised, he put his arm around her. "For what, sweetheart?"

"For loving me."

He smiled and swiftly kissed her cheek. "I've only begun, my love."

"How sweet a picture the two of you make."

They both looked up and Elizabeth's face went white.

"My lord of Warring," Tom said, a cold flame blazing into his dark eyes. "I was wondering if you would return to us."

Taliferro realized that Elizabeth had told him of their encounter. Tom could read that in the older man's knowing expression. He read there, too, Taliferro's secure awareness that Tom could not denounce him before the court without denouncing Elizabeth as well.

"What could keep me away from such pleasures as I have found here, my lord?" he asked with the most innocent of smiles, and Tom's expression tightened.

"Stolen pleasure always has its price."

"But one cannot steal what is freely given," Taliferro observed. "Is that not so, Madonna?"

Elizabeth shrank a little closer to Tom.

"Did you have some business with me, my lord?" Tom asked.

"I merely wished to inform you of my progress in Warring. I have distributed everything the king so graciously provided, save four wagonloads of wheat and another of sturdy cloth. Those are to go next week." Again Taliferro smiled. "I suppose you've not heard from the king, my lord?"

"Not yet," Tom replied coolly. There had been a message from Darlington just that morning saying there was yet no trace of Philip, but of course he did not tell Taliferro that. "When he returns, I have no doubt he will be pleased that the people of Warring have had their needs seen to."

"No doubt, no doubt," Taliferro agreed. "I pray, as I am certain you must, that his return will come soon. All the kingdom looks to his rule, and, in these troubled times, who knows whom the people might follow were he not there for them."

"There is One who knows," Tom said and Taliferro made a deep bow.

"Indeed. Well, I will bid you good night, my lord, and you, my dear princess." He smiled once more. "My dear, dear princess."

It was a long while after he was gone before Elizabeth could stop trembling.

CHAPTER

17

MARGARET CREPT TOWARD THE ALCOVE, UNABLE, UNTIL SHE was almost to it, to see the tall, angular figure waiting within.

"My lord Taliferro."

"Your majesty," Taliferro said softly, kissing her hand, and Margaret's eyes took on a cold gleam of satisfaction.

"You have arranged it, then."

"Brenden has agreed to give me public audience soon," he said with his thin-lipped smile. "Everything is in place."

"You have made certain of it all? You have been back but a week now. Have you taken time enough to see to everything? You know where it leaves us both if we fail."

"Doubts, my lady?" he asked sardonically. "Perhaps you have some qualms about this for the sake of your sister, the queen. Perhaps for the sake of the king and the Duke of Brenden, because they are the brothers of your first husband. Do you yet grieve for him?"

She laughed. "Grieve for Richard? I grieve that he died before he could make me queen, perhaps. Just like that pompous fool, Stephen, I married after him."

"I thought as much."

"As for the rest, I will swear faith to the devil himself before I kneel any longer to my younger sister and that over-proud Philip Ice-Heart!"

He smiled at the vehemence in her words. "Philip is gone, my lady, and soon, quite soon, everyone will be kneeling to you."

They said no more as one of the serving girls came down the corridor with a basket of dirty laundry so large they could only see her chapped hands, a few inches of skirt, and then her back as she tottered away from them.

"Soon," Taliferro repeated softly, once the girl was gone. Then he and Margaret went their separate ways.

Philip did not know how long he had been imprisoned. His cell was without windows, and even the door had nothing but a low slit, wide enough for a plate, showing just the unrelieved blankness of the corridor wall beyond. Only very occasionally did a quivering reflection of torchlight reach him, and often it was gone before he even noticed it.

When he had first been brought here, he had made frantic search for a window or a niche or something, anything that would let him keep track of day and night, but there was nothing. In frustration, he had lunged at the door, throwing his shoulder repeatedly against the rough wood until he feared he would jar the bone out of the socket. Knowing it was useless, he had finally dropped, panting, to the floor, sweat trickling down the line of his jaw.

"Oh, God, please."

It had hardly qualified as a prayer, but it had been wrung from deep inside him with the stark realization of his own helplessness. Here no threat or demand or plea could free him, and the only hope left to him was prayer, for there was no one to hear but God.

In the time since, he had prayed much, pleading for freedom, begging for some sort of purpose behind this confinement, and finally letting go of the need to understand, clinging only to the promise of God's faithfulness. He had trusted to God before and seen His hand leading him through. Even in this hopeless darkness, he knew it would be so again.

Sitting there now in the always-night, he passed his hands blindly over his unshaven face and wondered if Elandria would still find him so desirable. Perhaps, seeing him dirty and smelling of her dungeon, pale and thin from confinement and the near-fast she had imposed, she would have no more interest in the game and release him. He hardly thought that possible, though, knowing there was something dark and twisted in her nature that would likely be drawn by such rawness. But he did not try any longer to predict God's ways. In the past few days, he had felt more and more certain his release would come soon, though he could not yet fathom how. The possibility that it might come through death did not escape him.

If it is Your will—

He lifted his head at the sound of footsteps in the corridor. There was the scrape of a key in the lock. The door swung open and he was blinded by torchlight.

"I trust your time here has taught you the folly of willfulness, my lord king."

He put up one hand to shield his eyes and was able to make out Elandria's willowy silhouette.

"It has, my lady."

"Chain him," she ordered. "He's not to be trusted unfettered."

Two of her men pushed him up against the dank wall and locked the heavy manacles in place, forcing him to stand with his feet planted shoulder-width apart and his arms flung wide. The leg irons were immovable, set directly into the stone, but the ones at his wrists had short lengths of chain to secure them, allowing for variations in stature from prisoner to prisoner. Philip realized his height gave him a slight advantage because of it, a few precious inches of movement a smaller man would not have had. He found little comfort in the knowledge.

Her captive secure, Elandria took the key from her men and hid it in her bodice. "Now leave us."

Once the two of them were alone, she set the torch in the wall and peered into Philip's face. The sly, triumphant smile came to her lips.

"You have had enough, I see, of cold and hunger and darkness." She put her hand to his stubble-roughened cheek and he did not pull away. "You have been a worthy opponent, my lord." A tiny flame sparked into her black eyes, and she stroked her other hand down his hip to his thigh. "But to the victor the spoils."

"You mistake me, lady," he said, and she looked again into his face. There was no submission there, only calm, unbowed strength that needed no fury to bolster it.

"What do you mean?" she asked, her eyes narrowing.

"I have thought on you often, my lady, since we last parted."

"I knew you would," she breathed, nuzzling against him. But when she tried to press her mouth to his, he turned his face away.

"Lady—"

Incensed, she fixed one hand in his hair and clamped the other around his jaw. "I will have you!"

Her ravening kiss left his mouth bloodied, but it provoked in him no response but a slight, pitying shake of his head. A heavy slap from her jeweled hand bloodied his cheek as well.

"What is it you want from me, lady?" he asked, and she laughed harshly.

"Must I make it yet plainer?"

"It is for more than a moment of stolen pleasure that you have gone such lengths, I know. More than the prize, you crave the game, and you know the moment it is won, it ends. Should I surrender to you, you would soon need another game, another creature to break to your will. And when all were done, there would still be a howling, insatiable emptiness inside you, keeping you in helpless thrall to the lusts you serve."

She took a wary step back from him. "It is you who are bound helpless, not I."

"Am I?" He rattled his chains. "I am freer in these than you are as mistress of Warring. So long as I trust in Him, you have no power over me but what my God allows."

"Do you think I've not heard you crying out to Him for help? Where is He? Why does He leave you alone in the darkness?"

"It may be for your sake."

That surprised her into another harsh laugh. "What would your God have you do here for my sake?"

"Perhaps nothing more than tell you of His love for you."

"He would put you here in prison and in pain just for His whim?"

"I never said He put me here, only that He might purpose some good from your intended evil. I thank you, lady, for this time you have given me alone with Him. I am more certain now that, whatever comes, He is with me."

"And you claim He loves you, this Christ of yours."

"I know so. He has proved it oftener than I can keep count of."

"How proved?" she asked scornfully.

"A thousand different ways, but most in dying in my place, for the sins I committed."

"I can scarce believe such a staunch follower of His could sin at all."

He smiled a little at her mocking tone. "Often enough, lady, and blacker than you might believe. But, in His mercy, He's forgiven me and loves me still."

For a moment there was silence between them. Then her eyes narrowed again.

"And you claim He has such love for me as well?"

He nodded. "If you would accept it of Him."

"I had rather have yours," she purred, coming close again, close enough for him to feel her warmth in the cold cell.

"You cannot force love, lady. Even God Himself will not do that. He would have us willingly or not at all."

"I had hoped, in time, to make you want me just so willingly, just as I want you." Again she caressed his face. "You force me to keep you bound here, when I would have it be all pleasure between us. Allow me, and I will show you such love as you've never known."

"You know nothing of love," he said sadly, "only lust and conquest."

"We shall see." Serpent-like, she twined herself around him, and he closed his eyes, closed his mind to the suggestions of pleasure she was breathing into his ear, forbade his long-denied flesh to answer hers.

Think of something else, he told himself. *Think of Rosalynde*.

No, he could not think of her and stay cold to any woman's touch. He had to think of something that would sicken him, something powerful enough, something painful enough, to tear his senses from the pillaging force of Elandria's mouth on his.

The dream he had had of Kate, the hideous nightmare. It was vivid enough. It had come to him in loathsome perfection of sight and sound and smell. "My *sweet Philip . . .*"

He drew the apparition back from the cavern of memory where he kept it chained, called on it in nauseating detail. He saw again the blackened face coming toward him to kiss him with its lipless mouth.

Elandria could not have missed the revulsion on his face, and it seemed only to urge her on.

God, let my thoughts be only on You, he prayed, but he made no move to resist her.

"You know you want me," she whispered, her hands roaming over him, making his blood pound harder in his veins. "You know you do."

Please, dear God, do not let me falter in this. Please. Make a way out.

He tensed away from her. "Lady—"

"Stand away from him, my lady."

She sprang back and whirled to face the door.

"Cafton! Dare you order me?"

"In Baron Taliferro's name, lady, stand aside," Cafton charged, brandishing his drawn sword. "You pledged you would kill him when you'd done with him. Since you have not, I see I must do it for you. Even my own men think he is dead, and it is more than my life is worth to have the baron find out I did not carry out his command."

"Disobedience does merit death," she observed.

As Cafton stepped toward the prisoner, Elandria moved to one side, her body screening the furtive movement of her hand at her waist. Philip saw the jeweled dagger she now held almost concealed in the deep folds of her skirt.

"My lady, do not—"

He broke off as Cafton raised his sword. Before the blow could fall, there was a sudden glinting arc of golden light that stopped abruptly in the middle of the assassin's broad back. Elandria pulled her dagger free and, in pure reflex, Cafton turned and buried his broadsword to the hilt in her stomach. Her eyes widened in surprised rage, and she thrust her blade again and again into his heart.

He fell dead at her feet, and she looked up at Philip, tears streaming down her face as she tried in vain to wrest free of the tormenting steel. Sobbing and struggling, she fell against him, staining him with her blood.

"Do you—love me now—my lord?" she gasped out.

He strained against his shackles, fearing she would fall if he did not support her, and she took the key from its hiding place and pressed it, still carrying her warmth, into his hand.

"Where is the boy?" he urged, twisting his wrist as he struggled to open the lock. "Tell me before it is too late."

She shook her head. "Cafton—Cafton killed him—the day you—were taken."

She cried out for the pain. Then her arms tightened convulsively around him, and, blood bubbling to her lips, she kissed him for the last time.

"Do you love me—now that I have—died in your place—and you have your precious freedom?"

"My lady—Elandria, hear me. There is only one love that can save you, and it is not mine."

"Then I cannot be saved," she said with a cynical, bloody grin. She sagged emptily against him, and he knew she was dead.

He struggled again with the key, and finally the lock sprang open. In swift succession, he freed his wrists. Elandria's arms were still coiled around his neck, and he pulled them away, trembling, numbed to any emotion but release. After a moment, he lowered her to the floor and unlocked his ankles. Nervously, he licked his lips, and, tasting her blood, he felt a tremor of revulsion run through him, making him sway on his feet. But he knew he could not waste a moment on weakness now.

He retrieved Cafton's broadsword from Elandria's body and wiped the blood on Cafton's sleeve. Pulling the jeweled dagger from the man's chest, he wiped the blood from it, too, before slipping the weapon inside his own boot. Taking a deep breath, he stepped warily into the corridor.

It was empty.

Naturally light of step, he had no difficulty finding his way to the guardroom in perfect silence. Except for the soldier who lay in a sodden heap in one corner, snoring and reeking of ale, it, too, was empty. Elandria's men would not be expecting her to call on them for some time yet and Cafton would not have wanted his own men to discover his reason for coming to the dungeon. Evidently, they were all employed elsewhere. After so long, was he simply to walk free?

He opened the outside door just a crack and saw the stable not thirty feet away. Thinking his way clear, he started to open the door wider. Then he froze, hearing the low voices of two of Elandria's serving men. He gave them time to pass by and his heart time to slow, before he crossed to the stable, forcing himself not to run.

There was only forest and field beyond the wall, and the gate was hospitably open. If only he could get a horse—

"Who are you?"

A dark, dirty-faced boy stood in the stable door, threatening him with a pitchfork. Philip drew back, stung with a memory of Jerome. Then he moved carefully into the cover of the doorway.

"I mean you no harm, boy," he said quietly. "I only want the use of a horse and passage through that gate."

"Those are my lady's horses."

"Would you be free of her service, boy?" Philip asked, and he pulled the dagger from his boot. The boy thrust the pitchfork toward him.

"I will use this!"

"If I meant to hurt you, would I use a dagger over the broadsword I am carrying?" Philip asked. He held the smaller weapon out by the blade. "Look at it, all gold and jewels. Think what that would buy you along with your freedom."

He could see the idea was winning over any devotion to duty the boy might have had and he stepped a little closer.

"Just one horse and your silence. No more."

The boy backed into the stable and returned a moment later with a broad-chested bay.

"Leave the dagger on the ground, then," he said, still keeping the pitchfork between the two of them. Then he tossed Philip the reins. "Go quickly. It is more than my life is worth if Lady Elandria knows of this."

"You need have no fear of that," Philip said grimly, but he did not hesitate to take the boy's advice.

CHAPTER

AT TALIFERRO'S REQUEST, ALL THE NOBILITY WERE IN COURT, and a low rumble of uncertainty rose from them, filling the great hall. Tom looked at the baron and wished he could banish him from the palace, from the kingdom, so he would never again have to look at his smug face, never have to see the sly way he looked at Elizabeth and hear him turn what should have been the most innocent of courtesies into cutting innuendo. He was glad she had asked to be excused from attending today and wished Lady Margaret had chosen the same course, but Margaret was present, standing not far from the queen, ominously silent.

"Well, my lord of Warring, you have your audience. What would you say?"

"I've merely a tale to tell, my lord. One with which you are no doubt familiar, but in which these nobles might find much revelation."

"This is still King Philip's court," Tom told him. "He has never denied hearing to any man who speaks truth."

Taliferro bowed. "You bring me at once to my theme, my lord. I thank you."

"Go on," Tom said, his face taut.

"You speak of Lord Philip, the man who has always stood in this place as champion of truth and justice, and I have no doubt the lords assembled here would not dispute that nor stand idly by to hear it said otherwise."

A few low voices from the court attested to their loyalty to Philip, and Taliferro smiled.

"He has such reverence for truth that, even when his own father took the crown from old King Edward, young Philip spoke against that treason. Yet, being an obedient son, he did as his father wished and kept the kingdom and the throne, even unto taking the life of King Edward's rightful heir, Stephen of Ellenshaw."

The same lords who had spoken for Philip earlier began to object, but Tom silenced them.

"Tell your tale, my lord of Warring."

"As I before said, Lord Philip has always been a man of truth and justice. Would not such a man, once he had done his duty to his father's memory, once he had acquitted himself valorously on the field of honor, would he not in his honesty have to admit he had no true claim to the crown? Would he not, just as he has done, leave his wrong behind him so the rightful heir could have his place?"

"You have been cautioned to speak truth, my lord of Warring," Tom said.

"So I do, my lord. Can you say otherwise?"

"I can. All the world knows my brother is Lynaleigh's true king. Our father should have been made king when he was a boy, but they put in Edward, his uncle, instead. It was Father's method of taking the crown Philip objected to, not his right to it. Why should he leave it behind him now that we again have peace?"

"As I said, my lord, because he is a man of honor."

"And what man of honor would simply walk away from his duty, from his friends, from his home and family? Every man here knows how well he loves the queen. Why would he leave her? Why would he leave his own son and heir?"

"Because he is a man of honor," Taliferro repeated. "Knowing his marriage no more than a trumpery forced on him by his father, knowing his child no more than a bastard, would he not feel bound to return to the woman who had first claim upon him once he knew she lived?"

Rosalynde went white and Tom moved closer to her, keeping tight rein on his wrath.

"Yes, my lords," Taliferro told the dumbfounded nobility. "Doubtless you all remember the scandal not so long ago, of the waiting woman condemned to death for sorcery and for taking the life of poor Lady Margaret's child. They said she was our Lord Philip's mistress, but she was not, was she, my lord of Brenden?"

"No."

"Why, you are a man of truth as well, I see, like a good Heretic. In truth, then, what was the relation between them?"

"That has nothing whatever to do with—"

"Do you fear the truth, my lord?" Taliferro prodded.

"She was his wife," Tom admitted, "but that was before his marriage to the queen, long before the birth of their son. Katherine Fletcher's death ended his tie to her."

"Now there, my lords, hangs the question." Taliferro drew a crumpled piece of paper from the pouch at his waist and held it up for the court to see. "I see by your color, my lord of Brenden, that you recognize this."

"That proves nothing."

"Does it not? Shall we let the court decide?" Taliferro looked out over the astonished faces of the nobility. "This is the message brought to Lord Philip the day before he left us. Judge for yourselves, my lords, what a man of truth and justice would do on receipt of such a note. 'Katherine Fletcher did not die in Bakersfield as you were told,'" he read aloud. "'She is living in Ivybridge with her father. A righteous king and true knight would do right by her. You know the just claim she has on you.'"

There was only silence when he had finished.

"'A righteous king and true knight,'" Taliferro read over again. "Who can say that does not fit Lord Philip, especially knowing that 'just claim' she has on him? Can you truly say, my lord of Brenden, he did not go to her?"

"He went to make certain that message was a lie, as you no doubt know it to be, my lord of Warring."

"I, my lord? Faith, the only lies I know are his kingship, his marriage to the Lady Rosalynde, and the legitimacy of his son. Lord Philip himself has recognized his own unfitness for the crown. Doubtless he means that the nobility should as well."

"Let us, for just a moment, my lord, grant all your claims true," Tom said, looking more like his brother than ever, with his head tossed back and his eyes narrowed. "King Edward is long dead. So is his son, Stephen, and he was the last of the Ellenshaw pretense to the crown. Given my brother has abandoned his kingdom, given his son has no right in inheritance, who do you propose should rule here? One of Lynaleigh's lesser nobles? A baron perhaps?"

Taliferro smiled. "I only wish for the rightful heir to be acknowledged. True, Stephen of Ellenshaw is dead, but his child—"

"He left no child, my lord."

"I think I would best know that." Margaret stood up and smoothed down her skirt in front, showing the now-obvious swelling her heavy clothing had before concealed. "Your brother may have taken my poor Stephen from me, but I still have his child to carry the Ellenshaw right." She looked pointedly at her sister. "A *legitimate* child by my true husband."

Rosalynde fought tears. "Meg, please—"

"I claim the crown for my child's sake, now that Philip is gone."

"It seems strange that you've not spoken of this child before now, Lady Margaret," Tom said. "Stephen died some five months ago. You must have known quite a while now if you carry his child."

"I have known, my lord," Margaret said. "I feared what the man who murdered my husband might do once he knew there was to be another who held better title to the throne than he."

"Your husband made that challenge, Lady Margaret! Philip won it fairly and you cannot—"

"My lords," Taliferro protested, "can you dismiss the claims of this poor wronged lady out of hand, knowing what even the best of men might do for such a prize as Lynaleigh? Though we know Lord Philip to be a man of justice, can we fault her for her woman's fears? Her protection of her only child? Should we not all, in defense of the helpless, champion her cause and see the true heir of the kingdom restored to it?"

"If the king is gone," Lord Eastbrook said over the rumblings of the others, "then Lord Tom has the next right."

"Does he, my lords?" Taliferro asked. "If Philip has acknowledged his own unfitness to be king, is his brother, his *younger* brother, fit to succeed him? Besides, knowing the Duke of Brenden is as much a Heretic as his brother ever was, would you make him your king? We have seen already what tolerance of their practices brings. Would you choose him over the true heir, over one who would be guided by a good daughter of the church and raised in orthodoxy?"

There was an ominous buzz throughout the court, but Eastbrook's calm words stilled it.

"This is something that must be reasoned on carefully, my lords, before any rash decision is made. If our king returns—"

"But you know the truth of that as well, do you not, my lord of Brenden?" Taliferro asked. "You know your brother will never return."

Rosalynde dropped her head and put her hands over her face, muffling a sob.

"I know no such thing," Tom insisted, dogged stubbornness in his expression. "There is nothing certain from the reports I have had."

"Now you lie," Taliferro gloated. "Do you deny that the boy who went with him brought back his ring in proof? Admit it. Philip Chastelayne is dead."

"I think not."

There was a moment of stunned silence at the firm, quiet voice, and Rosalynde felt a sharp kick inside her abdomen. With a growing murmur of astonishment, all the court turned to face the back of the great hall, and she stood up, straining to see past the crowd of courtiers that finally parted to confirm her soaring hopes.

"Philip." She dashed away the tears that tried to blind her from what she had feared she would never see again. "Oh, Philip."

He quickened his stride, and in another instant his arms were around her, pressing her close as he breathed in her sweet scent. "Rose, my Rose."

Tom let the tight air out of his lungs. "Philip, thank God."

Philip looked up. "I am sorry to have left you to deal with this nest of traitors, Tom, but they'll not long trouble us."

Margaret went suddenly pale, and there was a grimace of intense pain on her face. She and Taliferro exchanged a glance. Then Taliferro smiled.

"My lord king, I am certain I speak for the entire court in saying how relieved we are to see your majesty safe. Now that you are returned to us, we have no need—"

"My lord of Ellison, have this man arrested," Philip ordered, "and put the Lady Margaret under guard as well."

"Your majesty!" Taliferro protested over the buzzing of the court. "I do not understand."

"Elandria is dead," Philip told him. "I think I need say no more."

The baron's black eyes smoldered with loathing, but he closed his mouth and kept his silence as he and the would-be queen were taken from the great hall. Still with his arms around Rosalynde, Philip looked out over the assembled nobility.

"I know you have questions." He put his hand on Rosalynde's barely-rounded stomach and let a touch of a smile lighten his grave expression. "I have a few of my own."

Her face turned pink at that, and the courtiers smiled among themselves, as if a great weight had been lifted from them.

"But you shall have your answers," Philip told them. "And if you find even one of them false, I give you leave to choose your own king."

"No!" they cried. "We have our king!"

He flashed them a weary, winning smile, and their shouts grew into cheers.

"God save King Philip! Heaven bless his majesty!"

Eastbrook held up one hand for silence. "If it please you, your majesty, we will hear your tale tomorrow. No doubt you would rather have a good meal and a soft bed and a moment with your fair queen before you tell it."

Philip smiled again. "I knew I need not fear for my kingdom with men of such perception to look to it. I thank you, my lord, and thank you all. Tomorrow then."

He walked down the corridor with his brother on one side of him and his wife clinging to his arm on the other and the muffled cheers of the courtiers still behind him. He pulled Rosalynde closer, smiling down at her and at the little bulge in her middle.

"We feared you dead," Tom said. "When the boy came back alone—"

Philip stopped short. "Jerome is alive?" He shook his head in amazement. "It seems we have no shortage of miracles today."

"He will be glad to know you are alive, too. He's not forgiven himself for not taking better care of you."

"He brought us this." Rosalynde took off the battered ring and gave it to Philip. "Even though it seemed a sure proof of your death, every time I looked on it I could only remember the miracle God made with it before. It gave me a little hope all this long while."

"Oh, God," he breathed in reverent thanks. He set it once more on his own hand. "Jerome must have thought me dead when he took this. I suppose I almost was, from a crossbow bolt I took in the side. The wound was a long while healing."

Rosalynde exhaled a little murmur of pity, touching his side with her free hand, and he squeezed her to him again.

"I am sorry to have grieved you, my lady, being gone so long. And you, Tom." He draped his arm across his brother's shoulders, and the three of them walked down the corridor again. "I can see you've not had an easy time of it here."

Tom laughed a little. "I'll not say there have been no difficulties, but your return settles the last of them, I think."

"And Robin?" Philip asked, turning to Rosalynde again. "I suppose he'll not know me anymore."

"He waddles all about now," Rosalynde said, the love in her eyes glowing a shade brighter, "getting into everything and saying 'no' to anything he's asked. He is more like you every day."

"I want to see him as soon as I've washed some of the road off me."

When they reached the king's chamber, he opened the door and stood for a moment looking around the room.

"I never thought I would feel so about any place but Treghatours, but it is good to be home again. All this wants now is for Rafe to be here to grumble at me."

"He's gone with Darlington in search of you, I fear," Tom told him. "I'll send messengers out for them straight."

Philip grinned and rubbed his chin. "I traded a good horse for a bath and a shave just before I reached Winton, but the barber must have been blind or drunk or both, and I swear he dulled his razor just for me. I'll be glad when Rafe can do a proper job of it."

"Well, I will leave you to yourselves awhile," Tom said. "You'll want to speak to your lady alone, Philip, and I know she has much to tell you. I'll want the whole story before long, though."

"You shall have it," Philip promised, and Tom gave him a brief, sturdy hug.

"I am glad you've come back."

"Thank you, Tom. For everything."

Watching him leave the room, Philip shook his head. "Has it been so bad here? He looks worn. Are things well with his lady?"

"Yes." Rosalynde smiled almost to herself. "They've made a true love match of it, I think."

Philip smiled, too. "I am glad of it."

They stood there for a moment, each of them drinking in the longed-for sight of the other. Suddenly shy, she reached up to touch the hair that was now to his shoulders.

"I see the barber neglected to cut your hair when you were with him."

"I did not want to waste so much time as that," he said, sweeping it back with one self-conscious hand.

"I wish you'd not stopped at all. You would have been home the sooner."

"I could not bring myself to stand before your beauty, my lady, looking as I did." He smiled again, a little unsteadily. "Or smelling as I did."

She put her hand up to his cheek. "You look pale, my lord. And thinner."

"It is not so with you," he said, slipping his hand down to her waist. "Faith, does every woman with child bloom so?"

"I wanted to be certain before I told you," she said, dropping her eyes. "Then the message came and I could not. I could not grieve you with what should have been joy."

"Poor, sweet Rose," he murmured, pulling her head to his shoulder so he could kiss her temple. "It is joy. To be alive and home and to have you and Robin and now to know we will have another child as well. It is all joy."

"But, my lord, about Katherine—"

He tightened his arms around her and kissed her mouth, a strong, intense kiss with no hesitation and no restraint, and she knew she need not wonder any longer. Tears filled her eyes and she held more tightly to him, savoring the solid reality of him and the knowledge that he belonged again to her alone. He drew her closer and closer, almost crushing her against him. Then, with painful effort, he stepped back.

"Forgive me, my lady. I know we've been a long while apart."

She took his hand and pressed it over her heart. "You've been no farther from me than this, love—not since that first day I saw you in Westered."

"Still, you will want some time—"

She put her hands on his face and brought his mouth down to hers. "I want nothing but you."

"Rose," he breathed, and she kissed him as she had long wanted to these cold nights alone, kissed him for all the time he had been away.

"My beautiful, sweet Philip," she whispered, caressing his cheek. "Sweet love."

He closed his eyes, clinging closer, and she felt a trickle of warmth touch her shoulder as he buried his face against her.

"How I love you, my Rose."

Philip was quick to settle any doubts of his right and fitness to be king. Although he told Rosalynde and then Tom everything he could remember of his captivity, to the court he made little of it, stressing only the part Taliferro had played and the baron's murderous intent. For Margaret's claim that she carried the true king of Lynaleigh, he had no answer save the preeminence of his own blood over her late husband's. In the eyes of the court and of the law, he needed no other.

He set Taliferro's trial for the next day, and Margaret was to be tried at the same time, if she was well enough. Since she had been taken from the court, she had been confined to her bed, racked with pains of a labor that was at least three months too soon.

When he knew there was no more he could do, Livrette sent for Philip to come to her.

"There is something wrong, my lord. Something that I think was caused by the way she destroyed the other child she was to have had. She has been in hard labor too long to last much longer. The child does not move at all. I fear it may already be lost."

Philip could hear her through the door already, screaming and cursing the pain. The sound only intensified when he went inside.

"Shh, Meg, shh," Rosalynde soothed, trying to cool her sister's face with a damp cloth, but Margaret only shoved her away with a curse.

Philip was unprepared for the look of death that was on his sister-in-law's face. Her hair was snarled and dulled with sweat, and her lips were parched and cracked. Only her eyes seemed alive still, and they blazed with more hatred than he had ever seen.

It took her a moment to notice him, but when she did she began fighting to get up, loosing on him the foulest maledictions he had ever heard. His first instinct was to take Rosalynde and himself out of the room, away from the death and hatred that seemed to fill the very air around the dying woman, but something stopped him. It occurred to him that, though he had pardoned her before the court, in the depths of his heart he never had.

Abruptly, he recalled the woman at the tavern who would have sold herself to him for less than his meal had cost, the women at court who had thought to buy renown with their poorly-kept chastity, the men who had thought to trade their wives and daughters for kingly favor, all of whom he had condemned with a glance.

He thought back on Elandria, too. How stern and unyielding he had been in resisting her temptations, and he had spoken to her of God's love and forgiveness just as sternly. How much more might she have heard and believed in their time together if he had spoken in love? Perhaps he had been meant to show her, and the woman at the tavern, and all the others like her, perhaps he had been meant to show them all God's love rather than his own harsh condemnation.

There were few he truly loved and how easy it was to love these, like Tom and Rosalynde, when they gave such love in return. But could he do as his Savior had done and embrace those who abused him, who mocked the pain they had so willfully caused, who cut him to the very heart? He had failed with Elandria. Could he, as Christ had done, lay down the pride and the righteousness of his self for the sake of such a one? For this spitting, howling devil who had brought into the world only pain and death?

He knelt beside her. "Lady Margaret—"

She flung herself at him with a shriek, seizing him by the hair with one hand and raking the nails of the other down his neck. He grabbed her wrists and pinned her back against the pillows until she had no more curses and no more breath to carry them. When he spoke again, his voice was low and gentle.

"My lady, there is great peace to be had in forgiveness."

She tried to break his hold, her eyes wide and wild. "I'll not hear of your God again! I'll not ask His forgiveness!"

"I mean to ask your forgiveness, lady. I have wronged you, and I would have it made right."

For an instant, she was too surprised to struggle. Then another pain tore through her and she tried to writhe away from him. "If my forgiveness would bring you peace, then die wanting it!"

"I'll ask it anyway, lady. I have carried hatred toward you a long while now, and I ask you, in the name of Christ—"

She began to laugh hysterically, still struggling and panting with pain. "So you hate me! At last I have hope there is truly a man in you somewhere past that puling piety."

He looked at her lying there, fighting death and hell and truth, and found he could hate her no longer. She was blind and lost and alone.

"God, send your peace here," he said softly.

"Such peace as Katherine Fletcher found in the flames!" Margaret screeched, and Philip only looked on her with pity, realizing that she had no more hold on him, no more power to wound.

"Ease her pain, Lord," he murmured, "and have mercy on the innocent life she carries."

"Never pray for that! As if the thing could have a soul!" she hissed. "Or, if it does, it is surely damned for murdering me!"

She arched her back and screamed, a drawn-out, hoarse cry of agony. Philip closed his eyes and held her there until it ended.

"Lady Margaret—"

"Oh, God," she sobbed, letting her head drop to one side, away from him. "It was sent to avenge that other life I took, Richard's child. It had just started to kick inside me, and I—" She turned her face back to him, a desperation in her eyes that had not been there before. "But it had to understand, if I did not destroy it I could never be queen. Now I have neither child nor crown nor redemption."

She screamed again, her eyes showing only the whites, her whole body straining. Still holding her wrists, Philip nodded his head toward her and Rosalynde came closer, to wipe the sweat and spittle from her face.

"Because of you!" Margaret howled, aiming a sharp kick at her sister's abdomen that did not connect. Then she went limp.

Philip still held her down, uncertain of what she might do, but she only lay there, still trembling. Then to his amazement, she began to sob again.

"Oh, God, I am damned. I am damned."

"You need not be, my lady," Philip told her. "I forgive you, truly. God will forgive you, too, and take you for His if you will but call upon Him."

"You should want me to be damned," she said, looking with a pitiful pleading into Philip's eyes. "After all I've taken from you. I tried to take your kingdom as well—but our claims are all pretense. Even the child—"

She broke off there, panting again.

Philip glanced at his wife and again at her sister. "My lady?"

"This child, this vengeance of God, it is not Stephen's child."

"Not—"

"Taliferro found a man, one of your soldiers, who looked enough like Stephen to give me a child that would convince the people. Then, when I knew I had conceived, we cut his throat and dumped him in the river."

"Mowbray," Philip said half under his breath, releasing his hold in surprise, and Margaret began to moan again, clutching at her stomach.

"I am damned for it all."

"Please, lady, take mercy," Philip pled. "Whatever you have done, you cannot go beyond what God's forgiveness will cover."

"Please, Meg," Rosalynde whispered, tears slipping down her cheeks.

"I cannot say the words," Margaret gasped, straining. "I know nothing to say. Oh, Jesus, I have sinned. Forgive me. Oh, Jesus, my Lord—"

She gave one sharp cry and then was gone.

CHAPTER
19

LADY MARGARET DIED IN GRACE," PHILIP TOLD THE COURT THE next day. Rosalynde, Tom and Elizabeth, and all the nobility were gathered for Taliferro's trial. Even Jerome, with Lady Marian watching possessively over him, was there, well recovered and pleased to be once more at his king's side.

After he had told of Margaret's treason, Philip had wanted his people to know of the mercy she had found. "Let us all remember that much of her and no more. She is at peace."

"Amen," Rosalynde whispered, holding to his hand. She had sunk, spent, against him in that first stunned moment after Margaret had died.

"I am sorry, love," he had murmured as he stroked her hair, but, behind her weariness, she had a look of deep gratitude.

"No," she had told him. "There is no sorrow now."

She wore black today for her sister but could not grieve for her. Not now.

Taliferro looked at the king and queen with a knowing grin as he sat, manacled and heavily guarded, before the court.

"I suppose the child went with her. How convenient for you, your majesty. Another challenger to your reign gone and, at least from the story, without your having to bloody your own hands."

"If you have a charge to make, man, speak it out," Philip said. "I fear nothing of the truth."

"What might any man say before this loyal company, your majesty? If your rival's widow and his heir are both taken suddenly, why we must see that as God's will and not springing from any man's intervention, must we not? Your own father was made king by just such a convenience, I have heard."

"That's not so," Tom began, but Philip stilled him.

"Your reasoning is flawed, Taliferro, on many counts, but mostly in that I would have no reason to wish harm to Lady Margaret's child."

"No?" Taliferro asked, amused. "No reason to dispose of a child with a better claim to the throne than you, majesty?"

"Stephen of Ellenshaw's child would never have had such a claim in law," Philip said calmly. "But, as you well know, the child was not even his."

The nobility exchanged startled looks, questioning each other over this revelation, and Philip had to lift his hand for silence.

"Lady Margaret, before she died, admitted it was part of the plot she and Taliferro had devised to find someone resembling her late husband, Stephen, and pass that man's child as Stephen's heir and claimant to the throne. Once he was certain of my death, Taliferro was to promote this child as the true heir to Lynaleigh and, through this child, was to rule with Lady Margaret himself. It did not quite unfold as you had planned, did it?"

Taliferro seemed unruffled. "A preposterous plot, my liege. It is easy enough to put words into the mouth of a dead woman."

"Indeed?" Philip asked. "And what of Darlington's aide, Mowbray? I suppose his murder was something I invented as well."

Taliferro shrugged. "You have no link to me in that. No link to me in any of this save what you claim were the circumstances of my sister's death. Perhaps she is not dead at all."

"She is dead, true enough," Philip replied grimly. "Her testimony, Mowbray's death, and Margaret's confession all agree together in condemning you. We even have proof that, instead of aiding the people in Warring with the goods we have given you, you have sold it all to your own profit."

Taliferro waved the accusation away with one negligent gesture.

"Hearsay. Nothing more. Bring a witness, my liege, just one, and I will dispute you no longer."

His expression grew uneasy when he saw the slight smile on Philip's face.

"I call Molly of Breebonne."

In a clear, steady voice, the girl from the laundry told the court everything she had learned since she had come to the palace. She told dates and times and names that, woven together with what Philip had said, closed an inescapable net around the would-be king.

"The girl's been schooled in this!" Taliferro protested. "What would some laundry wench know of such things?"

"Lord Tom asked me to keep what watch I could over Lady Margaret and my lord Taliferro," Molly said. Then she smiled a little. "Neither of them even noticed the laundry wench who often busied herself at windows and doorways, or who spoke to their servants, or who found the most interesting items while gathering laundry in their chambers." She handed Tom a piece of paper.

"Surely you cannot deny your own hand, Taliferro," Tom said, looking it over. "Here, I will read you a portion of it. It is addressed to Lady Margaret herself. 'Cafton brought me word that the deed is done. Once it is known, in the tumult, the court will turn to the claimant who best convinces them of his right. When the moment comes, I will see that claimant is the child you carry.' Shall I go on?"

Taliferro laughed hollowly. "The girl's his mistress!" he told the court. "All the world knows it!"

"Not so," Molly replied.

Her simple dignity and the smile Tom and Elizabeth exchanged were more damning to Taliferro's charge than any number of vehement protests would have been.

Before he and Elizabeth returned to Winton, Tom had explained his meetings with Molly, how she, while ostensibly collecting dirty laundry, could collect a great deal of information that he could never hope to come by any other way. Elizabeth had understood at last and realized her connection with Taliferro had prevented Tom from confiding this to her as well. His forgiveness had taken the sting of shame out of the memory for her, and now she could smile at the girl and, with great satisfaction, at Taliferro.

"I presume you can prove *your* charges, Taliferro," Philip asked, and, getting only a searing glare in answer, he smiled, too. "We all of us thank you, Mistress Molly, for your diligence. Your king rests in your debt."

Philip turned once more to the accused and his smile vanished.

"Simon Taliferro, former Baron of Warring, in the face of the overwhelming evidence against you, you are found guilty of treason against the kingdom of Lynaleigh and against the person of her king." Philip's voice was clear and steady as he, for the first time, condemned a man to death. "You will be executed at dawn tomorrow and your lands will be forfeit to the crown."

"I give them to you, my lord, in fond farewell," Taliferro said, smiling once more. "But only after I am dead."

"I trust you are aware that there is but one punishment for treason in Lynaleigh," Philip told him. "Hanging, drawing, and quartering. For Christ's mercy, and though you've refused all pleas to turn to Him, I will spare you the last two."

"Very gracious, my liege lord," Taliferro said, losing none of his smugness. "One thing more, your majesty, before sentence is carried out."

"What? What more could you possibly have to say in your defense that will bear the weight of truth?"

Taliferro looked at Elizabeth and smiled to see the horrified realization dawn on her face. Tom put his arm around her, glaring at his insolent adversary.

"Merely a small matter of betrayal," Taliferro said affably, "of treason, not against your majesty's person, but against your house—against his highness, my lord of Brenden."

Philip glanced at his brother and saw the stubborn determination in his eyes and in the tight set of his white lips.

"Treason against Tom? How?"

"By adultery."

There was a murmur from the court and Philip shot Elizabeth a hard look. She hid her face against Tom's shoulder and began to cry. Philip turned again to Taliferro.

"Your proof?"

"Only the most perfect proof that can be had on such a charge."

"Witness?"

"Participant."

Philip looked again at Elizabeth, but she was still huddled against Tom, shielded now in both of his arms.

"Do you answer these charges, Lady Elizabeth?" Philip asked stiffly, and Tom pulled her closer.

"Philip—"

"My lady?" Philip demanded.

"She can make no answer, my lord," Taliferro said. "None but her guilty tears."

"You know you condemn yourself in this confession, Taliferro," Tom warned.

"I am condemned already, highness. I lose nothing by this bit of loyalty I have shown here—to your own house, my lord."

"Loyalty," Tom spat, and then he turned to his brother. "Please, Philip, for mercy's sake and my lady's, dismiss the court. Let us speak of this in private."

They withdrew into the council chamber, the king and queen, Tom and Elizabeth, and the smug-faced former Baron of Warring. When the door was closed, Elizabeth swayed on her feet and Tom helped her to a chair. He stood close beside her, his arm around her still as she leaned against his side.

"Very well, Lady Elizabeth," Philip said, "you have heard the charge this man has brought against you. He is a proven traitor and mayhap he does this for no more than spite. It is only left for you to make answer to it." He saw the pain in Tom's eyes and a touch of pleading crept into his voice. "I will take your word over his, my lady. You have but to deny it. I will believe you."

Elizabeth did not even lift her head. "He speaks true."

Philip saw the telltale quiver in Tom's clenched jaw and the pitying tears in Rosalynde's eyes. His expression tightened.

Taliferro dared a smug smile. "As I said."

"Lady Elizabeth Briesionne, you are under arrest," Philip said, "for adultery and for high treason."

"Yes, your majesty," Elizabeth whispered, and she tried to pull away from Tom, but he would not allow it.

"Philip, for my sake, please—"

"She's confessed it, Tom. I cannot save her."

Taliferro laughed and Philip seized his arm, tight and high up, and hauled him out to the guard that waited outside the door.

"Keep him under close watch and send me two more of your men."

"At once, your majesty."

Philip shut the door on Taliferro's taunting laughter.

"You will be imprisoned until we can hold trial, Lady Elizabeth."

Elizabeth stood, but Tom did not loosen his arms from around her.

"Not prison, Philip," he pled. "You've known the shame of that."

"I know. Tom, if I—"

Philip felt a soft hand on his arm.

"Please, my lord," Rosalynde asked in that sweet tone he could never resist. There were still tears in her eyes. He could never resist those either.

"My lady, it cannot be otherwise. What would you have me to do? Have one law for my subjects and another for my kin?"

"There is no need to imprison her, my lord. There is no heart in her to flee." Rosalynde touched his arm in petition. "Let me have charge of her awhile, at least until the trial, if there must be one."

"There must. You know there must."

"But no need to put her into prison."

Philip looked from her pleading eyes to Tom's. "No. No need."

Tom hugged his wife closer.

"Go with her, Bess," he murmured against her cheek. "I will come to you soon."

"Tom," she sobbed.

"Shh. Go with her." He looked up at Philip. "There is a way, Bess. God will make us one."

Swallowing down more tears, she nodded and allowed Rosalynde to lead her away. Only once did she look back.

Tom turned to his brother when they were alone.

"Philip—"

"Do not plead for her, Tom." There was no harshness, no anger in his voice, just a pleading of his own. "I can do nothing to save her. Were she my own wife, I could not. Not with the truth of it coming from her own mouth. I have no choice, not in law."

"You can choose mercy."

"She has been false to you. I cannot pardon that."

"You've pardoned greater crimes. You pardoned Margaret the lives of Richard's child, of your own dear Katherine, and of the child she was to give you. Can you do so much and cannot pardon my wife's misstep?"

"Margaret's wrongs were against me, Tom. Lady Elizabeth has wronged you, and that I cannot so easily pardon. For your sake—"

"If you must do anything for my sake, Philip, pardon her for it. Love her for it."

"You know the law does not allow pardon in such a case. The threat to the sovereign line would be too great if adultery in any royal lady were winked at."

"Enough time has passed," Tom said. "She is certain now she does not carry his child."

"Still, you have every right to leave her to the law."

"I had rather forgive her and keep her than judge her and lose her."

There was a tenderness in Tom's eyes that Philip had seen time and again in the eyes of his own beloved Rosalynde, when he knew he did not himself deserve it.

"Tom—"

"You said yourself, Philip; she's confessed. If you had heard her when she told me of it, knowing how uncertain she's been, knowing her fears and how subtly Taliferro played upon them, you could only have pitied her. It was more so with me, because I love her so well."

"Then you've known some while now."

"I've known."

"And you do not care?"

"Not care? Please, Philip, never say that to me. Not care? It cut me so deep when she told me, I thought I would bleed to death. I've tried so hard to love her, to understand her, to make her happy, and then to know she was false to me? Not care? I—" He let his breath out slowly. "I had to let it go. She knows she was wrong; how foolish she was. I was in the wrong as well. Should we not forgive one another? Pardon her, if for nothing but my sake." Again his eyes pled. "What good is it that you are king if you cannot get me what I want?"

"She was accused before the court. If I should pardon her, there is still the public knowledge of her guilt. God may forgive it; even you might, but the people? Never. No child she bears you will escape the stain of it in their eyes."

"And if I could prove them her innocence?"

"She's confessed, Tom."

"Only before us. And God. The court heard only the accusation. Would it not be my right to make her honor good with my sword?"

"You would challenge Taliferro?"

"The law allows trial by combat. She would stand wholly innocent if I win."

"Taliferro is the very devil with a blade."

"I am a fair hand myself, if you remember."

"Not as he is. I've seen him. What good would it do you to die for this and her left still to face the penalty for her guilt—proven if he wins."

"It is a risk, I grant you, but I'll take it if it might hope to save her."

"Never do it, Tom. I will pardon her. I swear it."

"No, as you said, she would never escape the stain of it if she is pardoned guilty. My way makes her clean of all of it."

"I'll not allow it. I'll have you put away if I must until this is settled."

"As Father once did you?"

The stubbornness in Philip's face softened, and once more there was pleading there. "Tom, if you fail—"

"Would you not risk as much yourself for your Rosalynde? Would you not have for Katherine? Would it not have soothed you more than standing by helplessly and letting her be put to death?"

"May God protect you in this," Philip said softly.

"He has always."

"But in a wrong cause—"

Tom shook his head. "She's confessed her sin to Him and to me already. He has cleansed her of it. I do not champion the wrong."

After a long pause, Philip nodded. "For your sake, then, if you will have it so. Make the challenge. You know if you choose this course you will be bound by all points of the law and I cannot help you."

"I know."

"You know, too, that if he wins in this I cannot punish him for his other crimes. The law will adjudge him wholly innocent in heaven's eyes, and I can do nothing more.

"I know."

Again there was a silence between them and Philip looked intently at his brother.

"Do you love her so much then?" he asked finally and Tom smiled.

"Take the measure of my love by your own, Philip. Do you love your queen so much?"

Philip hugged him close and tight. "God grant you victory."

Elizabeth was in bed when Tom came to her, but he could see she had not slept and had not expected to. He said nothing as he undressed and got under the coverlet beside her. She, too, said nothing, but she did not take her eyes from him all the while, as if the sight of him was one she was not to have for much longer. He put his arm around her, and she huddled against him and still the silence reigned.

"I have spoken to Philip," he said after a time, the soft words coming with effort as he toyed with one mahogany curl. "He's granted us trial by combat."

She sat up. "Oh, Tom, no! Taliferro will kill you!"

He sat up, too, and tried to smile. "Do you think me so poor a swordsman, love?"

She did not answer that, except with tears.

"Bess—" Tears filled his eyes, too. "Bess—" He took both of her hands and bent to press his lips to them. "Let me do this, Bess. Let me love you the only way I am able, with all my life."

"Tom," she sobbed, pressing him against her breast, against her racing heart. "If you should die in this—"

"What would my life be to me without you, beloved?" He clasped his arms around her and then lifted up his head and looked deeply into her eyes. "It is what I am meant to do, Bess, whatever comes of it. If there were any other way—" He took a deep breath. "Bess, love—"

His voice broke, and she cradled him once more against her. After a moment, their eyes again met and then their lips, and they both tasted tears in the kiss.

They twined themselves together, holding tighter and tighter until they could be no closer. Then they lay still and silent. It was much later in the night that they made a wordless, passionate vow of love, a bittersweet blend of forever and farewell that was indelibly etched in both their hearts.

CHAPTER

THE RULES OF THE COMBAT WERE SIMPLE AND NEVER VARIED. THE winner was innocent of all charges brought against him or the one he championed. The loser was guilty and dead.

Once it began, no one could aid or even touch either of the combatants until the king himself gave a verdict and the trial was over. Afterward, no reprisals could be made against the victor, and the loser was to have no mourners.

All the courtiers were gathered in the great hall to see the outcome. Livrette was among the onlookers, ready in the event his surgeon's skills were needed at the end of the trial. The accusations were well known, and, though there were many who looked with pitying sorrow at Tom as he stood at Elizabeth's side, the glances cast her way were nothing short of murderous condemnation. It did not help that Taliferro stood at the other side of the area that had been marked off for the battle and smiled in knowing confidence at her. Seeing him, Tom merely squeezed her hand and spoke encouragement to her with his eyes.

Oh, God, she cried silently, *take my life before You take his. I cannot—*

"In the matter of charges of treason and adultery brought by Lord Simon Taliferro, Baron of Warring," the court scribe read aloud, "Lord Thomas Chastelayne, Duke of Brenden, Prince of Lynaleigh, stands here champion for the accused, Lady Elizabeth Briesionne of Aberwain. My lord prince, how do you answer?"

"Let her make answer for herself," Taliferro taunted. "She knows the truth of it."

"My lady will not dignify your charge with any answer, Taliferro," Tom said, drawing his sword. "I make answer here for her."

Taliferro grinned. "Because she knows herself guilty. She knows I have tasted freely of her sweet—"

"Let it begin," Philip commanded brusquely, and, grinning again, Taliferro saluted with a whistling slash of his blade.

Tom answered perfunctorily, his face all watchful determination, his rapier's movements tight and precise. Then the two of them began to circle each other, a slow, wary, graceful maneuver. Taliferro smiled all the while.

"You'll not be the first I've killed, your highness, who thought his life worth less than the reputation of a noble-born slut."

Elizabeth's face paled and Tom's jaw tightened, but he did not rise to the bait.

"I thought our weapons were to be rapiers, not barbed words."

"Even so," Taliferro replied, lunging as he did.

Tom sprang backwards and thrust at him, narrowly missing his arm. Taliferro shoved Tom's blade out of the way with his own and drew back, slashing Tom's side as he did, bloodying his shirt. Tom gasped but did not pause in returning the stroke, and the hall was filled with the whoosh and clang of swordplay. Soon the labored breathing of the combatants added to the sound, but otherwise there was silence. Then Taliferro's laugh rang out.

"You indulge me, your highness, allowing me such easy hits. Come, do not hold back."

Tom stood a few paces off from him, panting and clutching his thigh where Taliferro had cut him, deep and painful and darkly bloody. Livrette began rummaging through his things, readying himself for the task that lay ahead of him.

"Come on then," Tom said, straightening and lunging forward all at once. Taliferro spun away from him and slashed at his face. Tom jerked back from the blade, but it caught him under the chin, starting another stream of red that rushed down to further stain his shirt.

Elizabeth knotted her handkerchief, wrenching it mercilessly in her hands, fighting to keep herself from screaming. Beside her, Rosalynde was holding tightly to Philip's arm, her mouth moving in silent supplication to heaven, her eyes fixed on the combat. Philip, too, kept close watch, and Elizabeth was certain he was wondering if he would have to stand by and see his brother done to death by a scoundrel to whom this was all no more than sport—all for the sake of a faithless strumpet.

His eyes blazing determined fury, Tom swiped the back of his hand under his chin and advanced again, thrusting at his opponent, his strokes faster almost than the onlookers could follow, driving Taliferro back to the wall, leaving him able to do little more than dodge Tom's blade. There was no longer a smile on his face.

"Do I indulge you now, my lord?" Tom panted. Taliferro, too winded to answer, shoved him backwards and maneuvered him once more into the center of the hall.

The combat continued in a whir of rapier on rapier. Taliferro made a touch here and there, sometimes catching little more than Tom's clothes, occasionally darkening them with his blood, but buying each hit with a maximum of effort. None of his previous opponents had proved so stubbornly troublesome as this boy. He'd never had to work so hard to keep himself whole.

Tom's blade whistled past his ear, and, enraged by the insolence of it, Taliferro ripped his rapier across Tom's chest. Tom staggered backwards, and Palmer took his arm to keep him from falling.

"My lord—"

"Let me staunch that, my lord," Livrette insisted, coming up to his other side.

Tom pushed away from them and headed again for Taliferro. Palmer started to follow.

"My lord, please—"

"Stay back," Philip warned, and Palmer, looking into the anxious tautness of his face, obeyed. Elizabeth turned to her brother-in-law, her bewildered eyes meeting his stern ones for only a second.

Then he looked again toward the combat. Forcing her handkerchief into another contortion, she did as well.

The challengers fought on, exchanging stroke for vicious stroke, neither of them gaining or losing ground. Taliferro began to smile once more. Tom was turning pale, his sword arm was growing unsteady, blood was flowing still from his wounds. Taliferro feinted at his injured leg and raised his blade, meaning to cut him through the middle. Tom blocked with his forearm, and Elizabeth could not suppress a cry of pain as Taliferro's rapier razored through his sleeve and through his flesh. Tom grimaced and clenched his jaw more tightly, but that was all.

"It is not so easy now, is it, highness?" Taliferro asked, a glitter of triumph in his smile. He flicked loose the lacing on Tom's shirt with the tip of his blade, stinging Tom's chest as he did it. Tom's attempt to parry was slow and clumsy.

"Wounded so, you might have control enough for a broadsword," Taliferro observed, "but never enough for the nuances of a rapier."

Tom tried again to advance and Taliferro swiped at his face. Tom ducked the blow, but it left a gash over one ear, drawing blood enough to mat his hair and run down the side of his face, blood enough to make Elizabeth cry out again.

Tom made another unsteady thrust, and Taliferro slashed at his boot, laying it open from knee to ankle, along with the fabric and flesh beneath.

"Please, your majesty!" Elizabeth cried, her handkerchief now in shreds. "Stop it! He is toying with him, killing him by inches!"

Philip shook his head, his face set and stern, pain in his eyes.

"Yes, our king will keep the law, even to his own hurt," Taliferro said, blocking Tom's next stroke with an easy turn of his wrist. Then he ripped once again through Tom's upper arm, leaving his sleeve hanging in bloody ribbons. Tom staggered sideways, scarcely able to keep hold of his weapon.

"Your majesty, this cannot continue!" Livrette protested, but Philip did not even acknowledge him.

"Come, my lord," Taliferro taunted, flicking Tom's other sleeve and piercing his arm. "You cannot yet be weary."

Tom grimaced and pulled free, only to feel Taliferro's blade slash like a cat-o'-nine-tails over his hands and arms, his legs, his shoulders, but he made no sound. It was Elizabeth who made those wounded cries, watching him sink under each blow. Finally she turned away from the unbearable, condemning sight, but Philip dragged her back.

"Watch!" he commanded through clenched teeth, his grip bruising her arm, and she looked up to see Taliferro whisk the weapon out of Tom's slackened grasp.

Tom caught the next blow in his gloved hands, barely keeping it from cutting his throat. Taliferro whipped the blade free, slicing across his palms. Tom drew a hissing breath and fell to his knees. Taliferro was instantly on him, taking a hurting handful of his hair and forcing his head up for the coup de grace. Philip froze, not breathing, and Rosalynde hid her face against him.

"Stop it, please!" Elizabeth begged, falling to her knees before the king. "I will confess!"

"No!" Tom wrenched away from his opponent, leaving him with a fistful of blood-and-sweat-matted hair, and tackled him low. The two of them rolled over and over, grappling for control of Taliferro's rapier until it finally skittered across the stone floor and came to rest under one of the chairs. Still the combatants struggled, and Elizabeth sprang to her feet, seeing Taliferro fumbling for the weapon that hung at his waist. Philip saw it, too.

"Tom, his dagger!"

There was a flash of bright steel. Tom gasped and went limp. Taliferro lay on top of him, his dagger plunged into Tom's side.

"Tom!" Elizabeth shrieked, and Taliferro dragged himself to his feet.

"You would have done better to confess and be punished alone, Madonna," he taunted, winded and smiling still, "rather than to take this boy's foolish, innocent life." He reached down and twisted the blade out of Tom's side and held it out to her. "You may have this now. Surely this blood is on your hands as well."

"Tom!" she cried again, reaching toward his crumpled, mangled body, but Philip held her back.

"Livrette—" he said, but his voice broke, and Rosalynde hugged more tightly to him, weeping. "Livrette, see that—"

"No," Taliferro insisted, "you know the law. No one touches either of the challengers until the king gives a verdict." He stood there gloating, teasing his shirt front with the razor point of his dagger. "The law, your majesty."

The physician stood there helplessly, he and Palmer both making a visible effort to stay where they were. Philip pressed his lips together, pain and anger and tears in his eyes, but he bowed his head. *If this, too, is Your will—*

He looked up and spoke in a loud, clear voice. "Lady Elizabeth Briesionne, charged with the crimes of treason and adultery against her lord and husband, Prince Thomas, Duke of Brenden, is by this trial of combat proven to be—"

"No!"

There was a gasp from the entire court at Tom's hoarse cry. He lunged at his opponent, tackling him at the knees, toppling him forward, driving Taliferro's own dagger half its length into the soft flesh under his breastbone.

Taliferro landed on his forearms, bracing himself in the fall to keep the blade from being fully buried in him. There was fury in his face as he struggled to pull it out, but Tom's arms were around him like a vise. Tom's mangled hands were around his, holding the dagger where it was, forcing it by agonizing fractions deeper and deeper into his chest.

Taliferro's face contorted with pain, and Tom's turned harder and more determined. With a sudden wrench, Taliferro tried to throw him off, but he only succeeded in pushing the blade deeper and higher up, closer to his hammering heart. He tried twisting sideways, but he only jerked the blade still deeper and punctured his lung with the sudden movement, filling his throat with choking blood.

His eyes bulged as he fought for breath, and he wheezed out pinkish froth with every futile attempt. Tom pressed harder against his twitching body, ignoring the pain that shot through his own tortured flesh, his burning wounds, his nearly numb hands. Taliferro groaned and twisted once more in desperation, and again Tom's grip tightened.

"God, give me strength," he gasped, throwing all his weight against his opponent's back, and, with a jolt, the dagger sank to its hilt.

Taliferro died without a sound.

Tom put one bloody hand on his adversary's pulseless throat, then looked up at the king.

"Your verdict," he demanded. "Philip, say it!"

Philip nodded, shaken. "The lady is proven innocent."

Palmer was the first at Tom's side, helping him to his feet, as Livrette tried to assess how badly he was wounded. Tom pulled away from them and stumbled to where Elizabeth stood with her arms outstretched. He lurched to one knee before her and managed to raise his head enough to look into her pleading, remorseful eyes.

"You are free," he breathed. Then he fell into a heap at her feet. There was an utter stillness in him that froze her heart.

He is dead.

Livrette was immediately beside them, pushing Elizabeth out of the way, ripping open the bloody remains of Tom's shirt so he could listen for the faintest pulse of life. After a frantic moment, he looked up at Philip and slowly shook his head.

"Your majesty, there is little I can do now."

"No," Elizabeth whispered.

"We should take him from here," the physician said quietly. "Some of you men . . ."

White-faced, Palmer knelt at his master's feet, but something in the king's expression kept him from doing more. Without a word, Philip slipped his arms under Tom's shoulders and knees and lifted him up. Rosalynde laid her hand on his damp, bloodied brow, weeping and praying still.

"No," Elizabeth wailed, wrapping her arms around his legs, pressing her cheek against his thigh, her tears reddening as they mingled with his blood. "No, no, no!"

Philip shoved her back with his shoulder, pulling Tom away from her.

"No more," he said, his voice low and tight. "He's past your hurt now."

"I'll make ready a place," Palmer said in a gruff whisper.

He and Livrette left the great hall and Philip followed after them. Elizabeth sank to the floor, watching him walk away, able to see nothing of Tom but one torn, dangling arm and his head thrown limply back, exposing the defenseless, battered curve of his throat.

"Tom!" she shrieked as the door swung shut behind them. She struggled against Rosalynde's soothing hands. "Tom! Tom!"

There was no answer.

Rosalynde had sent for Nan and some of Elizabeth's other ladies to take her to her chamber, and Elizabeth had followed them numbly, not caring where they led her or what they did with her. Not now.

Sometime she fell asleep, and it was dark when Nan woke her.

"My lady, his majesty is here to speak with you."

There was pity, not condemnation, in the girl's eyes. It was unlikely the king would show such mercy.

Elizabeth stood up, her head feeling hot and heavy, her body aching as if it were herself Taliferro had ripped into pieces with his rapier. The door opened and she heard Philip dismiss her attendants. Then it closed. She dared not raise her eyes. It was as if she stood before almighty God Himself in all His wrath and glory, knowing He had a righteous judgment to mete out to her.

She managed an unsteady curtsey and then went to her knees. "Your majesty."

He did not speak and after a moment she looked up at him. His eyes were steadily on her, but they told her nothing except that he, too, had wept.

"I know it would make no difference if I told you how sorry I am," she said, her breath coming unevenly. "I have no words to express it even if you had the ears to hear it."

"And what would you say, lady?"

"I would say—" Her voice dropped even lower. "I would say that I had rather have died myself than let him die for my foolishness. I had rather he had never married me, never seen me, than have it end so. I had rather—I had rather—" She bowed her head. "Except I know he is in the heaven he deserves, I could not bear now to draw breath."

"And if you had it again to do?"

"I would love him as I should always have done. I would trust him and cherish him and never wrong him." She lifted tortured eyes to him. "Punish me how you will, my lord. My hands are guilty of his blood. I took his life no less than if I had wielded the blade myself."

To her amazement, Philip's expression softened. "You took nothing he did not willingly give. Most of the love that comes to us in this world comes undeserved." His mouth turned up at one side. "I know."

"You needn't remind me how little I deserved his love."

Philip shook his head. "I never meant it that way. I only meant that he loved you because it was what he wanted most to do. He never regretted that, whatever came of it."

"What came of it was nothing but pain."

"I have wanted to hate you, my lady. Each time I saw him hurting, I wanted to hate you for it, but I see too much of myself in you, myself before I learned merely to take the love that was offered me and not question it or try to constrain it. As hard as I fought it, it never let me go, and I am glad now for my second chance. You should have another chance as well."

"It is too late." There was no hope in her face, nothing but desolation in her eyes, and she dropped her head. "Too late."

Philip lifted her chin. "He is asking for you."

She caught her breath. "My lord?"

"He is asking for you." Again one side of his mouth turned up. "Where would any of us be without our second chances?"

"Oh, my lord," she murmured, and she pressed her now-wet cheek to his hand. "Oh, merciful God."

He let her cry for a moment. Then he helped her to her feet and led her down the corridor to Tom's chamber.

"Remember what you have said," he told her before he opened the door. "Love him, trust him, cherish him, and never wrong him.

He deserves it of you, and, believe me, you will find yourself well rewarded for it."

There was warmth in his expression, and she smiled the tiniest of smiles. "I will. I promise."

He opened the door and motioned for Palmer and the other servants to leave the room. Then he urged Elizabeth inside and left her there alone.

Tom was laid out on the bed, the coverlet drawn up just past his waist. His eyes were closed, there were tired little lines around his mouth, and what she could see of his body was bandaged or at least bruised.

"My lord?"

He did not stir.

"Tom?"

His eyes fluttered open and, seeing her, he smiled.

"My Bess."

She ran to him and dropped to her knees at the side of the bed. His outstretched arm was wrapped from shoulder to knuckles, and she cradled it against her cheek, bathing his hand with kisses and tears.

"I am so very sorry."

"I know, sweetheart. It is every bit worth it, having you with me now."

She flung herself into his arms, and he held her as close as he could manage, laughing and groaning, too, as she squeezed him tight.

"Easy, love."

"Oh, Tom!" she cried, pulling back from him, realizing she had hurt him yet again. But he would not let her up.

"Do not stop either," he said, nuzzling her hair, and she nestled there against him, holding him as closely as she dared.

She stroked his linen-swathed chest and remembered the deep wounds Taliferro had made in his side and across his heart, leaving his shirt sodden and heavy with blood. There was no blood now, only the clean white of his bandages, just slightly more pale than his face.

"I was certain he had pierced you to the heart with his dagger," she said, clinging closer to him, again fighting tears. "I was certain you were dead."

"Livrette said he's never seen the like of it, but he thinks the blade struck one of my ribs at just the angle to turn it from doing any real harm." He laughed softly. "He says he does not know how, except by some miracle."

She saw the pain even that low laugh cost him and knew his wounds were not so inconsequential as he claimed. Certainly it was only by a miracle that he was holding her now.

"You and Philip have made peace, I see," he said after a moment. "I thought never to see such a thing." Tom smiled. "He loves fiercely. There is no better ally, I can assure you, once you win him to you."

"Steadfastness must run in the Chastelayne blood," she said, caressing his cheek, pleased to see that, except for the shallow scratch under his chin, Taliferro's blade had missed his face altogether. She was glad. He had such a beautiful face. All of him was beautiful. Was.

She pressed her cheek again against one bandaged hand and began to cry.

"Shh, love," he soothed. "I will mend. Livrette said so, and he is never one to give out hope unless he is sure."

"Your poor hands," she sobbed, "your back, your side. The marks will never go away."

"They will, sweetheart, they will. Most of them will. I guess there are a few I'll carry awhile. I suppose they'll not be too pretty to look on."

"How can I ever look on them, knowing I put them there? They will always remind me—"

"If they remind you of anything, Bess, let them remind you that I love you." He used his free hand to fondle the gleaming bracelet that circled her wrist. "They say you can never love a thing by any more than the pain it has cost to win it."

She looked up at him in wonder.

"You must love me a great deal," she said, and he pulled her again into his arms.

"I do."

"How can you? How can you still love me and forgive me after I've hurt you so much?"

"Because I've been loved so," he said, "and been forgiven so." He stroked her flushed cheek. "Because there are hands that have been scarred for my sake and innocent blood shed to cover my guilt and because I've been given mercy rather than justice. That is the truest love I know, sweetheart, and the best I could give to you." He caressed the bracelet once more. "Do you believe now that I love you?"

"Oh, yes! Yes!"

"Then will you believe one more thing of me?"

"Anything," she breathed.

"However much I love you, and I *do* love you, He loves you much, much more."

She was silent for a moment. He had painted a picture for her, in his blood and in his scars, in his gentle eyes, of a love she was only beginning to comprehend, a love that could only come from God Himself. "*As Christ loved the church . . .*"

There was a sudden earnestness in her expression. "Teach me to know Him as you do."

He blinked back unexpected tears and cuddled her closer.

"Oh, Bess, Bess, love," he whispered, "I do truly love you."

It was not long before the spring came, touching the whole earth with green and gold, sweeping away the winter's browns and grays as if they had never been.

Philip knelt down among the newly leaved rose trees and scooped out a hollow place, not wide, not deep, just large enough for the small carved box, ornate and fitted with gold, that he had taken from the chest at the foot of his bed. Rosalynde was at his side, watching his face as he worked, praying God's blessing on what he did.

Elizabeth stood there, too, her hand linked in Tom's, her eyes frequently on him, as if she would assure herself that he was truly there with her. He was still somewhat pale, more so today than he had been recently, but he was nearly mended, and even Joan did not fuss over him much anymore. Elizabeth held him a little tighter when Philip dusted off his hands and opened the box.

"Kate," Philip said softly. He turned to Rosalynde, and she gave him the fragrant white blossom she carried, the very first saint's rose of the spring. He brushed it with his lips and nestled it in the braided coil of golden hair the box held.

"Tabitha," he whispered, almost too low for even Rosalynde to hear. "Innocent unborn."

He closed his eyes, steadying himself. He took a deep breath.

"I must let you go now, Kate. I love you. I love our child. I will never forget you, but I must let you go. You must let me go, too."

Once more, he touched the plaited gold hair and the white flower that lay with it. He closed the box and set it in the ground. With reverent hands, he laid the earth over it.

"I know there is only joy and peace in heaven where you both are. I have found that here in as great a measure as mortal man is allowed. Be happy for me, Kate." A single tear trickled down the side of his face. "I know you loved me. Be happy for me now."

Rosalynde put her arm around him, and he closed his eyes and leaned his head against the comforting roundness in her middle, still on his knees, there between the living and the dead.

"Lord God," Tom said softly, laying one compassionate hand on his brother's shoulder, "hallow this place as these we remember are hallowed already, through Christ Jesus. They are Yours and in Your hand of mercy. For that we give You thanks and ask no more." He held Elizabeth closer, feeling her silent weeping. "Be Lord of all that has gone before, and let us remember only Your forgiveness, Your love, and Your grace. Amen."

"Amen," Rosalynde and Elizabeth echoed.

"Amen," Philip murmured, the word muffled against the soft fullness of Rosalynde's dress. Then, after a moment, he stood up and took her into his arms, letting her spend the rest of her tears against his chest. His own eyes were still wet, but there was a fresh peace in his expression and even a touch of a smile.

"I thank you, Tom, for saying what I could not. I thank you both for standing by me today. It helps somehow."

Tom hugged one arm around him. "It helps us, too."

Elizabeth looked up at her brother-in-law, a trace of shy hesitancy on her tear-stained face, and he clasped her hand.

"Remember what you have promised me, Lady Elizabeth, and leave the rest of your past here with mine."

"I will. Thank you, my lord."

They shared a smile. Then he touched Rosalynde's hair with his lips.

"Shall we go on now, love?" he asked her softly, and, each with one arm encircling the other's waist, they went back into the palace.

"What did you promise him, Bess?" Tom asked, puzzled.

"*I am my beloved's and my beloved is mine*," she thought as she looked up at him. She pressed a tender kiss into the scarred palm of his hand.

"You will see."